KICKS & STONES

KATE ALBERTSON MYSTERY #1

KARL FIELDS

1

The chaos didn't really start until after I'd locked myself in the bathroom, but I'm skipping ahead.

Trammell Preston lived in Holmby Hills, where even the air reeks of money. That night, a gentle breeze swept in through the curved, sliding glass windows in the parlor, cascaded past the solarium and lower library, and came to rest in the ballroom, dispersing a creamy vanilla scent among his guests, courtesy of the sweet clematis lovingly planted in the garden.

The way I heard it, Trammell made his money the old-fashioned way: he stole it. According to his press release bio, he got rich off a patent for a movie camera trucking system used worldwide by production companies large and small. Ply the right person with enough alcohol though, and they'd tell you that Trammell swiped the design from a colleague.

In a town where actors and directors rub elbows with models and musicians, having "theatrical accessories architect" as one's claim to fame hardly captures the imagination (at least, not the attention of the aforementioned models). To compensate, Trammell threw parties—and lots of them—at the Ocean Club, on his one-hundred-fifty-foot yacht, in his VIP suite at Staples Center, and especially at his home, ten thousand square feet if it was an inch, with lobster and champagne flowing freely.

And it worked. With equal parts patience and cash, he scammed his way onto Hollywood society's A-list, and now an invite to a Trammell Preston soiree doesn't come easily.

I'd finagled mine through a makeup artist friend in exchange for a signed first edition of *Murder on the Orient Express*, which I'd "acquired" (ahem) for her. In return, she'd called in a favor from one of her friends, and there I was at Trammell's party, in a lava-red, off-the-shoulder cocktail dress and black, patent leather pumps with pyramid studs, slipping in between guests on my way to the bar. The bartender, a guy wearing a tuxedo shirt open at the neck and a spray tan, passed me a flute of champagne. I won't claim that I can rattle off the vintage the way James Bond can, but no doubt Trammell had sprung for the good stuff. It was a shame I didn't have time to hang around to enjoy more of it.

Along the wall was an unclaimed vintage wingback chair. The pale green upholstery did nothing for me, but the chair was comfy and provided a perfect view of Trammell's guests, though it did have a down side: wide, sturdy arms that offered just enough space to sit on should someone be so presumptuous—someone like the guy with the graying soul patch.

"Hello there. I'm Niles."

Niles looked like the kind of guy who thought he epitomized "L.A. cool"—maroon houndstooth blazer, white shirt open to the second button, jeans, and a pair of black, soft leather slip-ons. He could've been a producer or a car salesman —a real schmoozer either way; the type who thought his mere presence—and maybe the abundance of his cologne—was all it took to make a girl a swoon. If all else failed to impress her, he'd whip out his Amex black card, the thought of which drew my eye to his wallet. Perched on the arm of the chair, Niles appeared balance-challenged. Throwing him off kilter was a wallet so fat it caused him to sit at an angle. I had no idea what was in there, but ten-to-one, he was that guy—the type who constantly complained about women carrying too much stuff in their purses.

He edged closer, his proximity giving me the kind of itch that made me want to go after my skin like a scratch-off lottery ticket, but I kept focused on the scene playing out in front of me. A man with his shirtsleeves pushed up to reveal forearms covered in tattoos was chatting over drinks with another man in a black-and-white plaid tuxedo jacket. There was a time when the tats would've belonged to the actor or musician and the tux to the accountant. These days, who could tell? Nearby, a redhead wearing an up-do and a grey power suit was texting away, ignoring the guy on her arm. Tall, blond-haired, and broad-shouldered, he resembled a certain Nordic superhero. Off to one side, a cluster of guests was enjoying cigars, which apparently made every comment absolutely hilarious. And I counted eight men with dates young enough to be their grand-daughters.

"You're not ignoring me, are you?" Niles asked.

Angling toward him, I said, "As a matter of fact—"

"That's okay. You know, I hate to say this ..."

And yet you're going to.

"... but, seriously, I'm lost ... in your eyes. Do you think you could give me some directions?"

"Niles? Call me crazy, but I get the feeling you already have plenty of people telling you where to go."

He laughed and nearly slipped off his wallet. Then he struck up a conversation with an imaginary person on his other side. "I can't decide what I'm more taken by: her beauty or her sense of humor. Irregardless ..." He turned back to me, but his chances, skeletal to begin with, had officially dwindled to zero.

First of all, "irregardless?" Not a word. And second, he was wearing a hemp belt.

"Say," Niles continued. "I didn't get your name."

Give this guy a shred of information about me? Not happening. I scoured the room for anything that would prompt an alias: the marble pedestals supporting mixed flower arrangements; the glossy black baby grand piano; the silk drapes covering the floor-to-ceiling windows. No inspiration from any of those, but in the backyard was an array of aluminum patio heaters. *Heaters*. The letters danced in my head: *Saether ... Eratsha ... Are those even names?* I shuffled and reshuffled them until ... *Oh!*

"Theresa," I said.

"Theresa, that's a lovely name. Almost as lovely as your dress." He fingered the material near my shoulder then brushed a hand along my neck. "You know, Theresa, there's a truly wonderful spa in the sublevel ..."

Hopping up from the chair, I told Niles, "I have to take care of a little something, but hold that thought." I thrust my drink into his hands. "And this."

"Hey, you're not rushing off, are you? I want to talk to you about a part I think you'd be perfect for."

I nearly laughed out loud. The last time a guy used that line on me, I still thought platform flip-flops were cute. Sadly, lines like that probably worked. Why else would guys like him keep using them?

My skepticism must've been showing, because Niles reached inside his jacket and fished out a business card. "I know how it sounds, but I'm serious. I'm hoping to talk to some people here tonight about backing."

The card read: *Niles Wendelstedt. Producer. Atomic Sky Productions.* It was printed on high-quality stock, but that didn't prove a thing. Anyone could have a card printed, and besides, the only thing I wanted pawing at me actually had paws:

Whimsy, my three-year-old smooth fox terrier and the sweetest dog ever.

My glimpse of Amelia Preston, Trammell's wife, was what had put me in motion. Before I searched the house for a certain necklace, I needed to make sure it wasn't clinging to her ample — and almost certainly ersatz — bosom. When she passed me, I saw she was sporting a lovely string of pearls, not a diamond necklace, so the hunt was on. I headed down the hall toward the restroom but veered off at the kitchen and, with no one the wiser, I snuck up the staircase that spiraled to the second floor.

The beaded chandelier suspended over the stairwell lit up the foyer below, but the only thing brightening my path on the second floor was the moonlight seeping through partially open blinds. I removed a pair of gloves and a penlight from my clutch and followed the hallway past four bedrooms and a study before reaching the master suite—if the double doors were any indication—at the end of the hall.

Rich people and poor people own entirely different kinds of valuables, but they both tend to store them in the master bedroom. I twisted the knob—locked. If I'd been hosting a party at my mansion, I would've locked the door too, only with a much better lock. I took out a set of metal lock picks, and eight seconds later I was on the other side. *Shoot! Almost a new personal best.*

In the dark, the room felt bigger than my entire apartment. My tiny light played over a matching sofa and loveseat adjacent to a sixty-inch television mounted on the wall. Opposite that, a pair of French doors led to a balcony, while a mammoth four-poster bed dominated the back half of the room. I got to work, starting with the armoire. The cashmere wraps were tempting but not on tonight's shopping list, so I put them back and kept looking. A run through the dressers turned up nothing, so I moved on to the closet.

Like the rest of the room, the walk-in closet was spacious

and open, with racks full of clothing—his on the left and hers on the right. No less than a fourth of Amelia's wall was devoted to shoes alone, and not just any shoes, but the red Nicholas Kirkwood double sandals ... the silver, leather Christians ... a pair of black Alexander Wang strappies (a bit dom for Amelia, I thought) ... and—I drew a breath—the Manuel Andrioni crystal-embellished, peep-toe pumps that you couldn't even get stateside. I swear if those things had been my size (yes, I tried them on), I would've walked out with them.

Stay on task, Kate.

I swept aside the clothes on Amelia's half of the closet, revealing a blank wall, except for three letters from the Greek alphabet—lambda, phi, alpha—but no panel with a keyhole or a dial pad or anything to indicate a hidden compartment. I turned to the opposite wall, where I pushed past Trammell's suits and shirts. There were letters on his side, too—delta, rho, sigma. That was the fraternity he belonged to in college, so I assumed the letters on Amelia's side were her sorority. I briefly attended college and knew the Greek scene was a big deal to some people, but the wall safe next to the letters was of far greater interest to me. It was a silver panel with a digital keypad. I *love* digital safes. All it takes is a little fingerprint powder—the kind the cops use at crime scenes and that anyone in the, um, acquisitions business brings to any job— and *voila!* I could see which keys had been pressed. All I had to do was figure out the order. Despite a million warnings over the years about using obvious combinations—like birthdays or anniversaries—for things like passwords and PIN numbers, people can't seem to help themselves.

The powder highlighted fingerprints on the numbers 1, 2, 3 and 7. I entered anything that could be a date but came up empty. No matter which combination I tried, the safe's door wouldn't budge, which left me with Plan B.

The keys had tiny letters printed above each number— just

an "a" and a "b" above the 1 while the rest of the alphabet was spread among the remaining keys. As I focused, the letters seemed to float off the keypad and rearrange themselves into different possibilities—*begs ... char ... gate.* My gut told me that all those combinations were wrong, so I didn't even bother keying them in. Then I saw another possibility: *safe.*

Cute, Trammell.

Sure enough, the door popped free. Before pulling the door all the way open, I slipped on a mask (some people hide little cameras in their safes to get pictures of people like me) and then examined the contents.

On the top shelf sat passports, envelopes, spare keys, and insurance papers, but stashed below were several black and maroon jewelry boxes, the largest of which contained an interlocking diamond necklace. I held it up to take a look. Maybe it was the dim lighting, but I wasn't particularly impressed—the pyramid-shaped diamond didn't strike me as a very unusual stone—but mine was not to question why; it was to deliver the goods and earn a tidy payday.

I stuffed the necklace in my purse, closed the safe, and wiped the fingerprint dust off the keypad. Then I beat an exit from the bedroom and hurried down the hall. Half a dozen steps from the staircase, I froze. Footsteps were headed my way.

2

I backtracked, but without enough time to unlock the door to the master, I ducked into one of the other bedrooms and shut the door behind me. Sadly, this one didn't have a lock.

The room was nice, but smaller than the master suite, and judging by the canopy bed with the frilly curtains and matching throw pillows, it belonged to a girl. Looking around for a hiding place in case my unwanted company was headed this way, I chose the bathroom. Good thing too, because no sooner had I shut myself in (fortunately, *this* door locked) than someone entered the bedroom. With my ear to the door, I heard heavy panting and wondered whether one of Trammell's guests was about to pass out. I cracked the door open and peeked outside. A large, murky figure stumbled across the room, which was lit only by a shaft of moonlight coming in through the window. He edged closer, and I realized I'd had it wrong. It wasn't one guy, but *two*, and they were groping and tonguing like high-schoolers.

And they weren't just any two guys. The one with his back to me was wearing the black-and-white plaid jacket I'd seen downstairs—there couldn't be more than one of those at the same party—and he was kissing the Thor lookalike who'd been reluctantly attached to the woman texting her French tips off. He'd looked as if he wanted to be elsewhere, and now I knew where. Plaid Jacket must've had some serious coin to reel in a hottie like Thor.

I checked the time and groaned. If I didn't get out of here quick, I'd have to wait until tomorrow to get the necklace to Mel, and I really wanted to offload the merchandise tonight. Not one for voyeurism, I shut the door and waited, hoping it would be a quickie, but the chances of that went by the boards when they were still panting and petting a few minutes later. Out of all the rooms and studies and other places in this house they could've chosen for a rendezvous, they had to pick this one.

And what if one of them needed to use the bathroom? They had to be at least a little tipsy to think cheating on their dates in one of the upstairs bedrooms was a good idea, right? What if they started banging on the door when they found it locked? Loud is okay if you're in a band, but if there's one thing people in my line of work really hate, it's noise.

A check of my surroundings didn't yield much in the way of an escape—just a window that looked too small for even me to crawl through. Plus, I don't do the whole heights thing. I looked back at the door. Would they even notice me if I just walked out, or were they too busy getting busy? I could do it. I could totally do it. Just breeze right past as if nothing was amiss.

Don't mind me, boys. Carry on. Yeah, right.

When Amelia realized her necklace was missing, the Prestons would be asking all kinds of questions about who had been present in their house. I couldn't chance either Plaid Jacket or Thor remembering a little brunette in a red dress sneaking around near the scene of the crime.

Maybe it was the desperation that came with the bathroom

air growing stale, but I looked through my purse and found
Niles's business card. Just holding it churned my stomach, but a
better idea wasn't forthcoming. So I sent him a text, knowing it
meant handing him my phone number.

Hey, Niles?

A moment later, he answered.

Do I no u?

It's Theresa. We met a few minutes ago.

Oh yeh! 'sup?

Oh, wow. It should be illegal for anyone over forty to
use 'sup.

Do you really want to talk to me about a part?

Of course kitten.

Kitten? This guy couldn't decide whether he wanted to be
hip or retro.

*Okay, let's talk. I'm upstairs, in the fourth room on the right. Just
let yourself in. And don't take too long. :-)*

B rite there!!!

Seriously? Sure, people like to be brief when they text, but
did skipping the "e" in "be" really save that much time? And I
won't even get into that atrocious typo.

After I stashed my phone, I placed my ear against the door
and heard what sounded like kissing and the rustling of sheets,
but my heartbeat was echoing in my ears, making it hard to tell.
I took deep breaths to calm down and prayed to everything
from Nike, the Greek goddess of shoes, to the four-faced
Buddha that this would work.

A minute or so later, I heard the sound of footsteps entering
the bedroom, followed by a pause in the action on the bed. For
a split second, the only noise in the air was the muted sounds
of the party going on downstairs.

"Hey, dude!" someone shouted. My money was on Thor.
"What's your damage?"

"Me?" He sounded a little shaken, but I recognized Nile's

voice. He must've been treated to a real eyeful. "Where's Theresa? You're not …"

There was the flick of a switch, and light from the bedroom spilled underneath the bathroom door.

"… R.J.?" Niles said.

Sounds of a mad scramble filled the room, and I imagined Plaid Jacket and Thor dashing out of bed to find their clothes.

"Seriously, get the hell out of here!" Thor barked. I heard a door close, and then Thor asked, "You know that guy?"

"R.J." didn't answer. All I heard was the swish of fabric as they rushed to get dressed.

"Want to hook up later?" Thor tried again. "I'll ditch the hag and meet you somewhere more private."

R.J. cleared his throat and said, "Yes, I'd like that."

The door opened and shut a second time. Whoever was left in the room muttered something under his breath, and then I heard footsteps coming toward the bathroom. Perfect. He grabbed the handle and twisted, but I'd locked the door. He rattled the knob a couple more times before realizing it wouldn't budge, so he stormed out, flicking off the bedroom light.

I waited, drinking in several long, deep breaths, and when I felt certain everyone had gone, I unlocked the bathroom door and slipped out. The room was empty, as was the hall leading back to the staircase. A million butterflies danced in my stomach as I made my way downstairs, clutching the bannister for support. I really could've used a drink, but I headed straight for the front door instead. Once outside, I handed the valet my claim ticket and a ten-spot.

"Right away, ma'am," he said and vanished into the night.

While I was waiting, I took out my phone and checked the app connected to the camera in my apartment. Whim was curled up on the couch, taking a nap.

"I'll be home soon," I whispered.

A moment later, my phone buzzed with an incoming text.

WTF Theresa? Where r u?

Oh. My. God! I knew I'd regret letting him have my number. I just didn't think it would be five minutes later.

I replied: *I'm in the spa in the sublevel. Where are you?*

Very funny. So what does Niles have to do? Chase you down?

Ugh. On top of everything else, he talked about himself in the third person. That alone was reason enough for me to block his number, which I did happily. I put my phone away as the valet returned with my lemon-yellow Volkswagen Karmann Ghia.

"Sweet rig," he said as he held the door open.

"Thanks!" I hopped in, wished him a good night, and soon found myself navigating the tiny, winding streets of Trammell's neighborhood, the cool SoCal breeze in my face. At Sunset, I headed east toward downtown and pulled up to *Imeldo's* just before closing.

The neon pink sign proclaimed the restaurant as the home of Filipino fusion cuisine, although what the cuisine had been fused with was Mel's closely held secret. The few lingering diners sat at mostly cleared tables, nursing their drinks. Remnants of garlic, ginger, and lemongrass laced the air, reminding me of how long it had been since I'd eaten. Komar, Mel's teenage daughter, was at the host stand wiping down menus. Her ponytail had frayed and her grim expression said she'd rather be hanging out in Westwood or on the Third Street Promenade with her friends, yet she managed a smile when she saw me.

"Wow, Kate. That dress is hot! Where have you been?"

"I had to make an appearance at a party. *So* glad to be out of there."

"Better than being stuck here."

"Tough night?" I asked.

She rolled her eyes and exhaled upward, rustling her bangs. "Dad's got your order in the back."

"Thanks, sweetie." I gave Komar's hand a squeeze. "Hang in there."

My heels clicked against the sparkly, black tile floor as I made my way to the kitchen, pushing through the padded, black swinging doors. Two of the busboys were scraping left-over food into large plastic trashcans, and Tony, one of the cooks, was banging pots against a steel sink full of soapy water as he scrubbed away the grime. Like he did every time he saw me, he smiled and pointed toward Mel's office as though I hadn't already been there a dozen times before.

I knocked on Mel's open door, breaking his concentration from his computer. "Kate! Hello, my little friend."

A *Scarface* reference, and an ironic one at that considering he was all of maybe two inches taller than me.

He stood from his desk and greeted me with a hug.

I put my hands on his shoulders and stepped back. "But seriously, Mel? Making Komar work on Friday *and* Saturday night? You might want to let her have a little fun."

"She doesn't need to have fun. She needs to focus on school, not boys and shopping."

"You can't keep her on the farm forever, you know?"

Mel frowned. "What farm? This is Hollywood. I haven't seen a farm since I left Mindanao."

"Um, colloquialism. Sorry. Look, you don't want her to resent you, do you? She'll come home from college one Thanksgiving with a shaved head and a guy who plays bass in a death metal band."

He scrunched his face, adding a few more wrinkles to his forehead. "Really?"

"It could happen. But anyway ..." I opened my purse just enough to show him the necklace and said softly, "Taa daa."

Mel's eyes bulged and his mouth gaped. He gestured to the

chair opposite his desk and closed the door before taking his seat. "I can't believe you got it. And so fast!"

He retrieved an envelope from his desk drawer and slid it over to me. I passed him the necklace in exchange.

"Let's just say I was"—I peeked inside the envelope and saw it was flush with cash—"properly motivated." Noting the time on the faux brass wall clock behind Mel, I stood. "I gotta run, but hit a girl up if you get another special order."

We exchanged another hug, and Mel handed me a to-go order of chicken Adobo with noodles. On the way out, I gave Komar a wink and told her that I had a feeling she'd be getting a weekend off soon.

Back behind the wheel of the Karmabile, I made a U-turn across the middle of the street, drawing a horn blast from an oncoming Hummer limo, and doubled back to Fairfax. From there, it was a quick trip back to my neighborhood, a quiet area near Restaurant Row. My apartment was on the top floor of a new-ish six-story building near the end of the block. I pulled into the underground parking garage, my tires scrunching on the concrete as I steered into my spot.

When I opened the front door of my apartment, Whimsy bounded off the couch to greet me.

"Hi, Whim! Sorry I'm late. I got home as quickly as I could." I kneeled down to stroke her light brown head. Her tail, white like the rest of her from the neck down, was a blur. "Are you happy to see me? Or do you just have to go outside?"

She barked as if to say of course she was glad to see me. It certainly wasn't like she'd ditch me for some other owner, leaving behind just a lame note.

With Whim close behind, I moved to the living room and stored the envelope in the safe hidden behind a Monet reprint. On my way to the bedroom, I glanced toward the kitchen counter out of habit, looking for Terry's keys, but they were gone, just like they'd been for the past eight days.

I changed into sweats, grabbed Whimsy's leash, and out we went for her potty break. As we walked, a light rain began to fall, which I hoped signaled an end to the years-long drought, but all we ended up getting that evening was a few puddles' worth of water.

That done, I polished off the Adobo—Mel's a genius in the kitchen—while checking my Facebook page. Word of the breakup had gotten out. Shrevie had checked in to make sure I was okay and swore his allegiance to me.

"If Terry comes to me for as much as a fake promise ring," he'd written, "I'll tell him to stuff it."

I appreciated that, but mostly I was glad Shrevie hadn't reminded me that he'd cautioned me about people in our line of business living and working together. We'd made such a good team though; I knew diamonds and Terry knew alarms. Everything I know about beating security systems I learned from him.

Another friend, Jeremy, who owned a restaurant, had written: "If Terry has the nerve to show his face in here, I'll personally serve him a sneezer."

By the time I finished reading all the messages, I was feeling mildly better, then I noticed the friend request. From Broussard, of all people.

Uh huh. We can be friends again when the devil wears a parka.

Between Terry and her, when it came to choosing co-workers my track record left much to be desired. I wouldn't have been surprised if Terry had run off with Broussard, but that honor went to Julia, my best friend right up until the moment she decided to start sleeping with Terry. And yours truly was the last to know.

I deleted Broussard's request and called it a night. I hadn't realized how enormous the bed was when Terry and I picked it out; it always seemed just right. But now, as I chased sleep, I felt as though I were flailing about in the Pacific. Finally though, I drifted off, and when I opened my eyes again, it was to the kind of morning that made people drop everything and move to L.A.

The weather was certainly one of the reasons I'd moved here, happily ditching Texas's scorching heat and stifling humidity. I stretched and entertained thoughts of visiting the new coffee house that had just opened on Wilshire.

"Sleeping until ten forty-two?" said a voice from across the room. "Excellent work if you can find it, right Miss Albertson?"

3

A couple weeks earlier, Mel had called me saying one of his clients was interested in a certain trillion-cut necklace currently in the possession of Trammell Preston. I did some research and found news footage that had been taken at a fundraiser put on by former USC fraternity brothers from Delta Rho Sigma. That video was the first time I'd ever seen Trammell, standing next to his wife, who was wearing the necklace, and two other couples. The second time I saw him was that morning in my bedroom. He was sitting in the tan slipper chair by the window, legs crossed and wearing a navy blue blazer over a crisp, white linen shirt and gray slacks. Sipping from a red coffee cup with a white lid, he took in my apartment's view of the Hollywood Hills.

I pulled the bedspread up to my neck. "What are you doing here?"

Trammell whipped toward me as though I'd just appeared. He smiled. Sort of. "Oh, I think we both know why I'm here, but ..." He put his cup on the window ledge and crossed his other leg. "I'll humor you. I'd like my necklace back."

I swallowed, trying to push my heart back down my throat. "Necklace?"

"That's right, the necklace. The very expensive necklace. The very expensive necklace you removed from my home last night."

"What makes you think it was me?"

He looked pleased that I'd asked. "When I realized the necklace was gone, I asked around to find out if anyone saw anything suspicious. The valet said a woman matching your description dashed off in a hurry, leaving him with a nice tip and this." Trammell reached into his pocket, took out a card, and flicked it onto my bed. It was the one Niles had given me. In my hurry to get out of there, I must've gotten it mixed up with my money and the claim ticket. But how had Trammell realized that the necklace was gone so soon? Was he so paranoid that he checked on it every night before bed as though it were a sleeping baby? "I spoke to Mr. Wendelstedt. He also remembers you. Quite fondly, I might add."

There was a shocker.

"From there it was a matter of tracking you down through the guest list, but I won't clutter your pretty little head with the details. Just return my necklace. Please. After that, I'll be on my way."

I snatched my phone from the nightstand. "I'm calling the cops."

"That would not be wise ... for two reasons. First of all, as far as local law enforcement is concerned, I'm a Very. Generous. Supporter. There's also the matter of the little rodent."

I squinted at him. What was he babbling about? He was already caffeinated; if anyone should've been incoherent, it was me. "Rodent?"

"The one normally scampering about your apartment."

My eyes flew wide open. "Whimsy! Here, Whim!" When

she didn't answer, I felt my stomach slosh back and forth. "Where's my dog?"

"Whimsy is fine. Where's my necklace?"

"I don't have it."

"Then I suggest you rectify that *pronto*." Trammell stood and smoothed a wrinkle in his pants. He approached the bed and bent over, his lips inches from my ear, lifting the hairs on the back of my neck. "Or the dog gets it." He downed the last of his coffee and placed the empty cup on my nightstand. "I'll see myself out. Good day, Ms. Albertson."

I waited, listening to his footsteps cross the hardwood floor. When the front door closed behind him, I tore out of bed, hoping Whim had just gone into hiding because of the stranger in the house. I dove under the bed, spotting only a few dust devils and the oscillating dumbbell that promised to save me hours at the gym. I ripped aside the drapes and looked behind the dresser and in the closet. Coaxing and whistling as I went, I moved to the living room. Stepping around some of the dirt Trammell had tracked in, I peered beneath the sofa and behind the entertainment center. There was no sign of her in the kitchen or the bathroom. I turned the place upside down but eventually ran out of places to look and dropped onto the sofa. He really had taken my dog.

I was still in shock as I threw on jeans and a Lakers t-shirt and dashed out the front door, but I had to deal with the necklace.

Mel's place did decent lunch business, but the atmosphere was completely different from the evening. The crowd was older, quieter, and more interested in the food than which club they were headed to next. Mel was out front cleaning off one of the tables when I arrived and looked surprised to see me.

"Can we talk?" I asked as I breezed by, not stopping until I'd reached his office.

He shut the door and sat at his desk. "What are you doing here? I never see you in the daytime."

"When I woke up this morning, Trammell Preston was in my boudoir."

"Your what?"

I exhaled. "My bedroom."

"Oh. Why?"

"He wants his necklace back."

"How'd he know about the necklace? How'd he know where you live? *I* don't even know where you live."

"I don't know." I dug into my purse for the envelope. "All I know is I have to get that necklace back."

"It's too late."

"*What?*"

"I moved it already."

"Are you kidding? I haven't even had coffee yet."

"Maybe you shouldn't sleep so late."

"I got up early once. The whole worm thing is a lie."

"Kate, I wish I could help you, but—"

"You know what? You can. Just tell me who bought it and I'll take care of the rest."

He looked at me as if I'd parked a food truck outside his restaurant. "Take care of the rest *how*? By stealing it back? When someone buys from a fence, the merchandise is supposed to be stolen *before* they buy, not after. Who's gonna do business with me if I get a reputation like that?"

"But Mel," I pouted. "He kidnapped Whimsy."

"Who's Whimsy?"

I took out my phone and showed him the picture on the home screen, the one of Whimsy wearing a Superman cape. "See?"

Mel nodded.

"Trammell took her. He's holding her hostage until he gets his necklace back."

"That's terrible. But I'm sorry. I can't—"

I held the phone out closer to him. "Melll ..."

He gave me his coldest stare.

Three years earlier, a friend of Terry's owned a dog that gave birth to a litter of pups, and he was looking to find homes for them. As soon as I saw the puppies, I wanted to adopt them all, but I was drawn to one in particular; she was so much smaller than the others. Terry's friend said she was a runt and that the mother had initially rejected her, going so far as to put her outside of the crate more than once. She'd stopped doing that, but the pup was too weak to fight for her share of her mother's milk. Terry frowned when I said we should take Whimsy, as though there was something wrong with her.

When I was a toddler, I was diagnosed with Blount's disease, a growth disorder that caused me to be bowlegged, especially on my left side. Wearing a brace that ran the length of my entire leg eventually solved the problem, but not before half the kids in my neighborhood teased me to the point of me not venturing past the gate in the front yard.

The causes for Blount's are unknown, but it shows up sometimes in those of small stature. Maybe that was why I was so drawn to Whim. It took a lot of pleading before Terry relented —his willingness to turn his back on her probably should've been a red flag.

Point is: no one was getting away with snatching my dog. We runts have to stick together.

I matched Mel's stare with one of my own. Three seconds later, he sighed, snatched the top sheet off the tear-away pad on his desk, scribbled something down, and thrust the paper toward me. I examined what he'd written—*NOT TELLING* — and broke out into a smile.

"Mel, I love you. You totally get me." I jumped to my feet. "I owe you."

"You bet your sweet Beetlejuice you do." He jotted something else down on another square of paper and handed it to me. "I'll be expecting one of these."

It wasn't until my fourth visit to the restaurant—the time I delivered an eighteen karat gold watch—that Mel and I ventured beyond business. He confessed to a fondness for '80s movies, and I told him about my thing for word puzzles, especially anagrams.

I hadn't even buckled my seatbelt before figuring out "Not Telling" was a reference to one of Hollywood's foremost cosmetic dentists, T Ellington; the T stood for Tad. He'd separated from his wife of a dozen years after she learned that the good doctor had been drilling more than cavities. The pending divorce made a few of the gossip sites devoted to L.A.'s society scene, complete with a photo of Denise Ladd, the alleged other woman.

Shortly after ten a.m. on the Monday after Trammell's party, I accessed the doctor's Brentwood townhouse—Mrs. Ellington had retained the couple's primary residence in Santa Monica (as well as the services of a high-priced lawyer)—and gave it a thorough inspection. I started in the bedroom, where I came across several sets of frilly undergarments in one of the dresser drawers. Perhaps cross-dressing, and not infidelity, had been Mrs. Ellington's objection, but the more likely explanation was that Miss Ladd was a regular visitor at the townhouse. From there, I moved to a room that had been set up as a makeshift office. The furnishings were bare, with only a desk and computer, but Ellington had spared no expense on those. The desk was made of heavy, dark wood and the computer looked like the latest model to hit the market. I rifled through the drawers and, beneath some paperwork, found a red jewelry box identical to the one Mel had put the necklace in. I hurried to open it only to find it empty, save for a yellow sticky note.

For me? Okay, I forgive you! was written on it, along with hearts and a smiley face.

"Shoot!"

The note must've been the work of the mistress, who apparently now had the necklace in her possession. Fabulous. I cleared out of the townhouse, but as I approached my car, company waiting was for me: a thin, long-legged blonde in jeans and a t-shirt, with her hair pulled into a ponytail tucked beneath a white baseball cap. Even with sunglasses concealing half of her face, I had zero doubt about the identity of the woman sitting comfortably on the back of my car.

"Kate!" she said, smiling. "It's not like you to walk out empty-handed, girlfriend."

I tossed my bag on the passenger seat and got in on the other side. "Broussard, I intend to peel out of here with a severe U-turn, and I'll have no problem sending you flying."

To no surprise, she hopped off the bumper. Less expected was her hustling into the seat beside me and scooping my bag up onto her lap.

"Presumptuous much?"

"Come on, Kate. Is that any way to treat an old friend?"

I scoffed. "Show me one and I won't."

"Well, if you would've responded to me on Facebook, I wouldn't have had to track you down like this."

"Or you could've just taken the hint." Of course, that would've required her to stop being totally self-obsessed for two minutes, but this was Broussard. She'd once broken up with a guy for not asking about her day. "Look, I don't know what you're doing here, and I don't—"

"Glad you asked. I need a teensy, little favor."

"You have *got* to be kidding."

She pulled off her shades and locked onto me with those greyish-blue eyes of hers. Gone was her typical flighty expression, replaced by a look that would've been at home at a wake. "Can't you at least hear me out? For old time's sake? Come on …

Albertson and Broussard, the A&B Team. You remember that, right?"

"A&B Team? What I remember is you setting off Gregory Whittaker's alarm and then bailing without bothering to tell me, so why don't you *C* your way out of my car."

"You aren't still mad about that, are you?"

It took every bit of my self-control not to wind up and sock her. "I spent two hours and forty-four minutes hiding in a neighbor's giant recycling bin full of empty Budweiser cans. He must've hosted a poker night or something. To this day, the mere sight of a Clydesdale makes me twitch. And let's not even get started on how long it took me to get the smell out of my hair."

Broussard sighed. "I'm really sorry about how that went down, and if it makes you feel any better, I got pinched. Not for that; a few months later on a different gig. I did eighteen of a thirty-six."

Actually, that did make me feel better. Considerably. "Well, you know what they say about karma."

She dropped her head and started fidgeting with her hands. "That's why I'm here. To make amends."

"Uh huh. I thought you said you needed a favor."

"Well, it's both. Look, Kate, I've got a line on something huge, but I need a partner to pull it off."

"Why me?"

"Because ... you're the only one I can trust."

The feeling was so not mutual. "Broussard, I've got my own problems to deal with right now, and I really need to get going."

"Oh. Sure. I didn't mean to catch you at a bad time."

Right, because ambushing me on the street was bound to be the perfect approach.

"Will you at least think about it?" she asked.

"If I say yes, will that get you out of my car?"

She nodded, so I agreed, but any thoughts of resuming our

partnership were gone by the time I reached the end of the block.

FINDING ELLINGTON'S MISTRESS, DENISE LADD, WASN'T difficult, given her career ambitions. The girl's headshot could be found on any number of websites, including one casting site that, in addition to listing her credits, had failed to crop out her phone number. A Google search of the number turned up the related address, an apartment complex in Manhattan Beach.

A two-day stakeout of the place ensued, testing my patience, not to mention my resolve. But whenever the possibility of giving up entered my mind, I thought about Whimsy, all alone in some strange place without her blanket or her favorite toy, an octopus-looking thing that squeaked when she picked it up. That sustained me through both boredom and Subway.

I was rewarded in spades just after lunch on Thursday when the gate to the parking garage opened and a metallic silver Lexus convertible pulled out with Denise at the wheel. And I could've sworn she was wearing the necklace.

I crumpled the sandwich wrapper and tossed it in the bag as I promised myself two things: I was getting my dog back, and the cold cut combo? Never again.

The Lexus came to rest at an outdoor shopping center, where Denise, sporting a white, crocheted sundress and black sandals, got out. She combed a hand through her wavy blonde hair and began leisurely exploring the mall. First, she perused the front windows of several boutique clothing and shoe stores while I followed at a distance. A row of palm trees was planted down the middle of the walkway, their leaves rustling in a fresh ocean breeze. I pulled my hair aside and let the gentle wind caress the back of my neck.

When Denise stepped into Wick-ed Ways, a store that sold scented candles, I found a bench and took a seat to wait. She exited minutes later, bogged down by a large shopping bag. Was she really going to make it this easy? I donned sunglasses and started toward the mistress, and as I approached from behind, I called out. "Denise?"

She turned, and I was met by a face even more beautiful than the one I'd seen online. She was so striking it took me a moment to realize that the stone dangling from her neck wasn't the droid I was looking for.

"Do I know you?" she asked.

"Uh ... sure. We met on that Oakley shoot a few months ago." I pointed to myself. "Theresa."

Denise stared, trying to place me. "Oh ... yeah! How are you?"

"You know, same ol'."

"Right?"

Social convention calls for at least thirty seconds of small talk when only one of the parties can call the other by name, and at that mark exactly, Denise said, "Well, it was great seeing you again."

"Ohmygosh, you too!"

The necklace must have been back at her apartment. With one arm, I reached out to give her a hug while slipping the other into her purse in search of her keys. It was one of those bulky, leather drawstring bags, and it picked that moment to slip off her shoulder, cinching my hand inside.

Denise looked down and then at me. "What the hell are you doing?"

She snatched her purse away and my hand came free, but so did a pair of earbuds, wrapped around my arm. I untangled them and handed them back to her.

"I don't remember you from the Oakley shoot. Were you there spying on me? What are you, some kind of stalker?"

"I'm sorry. This is all a big mis—"

She whipped a tiny spray bottle out of her purse and aimed it at me. I didn't know what it held and didn't care to find out. I grabbed for the bottle and engaged her in a struggle before wresting it from her grip, then I turned and made a beeline for the Karmabile, covering about ten seconds' worth of mall walkway when, from behind, I heard a thud. I risked a glimpse over my shoulder and saw Denise, not giving chase, but lying on the ground in a heap.

Several nearby shoppers rushed to her aid. One person propped up Denise's head while another tried to revive her. A third looked toward me and, as more people gathered, pointed in my direction.

"Uh oh."

4

I fled the scene and returned home. I felt awful about causing Denise's fainting spell and then not sticking around to help, but panic had set in. Once Denise came back around, how could I have possibly explained what my hand was doing in her purse or why she'd tried to spray me? Better to leave the situation in the hands of those not already involved.

The apartment was too quiet without Whim running around, so I clicked on the television for a welcome distraction. I didn't get far in my channel surfing before the image of a shopping mall appeared onscreen. It looked like the one I'd just left, which the type at the bottom of the screen confirmed. A middle-aged woman was standing in the foreground, grim-faced and holding a microphone.

"... no apparent signs of foul play, but police stress the investigation is just getting underway," she said, and then the station went to commercial.

Foul play? I flipped through the channels until I found another station's local news and caught the story from the beginning. Earlier that afternoon, a young woman collapsed at the mall and was later pronounced dead at the scene.

I shot up from the couch. "Dead?"

No, please. No, no, no, *no!* This couldn't be happening.

But it was. The video proved it. A reporter, live on the scene, recapped what had happened, complete with security video that someone had leaked (sold) to the station. There I was on the blurry video, walking away from Denise after I'd relieved her of the pepper spray, or whatever it had been.

Seconds after I walked out of frame, she collapsed like a mine shaft. They cut from the video to an interview with a cop on the scene. He repeated what he'd learned from witnesses: the victim was seen calling after another woman; she was seemingly in good health; then she suddenly and inexplicably fell to the ground, where she "expired." That's police blotter lingo for you, making the poor girl sound like a coupon.

The interview ended and the anchor returned to the screen. "Police would like to question the woman seen having an altercation with the victim just prior to her death."

Altercation? It was two people grabbing for a plastic bottle and they were making it sound like something that should've been on pay-per-view.

"She's described as a dark-haired Caucasian in her mid-twenties to early thirties, five-feet, five inches to five-feet, seven inches tall, and weighing between a hundred and twenty to a hundred and thirty pounds," he said.

For the record, I'm twenty-eight, so they got that much right, but I'm five-two and weigh a buck-twelve. Probably because of cop shows, most people believe an eye witness is needed in order to solve a case when, truth be told, witnesses are wrong at least as often as they're right. Sometimes, they can be an outlaw's best friend.

"She left the scene in a yellow Volkswagen Karmann Ghia," the anchor continued.

Fine. They got that right too. Then again, the car did stand out.

"Police stress there is no evidence of foul play and that the woman in question is not a suspect at this point, but rather a person of interest.

Person of interest. I didn't care for the sound of that.

Language is beautiful, one of the best tools humans ever invented, although far too many people, like Niles, never bother to learn how to use it. Irregardless. *Pfft.*

Language can be direct, subtle, or a million different things in between. It constantly evolves, sometimes for the better and sometimes not (we've gotten so comfortable with dropping four-letter bombs that hardly anyone says darn anymore). It's like a living, breathing thing we can use to communicate ideas, express feelings, or just help someone get from Hollywood to San Pedro. And I love its diversity. Take the whole thank you/you're welcome exchange. After someone expresses gratitude, options at your disposal include: no problem, don't mention it, anytime, you got it, happy to help, my pleasure, no worries, and yep (if you're in Minnesota). One idea, many ways to express it.

Which was exactly my problem with that "person of interest" business. It sounded to me like double-speak for suspect, and I wasn't—a suspect, that is. I certainly didn't kill anybody. I've never once been violent—unless you count that time I broke a guy's pinky toe when I stepped on it with my stiletto, but that was an accident. I didn't even own a weapon, although waking up to find Trammell Preston in my apartment had me rethinking my philosophy.

The police hadn't identified the victim during the afternoon broadcast, but by the time the six o'clock news rolled around, the media had learned Denise's name, that she was an aspiring actress, and that she lived in Manhattan Beach. They'd found a picture of her beaming and snuggling a tiny Yorkshire Terrier against her face. That was when I lost it. I couldn't help it. The dog was adorable, and Denise looked so happy. Every bit of moisture in my body headed straight for my tear ducts, and I sat on my couch, sobbing like a lost, little girl.

What if her death *had* been my fault? What if I wasn't just a person of interest, but an assailant? A sickly feeling came over me, and I ran for the bathroom. I was hunched on the floor with my head over the bowl when, in between heaves, a voice blaring from the television caught my ear. I hurried back to the living room to find Trammell Preston's face splashed across the screen. He was going on and on about how talented Denise was, and he didn't know how he'd continue the shoot without her. They flashed his name across the screen, along with the title, "Producer."

Denise was working on a movie that Trammell was producing? The last part shouldn't have surprised me—in this town, if you don't want to produce, it's because you want to direct—but I couldn't see him as anything other than the guy with the movie camera accessory, and he'd come by that through questionable means. And what was the star of his movie doing with his wife's necklace?

"And to this person of interest," Trammell said to the camera. "Do the right thing and come forward. If you've done nothing wrong, you have nothing to fear, and you may have information that can help with the investigation. Clear your conscience. Please."

His eyes pierced the screen, boring a hole into my gut, so I turned the TV off and collapsed on the couch. Could I do it? Go to the police and tell them what I knew? Bare my soul like Trammell had asked? They might not have looked too kindly on someone who'd been in an "altercation" with the deceased. Besides, my M.O. generally included avoiding all things law enforcement. Me entering a police station voluntarily would've been like Kanye West behaving himself at an award show.

I ruled out the precinct confessional, but what next? Barricade myself in the apartment and wait for things to calm down? How long would that take? There was no way to know for sure, but probably longer than I could realistically stay cooped up inside.

Once the sun had set, I ventured back to my car and started across town. I kept to side streets as much as possible, checking my rearview mirror nonstop all the way to the sleepy, pothole-riddled street in East Hollywood that was home to a cash-only, no-questions-asked storage facility where I rented space. Built in the seventies, the building was dark green, with a narrow, flat roof. It had been divided into six compartments, each marked by a white door wide enough to drive through. I hopped out and, with my hands shaking, unlocked the door to my stall. I lifted the door, revealing bare, plywood walls and a pale blue, compact Chevy. I hopped inside and backed it out of the garage, then replaced it with the Karmabile.

After locking up, I eased my way down the crumbling driveway onto the street and headed home. Even though the Chevy's gas gauge was approaching empty, just being behind the wheel of something less conspicuous eased my stress. The Karmabile, in its yellow brilliance, turned heads. The Chevy, on the other hand, got about as much attention as an overweight plumber standing next to George Clooney. Thirty minutes after seeing the Chevy, some would say it was white, others would swear it was grey. One guy would say the car was domestic, while his friend would swear it was foreign. In other words, it was totally nondescript, and after today's media firestorm, nondescript was exactly what I needed.

According to the news report, there was no indication of foul play in Denise's death. Why then was I a person of interest? Why was Trammell pleading for someone to come forward? Something didn't add up. Were the police holding back information from the public? It wouldn't be the first time.

They could've had reason to believe Denise's death wasn't some random accident, but she seemed so harmless. Who would want to kill her? And why?

Those were great questions ... for a suspect. A real one, not someone who'd been in the wrong place at the wrong time. Maybe I was being influenced by my breakup with Terry, but whether it's murder or skipping out on the lease, it seemed to me that the best place to start was with the boyfriend.

5

Tad Ellington had set up shop in Brentwood, on the fourth floor of an office building that looked north toward Topanga State Park. I parked on a street a couple blocks away and trekked back. Suddenly, paying him a visit seemed like less of a good idea than it had just a few minutes earlier. There was no such thing as a good time to pretend to be a cop, but doing so while they were looking for me seemed especially dicey. Still, there's something about a badge that gets people to open up even when invoking the Fifth might be their best bet. That was why I'd swung by one of L.A.'s many prop shops on my way to Ellington's.

The elevator door parted to reveal a brightly lit hallway with gleaming white marble floors. A sign pointed me to the left, and I found Ellington's office about halfway down the hall. Throwing on my best no-nonsense face, I pushed through the glass door and entered the waiting room. The lone patient, a woman in jeans and a light blue peasant top, looked up briefly from her magazine. I approached the receptionist, a woman in her mid-thirties with short, sandy blonde hair and glasses.

When she asked if she could help me, I adopted what I hoped was a tough but non-threatening pose.

"Detective Flanagan to see Dr. Ellington, please." I cringed a little at my choice of surnames. An Irish cop? Could I have been any more stereotypical? But that, combined with the piece of tin I flashed, seemed to work. The receptionist swallowed and licked her lips while suddenly needing to straighten out some paperwork. So police made her nervous. Now why would that be? Could the faithful assistant have been Ellington's accomplice?

"He's ... he's with a patient at the moment," she finally managed to say.

"This will just take a moment. Unless, of course, he'd prefer to come down to the station."

I looked her in the eyes without wavering until she excused herself. She walked down a small hallway, disappeared into one of the exam rooms and returned a moment later wearing a tight-lipped smile as she opened the door to the inner office. We walked past a couple exam rooms where one patient was being x-rayed and another was fully reclined while a hygienist, armed with something sharp and metal, looked into his open mouth.

The receptionist stopped at a small office and pointed to a chair opposite the desk. "He'll be right with you."

I sat and took a deep breath. The all-too-familiar antiseptic aroma of dental products filled the air. Chemicals. Denise had keeled over like someone who'd been drugged. A dentist would know which ones were safe to use on people and, more importantly, which ones weren't. Suddenly, I was even more interested in Dr. Ellington .

"Detective Flanagan?"

Ellington was tall, tanned, and had dark hair graying at the temples. It was easy to imagine someone like Denise hanging on his arm. Dressed in light blue scrubs, he moved with confidence as he approached me and shook my hand before taking a seat at his desk. He smiled at me as if I were a nervous patient instead of a cop who had just dropped in unannounced.

"What brings you by?"

I struggled to regain my all-business persona. "You're acquainted with Denise Ladd?"

"Yes, we were seeing each other."

Were. With the loss of his girlfriend so fresh, I would've expected him to use the present tense, only to correct himself, but Ellington had already relegated her to the past. Interesting. "Do you have any idea who'd want to harm Ms. Ladd?"

"I've been asking myself that very question, and I'm not aware of a single enemy. As far as I know, everyone loved Denise."

He was cool, too cool. Rehearsed even. Clearly, he'd been expecting this little visit. "You say you were seeing Ms. Ladd, but you're married, aren't you, doctor?"

Again with the calming smile. "My wife and I are in the process of splitting up."

"In the process of," I repeated. In other words, he was fooling around. "How were you and Ms. Ladd getting along? Had you fought recently?"

"As a matter of fact, things had never been better."

Then why had Denise written a note saying she'd forgiven him? "When was the last time you saw Ms. Ladd?"

"We had dinner at DiMassi's ..." He paused to think. "Three ... no, four nights ago."

"That long? It doesn't sound to me like you were seeing each other."

He cleared his throat and looked away. It was the first chink I'd seen in his facade. "I'm sorry, Miss...?"

"Detective. Flanagan."

"Right. May I ask what that has to do with Denise's death, Detective Flanagan?"

"It's a routine question," I said, and then I remembered a line from a TV show. "I'm just trying to rule you out as a suspect."

"Perhaps I need to contact my lawyer."

He reached across the desk for his phone. Next to it was a computer with cables connecting him to the office network and a tiny, silver hub plugged into one of the USB ports in the back.

A couple years earlier, when a job took me to a diamond trader's office in Orange County, I saw those on the backs of all the computers. It turned out they were listening devices the owner used to check up on his employees. But Ellington wasn't some desk jockey; he ran the place. If anything, he should've been the one doing the snooping. So who had bugged his office?

I opened up the camera on my phone, put the shutter on a five-second delay, and laid the phone on the desk with the lens aimed at the back of Ellington's computer. Then I pretended to be hunting for something in my purse while the phone counted down to the moment it harmlessly snapped a picture of the hub.

Ellington had finished dialing and was waiting for someone to pick up. He exhaled, his forehead creasing.

"That won't be necessary," I said. "I have everything I need for now. Thank you for your cooperation, doctor. I'll see myself out."

He nodded, but it seemed more like an involuntary reflex than anything else. I followed the hallway back to the receptionist and thanked her for her assistance. There were a few more patients in the waiting room, and on the way out, I nearly collided with a guy in a suit making his way in. Unfortunately for him and the others waiting, I had a feeling Ellington would be running behind on his next few appointments. If my hunch was right, I also needed to hurry up and tap into that bug.

The elevator arrived to take me back to the ground floor,

and no sooner had I stepped aboard than the guy in the suit came bursting out of Ellington's office.

"Ma'am?" he shouted in a way that made it clear he was not in a good mood. "I need you to stop. Right. Now!" He pulled his jacket to the side. Clipped to his belt was a police badge, presumably a real one.

I stabbed the "close door" button repeatedly. The cop ran toward the elevator, but the doors thumped shut and the car began its descent. I just knew he'd be waiting for me at the first floor, but when the doors parted, there were only civilians in the lobby. I hurried out the door and down the street.

"You!"

I looked back and saw the cop running full tilt after me. My car was parked across the street, more than a block away. No way was I going to make it, especially if I waited at the intersection for the light to change. That left me with one option.

It wasn't really a break in the traffic—more like an awkward pause—but I dashed out anyway. Brakes squealed. Horns blasted. One motorist wondered, in very colorful language, what I was doing, but by then I'd reached the grassy median and was eyeing the traffic coming from the opposite direction.

A steady stream of sporty cars and jumbo SUVs whooshed by, whipping my dress in the resulting breeze. Behind me, the cop was taking a more prudent approach to running out into traffic. He stood on the curb, waving at traffic with one hand while holding his badge aloft with the other. Gradually, people got the hint. With his path clear, he started across, leaving me no choice.

I stepped off the median and into the nearest lane. A white convertible slammed on its brakes.

"LAPD!" the cop shouted. "Stop right now!"

Seeing me standing there, the drivers in the two other lanes stopped, and I dashed safely to the other side. But my car was still too far away, and I was on the verge of waving the white flag, when a blue Fiat came to an abrupt halt.

"Need a lift?"

Broussard. Of all the people to come to my rescue.

I hopped in and she floored it just as the cop reached the other side of the street. "Where to?"

"Just drive."

I took out my phone, pulled up the photo from Ellington's office, and zoomed in on the bug until I could make out the markings. It was a Vogler. My phone's signal was patchy, but I successfully downloaded the company's app and entered the bug's serial number from the photo. While the app struggled to connect, I untangled a pair of earphones from my purse and plugged them in.

"Come on," I muttered while looking at the little "I'm thinking" icon spinning away on my screen.

"What's up?" Broussard asked. Her outfit, jeans and a t-shirt, was similar to the one she'd worn two days earlier, but this time she was wearing a faded black hat featuring a San Francisco Giants logo. As an Angeleno, she should've been repping the Dodgers, but that was Broussard: a traitor, through and through.

"Just doing some homework."

I stuffed the buds into my ears. At first, all I heard was muffled traffic, then a male voice came through. The sound was tinny and kept breaking up.

"... I don't know ... just left ..."

It was Ellington. He was keeping his voice down, but even so, he sounded panicked. Was it my visit that had shaken him up, or the one from the real cop? Maybe the police were looking at him as a suspect in Denise's death after all.

"... still at her place ... I-I think—"

A shadow passed overhead and I lost my connection again.

I looked up to see that we were passing beneath the 405. "Broussard, speed up! I can't get a signal in the underpass."

She frowned. "Uh, you're welcome, by the way."

"Yeah, yeah. Much obliged and all that. But why were you following me in the first place? Or did you just happen to be in the neighborhood?"

She shrugged and punched the gas. Once we were free from the underpass, my phone regained its signal.

"... get it back." Ellington paused and then uttered a couple *mm-hmm's* before saying, "You're right. Just like Delta house."

Get what back? The necklace? Was that what was "still at her place?" I wished I could've heard the rest of the conversation, but the bug only picked up whatever took place in Ellington's office.

He ended the call and spent the next minute or so tapping at his keyboard before walking out of his office.

"Did you get what you need?" Broussard asked. We were on Santa Monica Boulevard, approaching the Century City mall.

"Pull in here!"

She did, and I had the door open as the car was rolling to a stop.

"Thanks. I got it from here."

"No problem. Soo ..."

I looked over my shoulder to see her beaming at me.

"... this means we're a team again, right?"

Ulterior motives. I should've known.

"Actually, I think this makes us about even for the alarm thing."

6

It was after lunch and the mall's outdoor food court had emptied, so I found a seat and tuned back into the chip, but if Ellington had made any more phone calls, he'd done so from somewhere besides his office. Based on the snippets of conversation I'd heard, I couldn't imagine he and whoever he was talking to had been discussing anything other than the necklace. But why? Hadn't it been a gift for Denise? Then why was a third-party involved?

Those were just some of the questions racing through my mind, but ultimately none of that concerned me. I just needed to get Trammell's necklace back, and Ellington thought it was still at Denise's place, so that's where I was going.

I called for a car that took me back to Brentwood, and after twenty nerve-racking minutes of watching the area for the cop who'd chased me, I decided it was safe to reclaim my car.

Traffic on the 405 totally sucked, and the afternoon was fading by the time I made it back down to Manhattan Beach. Of course that meant all the good parking spaces near Denise's building were taken. I found a spot about a half mile away and walked back to the complex, feeling every bit like the frazzled, weary cubicle jockey I was about to pretend to be.

A pair of palm trees flanked the entrance to the complex. Lanterns mounted to the walls above the trees provided the area with plenty of light, while a security camera kept watch over people coming and going through the front door. I lowered my head to hide my face and rummaged through my purse. I kept that up for a good two minutes before someone— a guy, thankfully—exited the complex.

As he opened the door, I gave him my best "pity me" face. "You're a lifesaver! I … I think I lost my keys."

He smiled, revealing a missing upper tooth, and held the door open so I could enter.

"Thank you so much!" I said.

"De nada," he replied. His hoodie obscured most of his brown, scruffy facial hair, and despite the hour, he was wearing shades—typical of the wannabe surfers populating the South Bay. Maybe he'd stand out in Joplin, Missouri, but you couldn't toss a slingback without hitting a guy like him in L.A.

Denise's apartment number was number 312, so I took the elevator to the third floor, and then followed the hallway, taking note of the locks on the doors. The door handle lock would be no problem—I can open one of those with a dull number-two pencil. Same with the dead bolt, but as it turned out, I didn't need to worry about either one. The apartment door stood ajar, and through the crack, I saw that a light was on. Slowly, I pushed the door open, and my eyes widened.

Someone had tossed the place. The couch was upside down and the coffee table was on its side, a handful of magazines and assorted papers scattered on the floor. A framed picture of the Santa Monica Pier at sunset lay on the ground, having been ripped from the wall.

"Hello?" I called out.

No reply.

My heart revved like a race car. After checking the hall, I slipped on my gloves and stepped inside, shut the door behind me, and was walloped by the smell. Someone had used the place for a toilet. I thought back to yesterday's news reports, recalling the picture of Denise holding a Yorkshire Terrier. The poor thing had been trapped in here with no one to feed it or take it outside for a walk.

Forgetting my original purpose, I stepped over and around throw pillows, plants, books, and some assorted clothes, looking for the Yorkie. There was no sign of it in the living room, so I moved on to the bathroom. None of the towels, shower bottles, or medicine cabinet contents were where they should've been. Whoever had paid the apartment a visit didn't do subtle. Finally, I gave the bedroom a shot. The mattress was lying askew on top of a beautiful cherry wood sleigh bed. The comforter and sheets were in a disheveled heap and partially off the bed. I kneeled to peek under the bed and spotted Denise's little Yorkie huddled in a ball and shivering as if it were fastened to a block of ice.

"Hi," I said gently.

The dog stared at me but didn't approach.

"Did I scare you?" Or had the previous visitor done that?

After a few unsuccessful attempts at coaxing the little one out, I returned to the kitchen. It was in the same condition as the rest of the apartment. Drawers were either hanging open or had been chucked aside, and the floor was littered with silverware, a wine opener, and a few broken dishes. Was this Ellington's handiwork—or the person he'd been talking to?—as he'd desperately searched for the necklace? What if I was too late?

An entire bag of dog food littered the kitchen floor, apparently having been emptied by the interloper. By the dog food's amber color and pyramid shape, I could tell it was Perfect Balance, the same organic brand I bought for Whimsy.

At the base of the wall opposite the dining table was a red

plastic double feeder, with both of its round receptacles empty. I picked it up. It was heavier than it should've been, and it rattled. I brushed the edges with my fingertips until I felt a tiny bump. When I pushed it, the bowl's false bottom popped open, revealing the necklace. Denise must have had a break-in before if she was resorting to such a clever hiding place.

I stuffed the necklace in my purse, then put food and water in the bowl, brought it back to the bedroom, and pushed it under the bed. The Yorkie eyed me for a few seconds longer before taking a tentative nibble and then another. While the dog ate, I took a moment to inspect the necklace. I was still underwhelmed, but clearly it did something for Trammell. No accounting for taste, so the saying went.

Once the Yorkie moved from its crouch, I figured out it was a male. What I hadn't figured out was what to do next. I couldn't just leave him here, but my place wasn't an option either, not once I got Whimsy back, which was my next order of business. She was pretty territorial and wouldn't take kindly to a stranger pushing her off her square, even one so harmless.

I operate on the belief that I use my hands to get in and my ears to stay out—out of a squad car. Or jail. Or trouble. No matter what I'm doing with my hands, my ears are somewhere completely different, doing their own thing. I can be deciphering the wiring of an alarm system and tell whether the faint wail several blocks away is a police siren or an ambulance. Or I could be sitting here feeding a dog that lost his mom and pick up on someone trying to sneak into the apartment.

The telltale sign was the faint click of the latch against the frame produced when you push on the door without fully twisting the knob first.

The Yorkie stopped eating and stared at me. I hoped feeding him had put me in his good graces, because right then the only hiding place had time to reach without being spotted was under the bed. I turned on my stomach and slid beneath the bed's wooden frame, an arm's length away from the once-again frightened Yorkie.

From my vantage point, I could see down the short hall and into the living room, but the comforter dangling off the bed kept me from seeing anything higher than a foot or so off the ground. Someone in jeans and sneakers crossed my field of vision, crushing a candle and some papers on their way to the kitchen.

Denise's place sure was popular tonight, and I doubted that was a coincidence. More and more, I wondered how such an ordinary piece of jewelry could be worth all the fuss. A trip to the jewelry district would've been much easier and yielded better results.

Finished in the kitchen, the apartment's latest visitor came back into view and headed down the hall. My chest, pressed to the floor, throbbed with every thump of my heart. The intruder's shoes — a pair of stained Nikes that had seen better days — paused at the doorway to the bedroom. With a sigh, the person backtracked down the hall and left as quietly as he'd come in. Time spent in the apartment: less than two minutes. I could only guess that one look at the damage had told him that he had been too late to find whatever it was he'd been after.

The Yorkie and I weren't in a hurry to come out of hiding. For my part, I was listening. Maybe he or she suspected someone was in the apartment and had only pretended to leave so I'd reveal myself. If that were the case, someone was currently in the living room impersonating a statue, but unless the intruder was a ninja or seriously into yoga, standing perfectly still for long would be nearly impossible. After just a few seconds, most people can't believe how stiff their joints feel, and their back muscles tighten up. For no reason, their neck starts to itch. A chair nearby looks *so* inviting. Then they decide to shift their weight, and that's when a knee pops or a foot slips. Not much, but enough to give them away.

After several minutes without a stray sound, I pushed out from under the bed. As I did, my foot caught on something and sent it skidding across the floor. A white, leather-bound book spun to a stop in the middle of the room. The cover was blank, but it looked like the one I'd owned in high school. I picked it up and quickly confirmed it was a journal.

Just holding it gave me a creepy feeling as I recalled the kind of stuff I used to write in my journal. I really didn't want to violate Denise's privacy any more than I already had. I knew she wasn't likely to complain given her current condition, but it still felt wrong. On the other hand, what if there was something in there that might explain all of this? Or any of it?

With a deep breath and a promise to volunteer at a soup kitchen or something to make up for snooping, I opened the journal and flipped through the pages.

As I'd feared, some of the entries were really personal, including entries about her grandfather's worsening diabetes, disappointment with an uncle who'd fallen off the wagon, and frustration over her career. I found the last one odd, but maybe she'd written it before Trammell had cast her in his movie. On several dates, all she'd written down were the initials T.E. and a time, like 8:00 p.m. or noon — her get-togethers with Tad Ellington.

Something else that appeared regularly — every two weeks, in fact — was "Payday!" Another smiley face or an LOL usually accompanied the note. I liked paydays as much as the next person, but they weren't something that typically inspired laughter.

I flipped through the journal, which was about two-thirds full — she was fond of adorning her notes with smileys, hearts, plus signs and other symbols. When I reached the blank pages, I found several glossy photos tucked inside. One was her head-shot, some were of her with her Yorkie, and a few more were of her and Ellington. The last item in the journal was a black business card with "Aubrey Hilliard. Accountant" stenciled in silver letters.

Something brushed my leg and I jumped. The Yorkie, out of hiding, was standing with its front paws on me. I reached down, and after the required sniff of my hand, he gave it a lick. Go ahead and call me crazy, but I swear he smiled at me.

"Okay, fine." I bent down for a closer look at the shiny, silver tag on its collar. "Yoda? You're coming with me, but only until I can figure out what to do with you."

7

The next morning, I was a girl on a mission. Several of them actually.

First, I fed Yoda and took him for a walk. He was a head-turner, drawing no fewer than four compliments in the short time we were out. Back in my apartment, Trammell called, from a blocked number no less.

"Good morning, Ms. Albertson!" He was awfully chipper for someone who'd just lost one of the stars of his movie. "Do you have the item?"

"I do."

"What say I swing by around noon and pick it up?"

"What say we meet somewhere public?"

He chuckled. "Prudent. How about Hollywood and Highland? It's out in the open with plenty of people around. You should feel safe there."

"Perfect," I said, then changed the subject. "I didn't know you were a filmmaker, Trammell. When did that happen?"

His end of the line grew silent, and I nearly repeated the question.

"It's a small project," he finally said. "Noon, then?"

"Yeah. Sure."

He'd been so pompous during his unannounced drop-in at my apartment. Same thing when he showed up on the news — like someone who had trouble shutting up — but now he was giving me the brush-off? It was odd, but I didn't have time to dwell on it.

I swung by the vet-slash-groomer's office where Jill, who always took good care of Whim, worked. She was surprised to see me, especially with a dog that wasn't mine in my arms.

"Hey there, Kate! Who's this?"

I stroked Yoda's fur as I introduced him. His spirits had lifted since I found him huddled under Denise's bed, and he'd eaten that morning as though nothing was wrong.

"I think he's lost and I was wondering if you could see if he has a microchip. There's a phone number on his ID tag, but no one's answering."

Jill pursed her lips. "No problem. I'll have one of the techs scan him. Sometimes people list a second contact number for emergencies and stuff."

That's exactly what I was counting on. As I handed Yoda over, I promised I'd be back for him, and then headed for the Santa Monica address listed on the business card I'd found in Denise's journal.

On the way, I turned on the radio and was greeted by one of the morning shows that are usually off the air by the time I get out of bed. I hadn't been missing much. The hosts were DJ Saul, who reminded me of a guy in high school who thought gluing lockers shut was funny, and Laura Pepper, hence the show's name, Saul 'n Pepper in the Morning. With her husky voice, Laura was going for sultry, but I just thought she sounded like someone in need of a cough drop. Normally, that sort of shtick would've held my attention for about eight seconds, but they too were getting in on the media frenzy surrounding Denise.

"Isn't it bizarre-o?" croaked Laura. "The way she just keeled over like that?"

"Well, have you heard the latest?" Saul asked.

"What?"

"An anonymous source at the medical examiner's office told TMZ the police will probably be treating her death as a homicide."

Laura gasped. "No way!"

"I know it's TMZ, but they get it right a lot of the time."

"Wow! I bet the cops really want to talk to that *person of interest* now," Laura said, in a way that likely involved exaggerated air quotes.

I turned the radio off but couldn't get Laura's voice out of my head, and not just because it annoyed me. She had a point. As far as the cops knew, the only thing connecting the drop-dead gorgeous Denise and the Denise who dropped dead was me, and they were bound to investigate that link.

Aubrey Hilliard's office was in a small, older two-story complex at the top of a hill, with about eight units total. The building had a view of the ocean, and with its nearest neighbor —a white, rectangular apartment building—about a hundred yards away on another hill, it was probably pretty quiet too.

The third unit on the ground floor belonged to Aubrey. I knocked and poked my head inside.

The office was small but bright, with a boatload of SoCal sun streaming in through a large picture window. Just in front of the window was a cherry wood desk, and sitting behind it was a pretty, auburn-haired woman about my age.

She was working at her computer but stopped to give me her full attention. "Can I help you?"

In a long-sleeved, blue-and white-striped t-shirt and jeans, she didn't exactly look like an accountant. Or sound like one. There was a duskiness to her voice. Unlike the woman on the radio, Aubrey's was a voice I wouldn't have minded listening to.

"You're Aubrey?" I asked.

"So it says on the lease. And you are?"

I sat in one of the two guest chairs facing the desk. "I'm Kate."

"Okay. And what can I do for you, Kate?"

"Well ... I was wondering what you can tell me about Denise Ladd."

"Denise Ladd?"

"She died yesterday at the mall."

"Right. I heard about that on the news." Aubrey shook her head the way people do whenever they want you to know they're sympathetic. "It's just awful, but what makes you think I can tell you anything about her?"

"She's got the cutest little Yorkshire Terrier. Have you met him?" I asked.

"No, I haven't."

"After I heard about Denise, you know, dying, I thought I should check in on him. When I was at her apartment, I noticed she had one of your business cards."

Aubrey remained silent, processing what I'd just told her. I wasn't being completely forthcoming, but I hadn't exactly lied to her either.

"So," she said, "you're a friend of Denise's?"

"Yeah, we worked on some shoots together." *Now* I was lying.

"You're kinda short for a model, aren't you?"

I shrugged. "I just go where the agency sends me."

She gave me a sideways look that suggested she wasn't convinced. "Suppose I do know something about her. Why should I tell you?"

"Because I'm about to tell you how you can keep all of this nice office equipment from constantly walking off."

Aubrey's eyes grew as big as ostrich eggs. "How do you know about that?"

I pointed at the heavy-duty cable locks anchoring her computer, monitor, printer, and a few other things. "Nobody buys those unless they're having a ... security issue. Probably on multiple occasions, right?"

She nodded.

"And every time it happens, there's no sign of forced entry. Right again?"

Another nod.

"What you need aren't these silly locks. It's a privacy screen on that big, beautiful window behind you."

She turned, inspected the window, and spun back to me. "But how—"

"It's like this: you have an awesome view of the ocean, but the rest of the world has an awesome view of your office, including your security alarm panel." I directed her attention to the panel mounted on the wall just inside the door. "Someone's been watching your office, and when you get here in the morning or come back from lunch—"

"I walk through the door, punch in the security code."

"And now whoever's got eyes on your building knows the code. All they have to do is pick the lock — which should take a halfway competent thief about thirty-two seconds — and they're in. That's the problem with these older buildings. I'd guess that the perp is in one of those apartments across the way."

Aubrey stared out the window again. "Way over there?"

"You'd be amazed at the range of certain binoculars. Some even have cameras. The management here really ought to replace the windows, but if they won't do that —"

"Privacy screen." She sat back in her chair and looked me over. "How do you know all this?"

"It's an area of interest," I said.

"Uh huh."

"So, Denise?"

She sighed. "I wish I could help you out, but I can't. I ... I could lose my license."

"Um, Aubrey? That already happened."

As a young, impressionable certified public accountant working at one of the studios, Aubrey Hilliard got mixed up with an exec who screwed up big time on a deal he'd cut with some overseas investors. He persuaded Aubrey to cook the books so things wouldn't look so bad, promising to leave his wife so the two of them could be together, as long as he got the deal to work. In the end, the money guys discovered they'd been had and told someone at the Times. The exec and Aubrey got canned, but the exec landed at another studio while Aubrey, having lost the "certified public" part of her title, had to accept whatever bookkeeping work she could find. It was probably a lot easier hiding little indiscretions like hers before Google happened.

I told her I knew her story and quickly added, "Hey, I'm not judging. I just want to piece some things together."

"Why are you so interested? And don't give me some BS about knowing Denise from a photo shoot."

"All right, fine. But do you swear this is just between us girls?"

She nodded. I had a good feeling about her. She'd done something stupid and had paid a heavy price for it by throwing away a career she'd spent years training for, and for what? Some guy who probably wasn't fit to be stuck to the bottom of her shoe? Despite all that, she didn't come across as bitter. This is going to sound like one of those California things, but she had good energy, so I decided to be straight with her, hoping she'd do the same.

"I work in ... acquisitions."

Confusion arrived on her face but slowly gave way to realization. Her jaw dropped open, then she snatched her purse from the desk, threw it in a drawer, and slammed it shut.

"Oh, please," I said. "I'm not some meth-addled klepto. I'm a professional. That's why I gave you the loss-prevention tip. You're welcome for that, by the way."

"How do I know you're not the one who's been breaking in here?"

"Because instead of saying anything, I would've kept on robbing you blind."

She smiled and some of the tension left her shoulders. "Thanks for your help, Kate, but I don't know what I can do—"

"I'm in the middle of a job that you could say has gone a tad askew, and now the cops think I had something to do with Denise's seriously untimely demise."

Aubrey's hand flew to her mouth. "You? You're the one on the news?"

"Yeah, and it's fifteen minutes I could do without. I'm more of an under-the-radar kind of girl."

"I bet."

"So, if there's anything you can tell me about her, I'd really appreciate it."

"Look, I still have a few studio contacts. A while back, one of them sent Trammell Preston my way. He needed someone to keep the books for this movie he's producing. I handle payroll, see that expenses get paid, that sort of thing. Pretty basic stuff, but it helps keep a roof over my head, you know?"

I nodded. "And Denise was on the payroll? That's what I gathered from Trammell's speech on the news last night."

"She sure was. Got paid every two weeks like the rest of the cast and crew."

"What kind of movie is this?" I asked out of curiosity more than anything. My guess was a slasher. Denise had seemed perfect for the role of the home-alone girl who gets whacked in the second-to-last scene.

Aubrey shrugged. "All I know for sure is that, based on expenses, it's pretty low-budget."

"So Trammell wants to make movies, but he's not putting too much of his fortune at risk."

"Trammell's not putting any of his fortune at risk. The money is coming from a couple other guys. Ellington —"

"Ellington? Tad Ellington?"

"That's him."

The same guy who'd purchased Trammell's stolen necklace was helping finance Trammell's movie? What were the odds of that?

"And the other guy?"

"Richard Spencer. Anyway, Kate, that's what I know."

Whether she'd given me anything to work with remained to be seen, but at least I knew something I hadn't when I'd walked in: the names of the people funding Trammell's movie. I stood and took in the view from Aubrey's window of the waves splashing ashore. "I really appreciate your help. We should do happy hour sometime. My treat."

"Yeah?"

"Yeah. We'll have margaritas and check out cute boys."

She laughed. "It's a date."

8

I parked the Chevy at a grocery store and had a car take me to Hollywood and Highland, an outdoor shopping complex popular with visitors despite its gaudy mash-up of architecture. I arrived at the shopping center a half hour early and used the time to look around — no sign of Trammell, but there were plenty of tourists buying overpriced leather goods and sunglasses — before settling into a quiet section on level three that overlooked the area below where we'd agreed to meet. He was turning out to be a real wild card. One capable of murder? I couldn't rule it out, and no way was I letting him sneak up on me again.

Business was good and the shopping center was packed, but Trammell — right on time — stood out among all the people streaming back and forth. Once again, he was wearing slacks and a blazer, rather than the shorts and t-shirts favored by most, and his hands were free of shopping bags. Looking down at him, I saw that his light brown hair was thinning on top.

He stopped in front of the rendezvous point, a boutique that specialized in trendy French shoes. I didn't see any sign of my dog, which told me I'd been right to be suspicious. I looked around for an accomplice — someone trailing him or standing off to the side — but if Trammell had a partner, he was keeping to the background. He spent a few seconds searching the crowd before checking his watch and then making a phone call. I thought he might be calling me to ask where I was, but my phone didn't ring. After a few more minutes, I took the escalator down to the second level and again surveyed the area for signs that something was amiss before walking up behind him.

"Where's Whimsy?"

He jumped but quickly regained his composure and smiled. "Do you have my necklace?"

"I'm here, aren't I?"

"No need to get testy. I just wanted to be certain," he said. "After all, you are known for dealing in deception."

This from the guy who'd swiped someone else's patent, which I absolutely believed at this point. "Pot? Meet Kettle."

He laughed again. "It's too bad we couldn't have met under different circumstances."

Circumstances like him tied to a fire ant mound and me holding a bottle of syrup? "Can we get on with it? I've got things to do."

"I'm sure. You're in high demand these days."

He briefly looked past me before reestablishing eye contact. It could've been nothing — maybe just a hot girl in a mini dress — but I got the sudden urge to know what was going on behind me. Looking at the reflection in the shoe store's window (and barely noticing those suede, polka dot pumps), I indeed noticed a hot girl— in jeans and stilettos, though — but to her right, two cops were heading my way.

"Trammell!"

He reached for me, but I slipped his grasp and ducked in between shoppers. The cops, previously walking, graduated to a run. I took off, bumping into a middle-aged couple coming out of the shoe store. In an instant, chaos erupted, with Trammell coming at me from one direction and the cops from another, while dozens of people holding Starbucks cups or Victoria's Secret bags tried to figure out what was happening.

I hurried toward the escalator. If I could make it down to the street level, maybe I'd get lucky and snag a waiting cab. I got to the escalator, but it was full of passengers. Even if I pushed my way through, it would've taken forever to reach the bottom. The other side was just as crowded, so running down the up-escalator wasn't an option either.

One of the cops, a little overweight and not looking happy about having to run for something other than donuts, shouted, "Police! Surrender yourself now!"

As he and his partner closed in, he added, "That's an order!"

Oh. Well that changes everything. Not.

A strip of polished silver connected the two escalators, sloping toward the ground floor like a giant playground slide. I hopped aboard, pushed off, and sailed between two streams of stunned escalator riders. Approaching fast was the first of several round, metal speed-bump-type things, probably designed to discourage people from taking this very route. Pushing up with my hands, I lifted my butt and did a little bunny-hop over the first speed bump. A half-second later, another bunny-hop, and then a third, and so on until I reached the ground level, where some people actually clapped for me. You have to love L.A.

I dismounted from the slide and wasted no time getting to the street. Not a cab in sight.

"Shoot!"

Back upstairs, the less portly of the two cops — he probably preferred protein bars to pastries — was preparing to slide down the way I had, while his partner excused his way through the cluster of shoppers packed onto the escalator. I took off down the block, but even with a head start and sensible shoes, I couldn't outrun them for long. At the corner, I thought about turning right, but a little voice told me to keep going straight.

I listened to the little voice. She's usually right.

Ahead, a street vendor was selling t-shirts, hats, and sweats. A pink hoodie, spread open to reveal "Hollywood" written in graphic print, sat atop a stack of folded merchandise. It looked about my size, so I grabbed it.

"How much?" I asked the vendor, a teenage kid wearing a backwards ball cap.

"Fifteen or two for twenty-five," he said.

The first bill I found in my purse was a twenty. "Keep it."

I was temporarily blinded as I tugged the shirt over my head, but I kept moving. The fit was loose, and it wasn't much as far as disguises went, but it might be enough to throw them off.

Or not.

I chanced a look back through the tangle of humanity and saw Officer Protein Bar jostling his way past pedestrians, gaining ground. I froze, but just for a moment. I was near the subway station. That's what the little voice had been trying to tell me.

I ran for the entrance and flew down the escalator steps, nearly losing my balance on the way to the subway platform. I was in luck. According to the overhead monitor, the south-bound train was less than a minute out. Stepping around a homeless guy, I shoved money into the vending machine, snatched my ticket, pushed through the turnstile and hurried down the escalator. A small crowd gathered as a gust of wind blew from the tunnel ahead and then light from the oncoming subway appeared.

When the train arrived and its doors opened, everyone lurched forward. My insides turned as I kept watch on the escalator, expecting to see Officer Not-So-Friendly at any second. Moving with the crowd, I shuffled toward the door when it hit me: All the cops would've needed to do was radio ahead and there'd be another boy in blue at the next stop, waiting to fit me with handcuffs. I ducked out of line and scanned the station for another option, a place where I could disappear.

Nearby, a homeless guy reclined against a concrete pillar. He looked as if he hadn't bathed in weeks and smelled even worse, but at that moment, he might as well have been Prince Charming.

"Hey," I said.

He looked up at me with glassy eyes.

"Want to make—" I rifled through my purse again. "Thirteen dollars?"

Just like that, he sobered up. "Hell yeah." He sounded as if he had rust on his vocal chords.

I tore off the hoodie and handed it over. "Put this on and get on that train."

Getting to his feet was a chore. I checked the escalator again. No cops, but a voice from the loudspeaker announced that the train's doors were about to close. He slipped the hoodie on and held his arms out. Yes, he actually checked himself out. The sleeves were a little short, but otherwise, the fit wasn't bad. I pulled the hood over his head, then pressed the ticket and money into his hand. "Go. Hurry!"

Hurry wasn't exactly in his vocabulary, but with a crooked smile, he shuffled across the platform and boarded the train seconds before the doors slid shut.

I took refuge in a corner behind a row of vending machines just as Protein Bar came bustling down the elevator stairs. He looked left and right, then at the train, which pulled forward and gradually disappearing into the tunnel. He peered through the windows of each passing car, and in the second-to-last one, spotted a lone figure slumped in a seat, wearing a pink hoodie.

The cop stomped his foot and swore. He turned toward the

escalator, nearly bumping into his slower-moving partner, who had just arrived on the scene.

I stayed put until well after they'd vacated the station. Then I bought another ticket and, three minutes later, boarded a train headed in the opposite direction.

9

No wonder Trammell had been so willing to meet in a supposedly safe location. The whole thing was a set up.

I'd avoided drawing attention to myself, and I doubted the two cops had recognized me based on that less-than-flattering security footage from the Manhattan Beach mall. So the question wasn't whether Trammell had tipped them off — probably with the phone call he'd made after reaching the rendezvous point — but why? He didn't have any reason to believe I'd double cross him, so why bring cops into this? If they'd grabbed me, his necklace would have then been in their possession, at least temporarily while it sat in an evidence locker. Had he overlooked that part?

The train took me to North Hollywood, and from there I returned to the grocery store where I'd left the Chevy. The interior was warm from the afternoon sun. I drove back to the vet's office to see what Jill had found out. When I walked in, she was busy clipping the nails of a German Shepherd, so I took a seat near the window and waited. When she finished, she came over to me, carrying a computer printout.

She took the seat beside me and said, "It looks like your little friend belonged to someone named Denise Ladd."

I nodded. I knew all about Denise, but I'd been hoping for some additional information.

As I looked at the printout, I said, "That's the same number as the one on his ID tag."

"But there's a second number in the database." Jill pointed farther down the page. "An emergency contact: Michelle Ladd."

Bingo! "That must be her mother, or maybe her sister."

Jill shrugged. "That's what I thought."

"Would it be all right if I delivered the good news?" I asked.

Jill handed me the printout. "Sure."

"Thank you so much!" I gave her a hug and started for my car.

Before I reached the door, Jill called out to me, "I'll see you next Thursday for Whimsy's shampoo next week."

"Right. Thursday. See you then." Assuming I had her back by then.

I took Yoda to my car and promptly called the emergency number on the printout — an 818 number. The Valley. After a few rings, someone picked up.

"Hello?" a woman answered. She didn't sound especially young or old.

My stomach tumbled. "Hi, is this Michelle?"

Following a brief pause, she replied. "Yes. Who is this?"

"My name's Ka ... Theresa, and I have a little Yorkshire Terrier that—"

"Yoda?" she cried. "You found Yoda?"

"Well, I ..." Found wasn't exactly accurate, but this wasn't the time for semantics. "Yes. I took him to a vet and they scanned his microchip. You were listed as an emergency ..."

I heard sniffles.

"Are you okay?"

"I'm sorry," she said. "I just can't believe what's happened …"

I wanted to tell her she didn't have to apologize, that I was the one who was sorry for calling during such a horrible time, but I couldn't let on that I knew about the murder. As far as Michelle was concerned, I was just a Good Samaritan and not the woman wanted for questioning.

"You mean Yoda?" I asked, playing dumb. "Did he run away?"

"No, it's … it's a long story. But thank you. I'm glad you found him."

"I … If you want, I could bring him to you."

"Oh, that'd be wonderful!" she said, sounding happy for the first time since we'd started speaking. "I'm in Woodland Hills, though. I couldn't ask you to drive all the way out here."

"It's okay," I said. "It's the least I can do."

Michelle asked if I was sure and then gave me her address.

I hadn't been to the Valley in months, and now I was making my second trip of the day. Yoda and I crept through the gridlock that was the 405 before spooling through the interchange that put us on the 101. Even with the windows up and AC on, I could feel the temperature rising as we drove west toward Woodland Hills.

Michelle lived in a townhouse a few minutes off the freeway, and as the nav on my phone told me the address was a quarter mile away on the right, Yoda stood with his front paws on the window, his tail whipping back and forth as though he recognized his surroundings, which I took as a good sign.

I pulled up to a gated entrance and buzzed Michelle through the intercom.

"I'm in building J," she said.

She gave me directions as the gate slid open, and I followed a narrow path to the building. She was standing out front in jeans and a beige tunic. I would've bet money that Yoda had already maxed out his tail-wagging speed, but he grew even more animated when he saw her and, for the first time, I heard him bark.

I opened the door and he bounded across my lap, scurrying right up to Michelle.

"Yoda!" She gathered him in her arms and hugged him tight while he squirmed and wiggled, trying his best to lick her face. "I thought we'd lost you."

She gave him another squeeze before turning to me. I could see the resemblance between her and Denise: blonde, with the same pointed chin and pert nose, although Michelle was a little older, probably in her early thirties. She gave me a smile, but it was the kind that had to force its way out, and who could blame her? Two days ago, her sister had been alive and well and starring in a movie. Now, she'd been reduced to another sensational headline.

"Thank you so much," Michelle said, on the verge of tears.

"Really, it's nothing. I'm happy to do it."

"Where did you find him? After I talked to the police, I automatically assumed the worst — that someone had taken him ... or ... worse."

I nodded and then remembered I was supposed to be someone doing a good deed and that Denise's murder was news to me. "Police?"

"My sister was ... murdered. It's been on the news."

My jaw dropped, and it wasn't an act. As I looked into her weary eyes, reality came crashing down: Michelle wouldn't see her sister again. Ever. And the way she clung to Yoda gave me the idea that he was the only connection she had left to her. I blinked back tears.

"I'm so sorry," I said, and I meant it. I was sorry she'd lost her sister and that Yoda had lost his mom. I was sorry for my part in it, no matter how small.

The tears came faster than I could brush them away. My

outburst must have taken Michelle by surprise. She looked uncertain for a moment, then reached over and, with one arm holding Yoda, gave me a hug.

"This must be so awful for you," I said. "Do you have any other family here?"

We parted and she shook her head. "Our ... my parents live up north. Fairfield. They always hated us being so far away."

She told me she'd attended UCLA and had planned to go back to the Bay Area after college, but ended up staying when Denise had moved down looking to get into movies.

"She finally caught a break and then ..." Michelle's eyes welled up, but she didn't cry, thank goodness. If she had, I would've been a lost cause, too. "The police investigator asked me if I had any idea who would've wanted my sister dead. He even acted as if I'd done it, asking where I was when she died, whether we'd been fighting ..."

I put a hand on her arm to let her know she didn't have to go on. I knew how it felt to be wrongly accused.

"I loved my sister. She was a good kid. It was my birthday the other day, and she took the day off from her movie and flew me to Vegas. That's just how she was, you know?"

I nodded, even though my last birthday surprise was a balloon avalanche inside the Karmabile.

"I should probably get going," I said. "Traffic's going to be —" Jeez, I almost said murder. "Awful."

"Oh, of course. Thank you again. Really." She juggled Yoda while reaching for her purse. "I don't have much, but will you take—"

"I most certainly will not." I didn't even know how much she was going to offer me, and I didn't need to. "I'm just glad he'll be all right. He's such a sweetie. Bye Yoda."

The little Yorkie's eyes sparkled and he barked what I'm pretty sure meant, "Thanks for helping a dog out." Watching

Michelle cradle Yoda reminded me of Whim. I missed her and had to get her back.

I envied the bond Michelle and Denise had shared. I'm an only child, so I've never experienced any of the sister-to-sister moments like Michelle had on her birthday.

The way someone had taken Denise from Michelle and her parents, not to mention little Yoda, was all so wrong. My guess was that the lousy job of breaking the news to her family members had landed on Michelle's shoulders. What a terrible thing to have to do. I pounded my steering wheel. I didn't know who was behind this, but I couldn't believe Denise had done anything to deserve it. My tears threatened to return, but this time, anger was behind them. Finding out who had killed Denise was no longer just about getting myself off the hook.

I had no idea what move to make next, and I couldn't figure it out now. I was exhausted. All I wanted was a shower and a good night's sleep. Come morning, I'd deal with everything I'd gotten myself into.

Navigating traffic back to my neighborhood, I rounded a corner just off Wilshire and saw my street ahead. The mere thought of hot water cascading over my shoulders and down my back did wonders for my mood. I slowed for the turn and slammed on the brakes. The driver behind me leaned on the horn and swerved around me, calling me an idiot, modified by an obscene adjective, on his way by.

Twilight was setting in, but there was no mistaking what was parked in front of my apartment building: a squad car belonging to L.A.'s finest.

10

I drove past the intersection, circled the block, and came back for another look to make sure the cop was parked in front of my building and not the one next door. He could've been there for any number of reasons — domestic disturbance, a suspicious package, breaking up a party, though probably not at six in the evening — but given my brush with his colleagues just hours earlier, the smart money said the police were keeping an eye out for me.

The cop was just sitting there, staking the place out, so I drove to Jeremy's restaurant, a little pub in Fairfax. My last meal had been breakfast, and with everything that had gone down today, that half bagel felt like an eternity ago.

There was already a decent crowd on hand, but the second he laid eyes on me, Jeremy — his chef's coat open to reveal a worn, Jimi Hendrix t-shirt — guided me to a quiet table not far from the kitchen and then vanished, only to return moments later with a glass of white wine.

"I don't know what you've been up to, but you look like you need this."

"Thanks, J." I breathed in the light citrus scent before taking a sip. Pinot Grigio. The wine was a delicate mix of spice and fruit that warmed me from head to toe. "You're right. I needed that."

He left me with a menu and a plug for the special: hibachi grilled halibut.

The restaurant was animated, with conversations coming from every corner, but the couple sitting at the table across from the bar was talking more intimately. They leaned in toward each other as they spoke and exchanged smiles that could best be described as coy. It could've been a first date, but I imagined they were having an affair, like the one Denise had had with Ellington.

I was still an anonymous figure as far as everyone else was concerned, but Trammell knew my name and where I lived, and he'd all but admitted to paying off the department, so it must've been him who had set the police on me. All of a sudden, that was more important to him than his necklace. Maybe he'd changed his mind and didn't want it anymore, but I wanted Whimsy back — pronto. I didn't know what insanity I'd gotten myself mixed up in, but I needed to get busy sorting it out.

The halibut was otherworldly, and I left the restaurant feeling better by a mile, but the warm fuzzies didn't last. The cop was still camped out in front of my apartment, and that was really beginning to annoy. Was a quiet evening at home really asking too much? As I kept driving, I weighed my options and discovered that, sadly, I didn't have many. I could've called a friend and asked to spend the night, but as the subject of an APB, I thought it best not to drag anyone I knew into this mess. I also scratched the idea of sleeping in my car. Even if I parked in a filthy rich neighborhood like Trammell's, a mugger or, maybe worse, a meter maid could happen by while I was snoozing. That pretty much left me with springing for a hotel, only that would've meant providing my ID. Again, not something I wanted to do while the cops had me on their radar. There were some by-the-hour no-tells in Hollywood, but none were the kind of place I'd want to lay my head.

The Westcott in Beverly Hills, however, was exactly the kind of place I wouldn't mind spending an evening.

Using my phone, I looked up a local events website and found that the Westcott was hosting a cinematography conference, with a reception scheduled for that evening. I bypassed the valet in favor of the parking garage, took a ticket from the dispenser, and parked on the fourth level. An elevator carried me back to the ground floor and a side entrance led me into the lobby.

The lobby was oval-shaped and spacious, with a sweeping ceiling and a bronze marble floor polished to a high sheen. Dozens of men and women mingled about, chatting over drinks and appetizers that the serving staff shuttled back and forth. Adjacent to the lobby was the registration desk and to its left, a curved staircase, outfitted with a red, plush carpet, reached up to the second floor. I scanned the crowd and quickly spotted who I was looking for: a security guard. Watching over the crowd with less than a passing interest, he was at least six feet tall and thickly built. He wore a basic Men-In-Black ensemble, minus the shades, and an earpiece to stay in contact with the other suits.

I grabbed a drink and strode through the crowd. As I approached, he glanced down at me before returning his attention to the painful monotony of his work.

"This is beautiful," I said, taking in the surroundings.

"Hmm?"

"This is my first time here. I can't believe how beautiful everything is."

He nodded and tugged gently at the lapels of his jacket.

"I guess it's no big deal to you." My fingers traced a squiggly, bone-white sculpture. It didn't look like it'd be worth fifty bucks to any of the fences I knew, but I pretended to be intrigued. "You're probably used to all this by now."

"I suppose."

Okay, no one would ever confuse me for a Victoria's Secret model, but I like to believe I come in a reasonably attractive package. Plus, I was being friendly enough, yet Mr. Secret Service was giving me nothing. In hindsight, I should've tried asking him how much he bench pressed. He tugged again at his jacket, this time wincing as he did.

"Is everything all right?" I asked.

"It's my shoulder. Something wrong my circulation or something."

Hey, complete sentences! Sort of. Now that wasn't too hard, was it?

"Well, you're pretty muscular. You probably need a bigger jacket."

"I tried that, but it don't help."

I sighed. Language gets no respect. "Maybe you should try acupressure."

"What's that?"

"It's a time-tested healing art that uses the fingers to stimulate the body's natural ability to heal itself. Great for relieving pain, tension, and all that."

"Seriously?"

I nodded. "Seriously. You'll never fear formal occasions again."

A crooked grin crossed his face, calling to mind a jack-o-lantern. "That's funny."

Now that we'd bonded, I excused myself and crossed the lobby to the reception desk, which was staffed by, according to the name tag on his blazer, a college-aged kid named Scott. Unlike the security guard, the fit of his jacket wasn't giving him any trouble.

"Good evening, ma'am. Welcome to the Westcott. How can I help you?"

I reached into my purse, took out my wallet, and flipped it open, once more displaying my prop-shop badge. His eyes widened. To a twenty-year-old who'd seen the badge for all of two seconds, it looked legit.

"I'm Detective Theresa Flanagan, Vice. I hate to interrupt the festivities, but we have it on very good authority that a high-priced escort service has several of its girls here in attendance with the intention of targeting the conference's attendees."

"Oh."

"Yeah, it's a real high-class operation, Scott." I hoped I sounded appropriately tough. "I'd like to run a little sting oper-ation, with one of my male officers posing as a guest, and see if we can't make a few arrests. Their lawyer will have them out on bail tomorrow by lunchtime, but in the future they'll think twice about doing their business at the Westcott ... Scott. Anyway, we just need the use of a room for the evening. I've already cleared it with house security."

I glanced back at the lobby, made eye contact with my new muscle-bound friend, and waved. He waved back.

"Nothing too fancy. Your basic suite should do the trick. Can you take care of that for me, Scott?"

"Yes, ma'am. Right away." He entered information into his computer, activated a plastic keycard, and handed it to me. "You're in 1608. It overlooks the pool. I hope that's all right."

"It sounds perfect. I'll be sure to mention your efficiency in my report. And Scott? Keep this on the down, will you? Loose lips sink ships and covert operations."

He sealed his lips with an imaginary key and pointed me toward the elevator.

The ride up to the sixteenth floor provided a spectacular night view of L.A.'s west side, courtesy of the glass-walled elevator attached to the hotel's exterior. The Ferris wheel at the

Santa Monica Pier was ablaze with yellow and orange lights, and boats dotted the harbor.

Off the elevator, a sign on the wall directed me left, and I found my room near the end of the hall. I slipped the card into the reader on the door, a little green light flashed, and the door clicked open.

I stepped inside and whistled. "Well done, Scott!"

The room was an oasis of parquet marble flooring, a sitting area with matching leather couches, and a sprawling California king-sized bed draped in the fluffiest white linens imaginable. There was also a small work area with a computer. According to a pamphlet propped against the keyboard, the Westcott was pet-friendly and had personalized towels and beds for dogs. That settled it. As soon as I got my baby back, we were celebrating with a night at the Westcott, although it might mean nicking another necklace to cover the bill; the suite easily went for a grand a night.

A pair of French doors led out to the balcony, where a cool evening breeze did its best to wash away what had easily been the craziest day ever. I stood on the terrace, plotting my next move, before deciding it was time for that shower. But first, I ran downstairs to the gift shop for a change of clothes. I picked out a navy blue sweatshirt, gray sweat pants, and some underwear. Okay, I get plastering the hotel logo on the shirt and sweats, but the panties too? Seriously? Were flashers corporately sponsored now or what? As tacky as the underwear was, the only other option was going commando. Veto.

The damage for the sweats, socks, and the awesome underwear came to nearly two hundred dollars, which put a hurt on my now-dwindling cash supply. The gift shop had an ATM, but electronic surveillance being what it was, using it would've been like inviting the police, to come and get me. I really wished I could have charged my purchases to LAPD. After all, they were the reason my own home was now off-limits to me.

Finally, I took my shower. Whether it was because of the speaker system piping in new-age music, the towel warmer, the fluffy robe waiting for me when I was done, or the fact that I was completely drained, I'd never enjoyed a shower that much.

Next stop: bed. When I collapsed onto the mattress, it was like snuggling up with a masseuse. A yawn hit me right on cue, but before calling it a night, I turned on the television — the latest in flat-screen technology, of course — to see if there were any developments in the case. The day before, Denise had been the lead story, but today, she didn't even rate a mention during the first several minutes. In fact, the station went to commercial, leaving me thinking they had nothing to report. Boy, was I wrong.

After the break, there was a story about a failed prison escape, and then the anchor — complete with a you-know-what eating grin — said, "Meanwhile, today in Hollywood, there was an escape of a different kind that was a bit more successful."

I sat up, my heart quickening. *No.*

"Remember the woman wanted for questioning regarding the death of actress Denise Ladd?" the anchor asked. "She fled the scene following Ladd's death yesterday at the Manhattan Beach Mall, and she was at it again today at Hollywood and Highland."

My hand covered my mouth as, once again, I watched myself on the news. Someone had captured video of me sliding down the escalator divider while shoppers and tourists cheered me on. I looked ridiculous, bouncing over those metal stumps. Luckily, the video was shot from far enough away that I wasn't recognizable, but after being caught on video at a mall twice in two days, I swore on my Manolo Blahniks that I was done with shopping centers, at least until this entire episode was over.

The anchor said the police hadn't released an official statement, but a source confirmed that the woman on the video was the same person of interest in the Ladd murder case. Then he quit smiling and adopted his obituary-face. "We've also learned that the name of the woman in question is Kate Albertson. Anyone with information regarding her whereabouts is asked to contact the police immediately."

11

S o much for a good night's sleep. I turned off the TV and stared at the ceiling, and when that got old, I threw off the covers and started pacing.

Why was Trammell working so hard to have me arrested? He must've been the one behind this, but what had I done to make him so angry? I was perfectly willing to live up to our agreement, so why go for the nuclear option? It would be one thing if I'd posed a threat to him, but that was impossible. It wasn't like I had any kind of dirt on him. I knew what everyone else in town knew: he was loaded and he might have stolen the idea responsible for his riches. I also knew he wanted to be in the movie business — par for the course in Los Angeles, except for the part about one of his backers being the same guy who'd bought his wife's stolen necklace. Other than that, Trammell was simply the guy holding my dog hostage.

I sat at the desk, fired up the computer, and spent the next few hours Googling my brains out. I learned plenty, and not only about Tad Ellington, but also about Richard Spencer, the other guy funding the movie. He came from a prominent family, the kind with hospital wings and parks named in its honor.

I also found my way to Denise's Twitter feed. Besides the picture of her with Yoda, which had been shown on the news, she'd posted pictures taken at the beach, another one with her eyeing chocolate-covered strawberries, and several of her glam shots, but the most recent ones were posted a day before she died. They showed her with a group of people about her age at some kind of formal event. They were laughing, dancing, and mugging for the camera, almost always with a cocktail in hand. Denise's drink of choice was a blue-green beverage served in a martini glass.

Eventually, eye fatigue sent me back to bed, and I was able to grab a few hours of sleep before clearing out of my posh surroundings. Whim and I were going to have a blast here, whenever that time came.

After stopping for a caramel latte, I took Wilshire across town to a strip center east of Hancock Park. There were no five-star hotels or gourmet grocery stores in this part of town. People in Trammell's neighborhood probably rode horses while wearing those super tight pants and funny-looking hats, but around here, equestrian was something you asked.

I parked at the far end of the lot and walked back, past the SoCal Divaz Nail Salon and On A Roll Sushi, to the Spyder James Investigative Agency. The front window featured the name of the business printed in red block letters. Beneath that was a picture of a black widow spinning its web. I peeked inside and saw a guy at a desk, so I pushed the door open. He looked up as if startled to have company. He had a medium brown complexion, closely cropped hair, a clean-shaven face, and eyes filled with suspicion.

I gave him my best smile and approached his desk, hand out. "Hi. You must be Darius."

We shook. "Spyder."

"Right. Like it says there." I thumbed back at the window. "You, um ... you know you spelled it wrong, right?"

He sighed. "What brings you in, Miss...?"

I took a seat across from him. "Albertson. But you can call me Kate."

"You're a long way from the Westcott, Kate. You get lost?"

I looked down at my outfit. Geez, I was a walking billboard for the hotel. Fortunately, this wasn't a social call. I would've hated for that getup to be my first impression.

"No, see, the reason I—"

He put a hand up to stop me and reached for a pile of newspapers on the corner of his desk. As he flicked through the stack, he asked me to stand. I humored him, but he didn't seem to notice, preoccupied with his copies of the *Times* and *Variety*. Once he found what he was looking for, he began reading out loud.

"Ms. Albertson is described by witnesses as a petite brunette ..." He looked me over and nodded. "Twenty-five to thirty years old ..." He examined me again. "Standing approximately—"

"Okay, okay, you've proven you're a detective. Bravo, Mr. James."

"Spyder."

"I have to say, I'm not really interested in calling a grown man Spyder, nor would any other self-respecting woman. Can't we just go with Darius?"

He looked at his wristwatch — black with a black band and a Swiss logo on the face. A decent watch but nothing worth taking, if I'd been of such a mind.

"I hate that name ... ever since I was a kid."

"Well, you could at least do something about the spelling of your nickname, or is that some sort of street cred thing?"

After a few seconds of staring at me as though trying to determine my species, he reached for the cell phone on his desk, punched in some numbers, and put the phone to his ear.

The base of my spine tingled. "Can I ask what you're doing?"

"Calling the police."

Never in my life had I moved faster than when I reached across the desk and snatched the phone from his hand.

"Oh my God! Why would you do that?" I ended the call before anyone could answer.

"Does the phrase 'aiding and abetting' mean anything to you?" he asked.

"Please. I'm not a fugitive. I'm a person of interest."

"And we both know all that means is they can't prove you did it ... yet. Besides, there might be some reward money involved, which — and I think you'd agree — would come in handy up in here."

The office was a far cry from Aubrey's tony digs overlooking the cliffs in Santa Monica. His desk was a basic brown rectangle littered with scuff marks; same with the filing cabinet, although it was a darker shade of brown. The chair I was occupying was made of tough plastic that had originally been white but now bordered on gray, and its mate was the same model but in black. I had to admit though, he kept a neat office, even if the furnishings were late-twentieth-century Ikea and the view was of a guy in a chicken suit standing on the corner trying to drum up business for the taquería across the street.

"You really should consider some new chairs. These are about as comfortable as crumbs in your bra." As soon as the words were out of my mouth, I realized he might not be able to relate. "Can I just ask you a few questions?" I asked. "It'll only take a few minutes, and then I'll be out of your hair. Promise."

After another time check, he stood. He was taller than I'd thought—six-one, maybe six-two, with a solid build.

"Actually, I gotta do something." He held out his hand and I gave him back his phone. "I ain't real sure why I wanna answer your questions anyway. You're the one supposed to be answering questions."

"Not if they're about Robin Castro."

He froze. "What about Robin Castro?"

∾

ONCE DARIUS REGAINED HIS COMPOSURE, HE TOLD ME TO COME with him, so I followed him outside to his car, a black Mustang with tinted windows. As we stood on opposite sides of the car, I asked, "Are you sure about this?"

"You want to talk? We'll talk on the way."

The sun had risen above the buildings and its glare made me squint. "Do you promise you won't run me in?"

"Run you in? The hell's that even mean?"

"You know, turn me over to the cops."

He shook his head as he unlocked the doors. "Girl, are you coming or not?" He climbed inside his car and fired up the engine. I opened the passenger door expecting to see fast food containers or at least some random papers covering the seat and floor, but didn't find a single piece of debris. I'd just clipped my seat belt on when Darius pulled out onto Wilshire and headed toward downtown.

"Where are we going, by the way?"

"To find somebody who doesn't want to be found. Shouldn't take too long," he said, before changing the subject. "How'd you get yourself mixed up in this Denise Ladd business anyway?"

I exhaled. "I've been asking myself that same question."

I told him the story, starting with Trammell's party and finishing with my dubiously legal impersonation of a police officer (hey, I never said I was with a particular department; Scott, the front desk clerk, just assumed).

"I swear, the first time I stole the necklace, Whimsy got dognapped. The second time I stole it, someone died. I don't even want to think about what'll happen if I have to steal it again."

"Sounds to me like you need to quit stealing."

"Well, I'm *trying* to give it back. That ought to count for something."

His phone rang with an incoming call. A check of the display resulted in a huge smile, and he put the call on speakerphone.

"Hey, Spyder," a woman on the other end purred.

Ugh.

"What's up, beautiful?" he said, giving me a wink.

I looked out the passenger window while the two of them engaged in idle chatter about some sunglasses she may or may not have left at his place, to which he said he'd look for them and let her know. As soon as their conversation ended, he looked at me and grinned. "What you got to say now?"

"What I *have* to say is that she uses a lot of double negatives."

"She also called me Spyder. You said no woman would ever call me Spyder."

"First, I'm pretty sure I said no 'self-respecting' woman. And second, if you ever put one of your women on speakerphone around me again, I'm launching straight into psycho-girlfriend mode. '*Darius?*'" I shrieked. "'*Who is that? Let me tell you something, witch. Don't you come around this house unless you want to get cut!*'"

His smile evaporated. "That was ... damn near authentic."

"Don't you forget it."

"So how do you know about Robin, and how come you're showing up three years after the fact?"

Robin's name had come up during my research the night before. She was a junior at USC, majoring in journalism while working part-time in the library to help pay for school, with student loans taking care of the rest. She came to L.A. from Fresno, where her father taught high school and her mother was an administrative assistant. Her older brother enlisted in the army after high school, and her younger sister opted for junior college. She was solidly middle class all the way, until she fell in with a group of rich kids. She must have been loving life, right up until the moment it was taken from her. Robin Castro had died suddenly and under mysterious circumstances. Just like Denise Ladd.

"That's a pretty strong coincidence, don't you think?" I asked.

"What are you telling me, Kate? There's some kind of connection?"

"Think about it: the way they both died is eerily similar, and they also both had ties to the Preston-Ellington-Spencer crowd."

"And this crowd goes around killing people?"

"I'm not saying that. It's just ..." I'd driven across town with the hope that Darius could tell me something, anything, that would help me find answers rather than turn up more questions. There had to be more to the murders than chance.

He made a left on Normandie, which took us to a little neighborhood just past Koreatown. He turned onto a smaller street lined with older apartment buildings, all of them candidates for one of those home makeover shows, and stopped in the parking lot of a three-story building with kids riding their bikes out front. One of them, a boy wearing a grey hoodie who looked around eleven or twelve, stopped what he was doing and nodded.

"That's my cue," Darius said.

"Cue for what?"

"Earlier, when you said you weren't a fugitive? Well, Victor Stanton is. Escaped custody a week and a half ago in Palmdale.

Something always brings these guys back to their old neighborhood like a damn homing pigeon." He reached into the center console, took out a fairly large handgun, and opened his door. "Wait here."

Examining the building's barred windows and graffiti-tagged walls, I said, "Um, yeah. That's a promise."

He got out, tucked the gun into his waistband, and took the stairs up to the second floor, carefully approaching one of the doors. I picked up movement in the corner of my eye and glanced back at the street. The boy with the hoodie had his phone out and seemed to be texting.

Back upstairs, Darius stood to the side of the door and knocked. A few seconds later, a woman in cut-off denim shorts and a baby blue tank top opened the door. After a brief exchange, punctuated by her repeatedly shaking her head, he moved her aside and entered the apartment. As soon as he did, a window flew open and someone dove out, landing smack against the concrete walkway. Victor Stanton, I presumed.

He picked himself up and ran to the stairs, taking them three or four at a time. Darius burst out of the apartment, giving chase. When Victor reached the bottom of the staircase, he looked for an escape route and chose the path straight ahead ... *toward me.*

Darius followed, but because of Victor's flying start, he was trailing by a good ten yards. Victor and I made eye contact as he sprinted for the car, toward my side of it to be precise. I swallowed and told myself I could do this. I'd seen it in the movies. I grabbed the door handle and waited for him to get closer ... and closer ... and at the last second, I leaned on the door with all of my one hundred and twelve pounds, flinging it open into the fugitive's path.

A grinning Victor lunged to his left, sidestepping the door, but a split-second later, he stopped grinning and started screaming. He grabbed the back of his left leg and tried hobbling away, but Darius closed the distance and tackled him, knocking him over like a domino. They landed with a thud, which caused Victor to howl with agony as he writhed on the ground. People really should stretch before attempting any serious physical activity, like fleeing. Pulled hamstrings are a serious problem.

Darius yanked a pair of cuffs from his back pocket and shackled Victor. He took a moment to catch his breath and then looked up at me, smiling. "Thanks for the effort."

12

I waited at a coffee shop a couple blocks away from the police station while Darius escorted Victor inside to be processed, booked, or whatever. Never having been arrested, I had no idea how it all worked, and with my name all over the news, keeping that record intact was going to present a challenge. Darius had said that Victor's apprehension came with a two-thousand-dollar price tag, which wasn't bad money, but I much preferred my way of pulling in a grand or two.

He joined me after concluding his business, wearing a huge smile as he slid into the opposite side of the booth.

"So the check is in the mail?" I asked.

He nodded. The server swung by, poured him a cup of coffee, and took his order: toast and a spinach mushroom omelet.

Once she'd left, he said, "I wasn't expecting you to get involved like that. I figured you for one of those don't-break-a-nail types."

"I'm just full of surprises. Speaking of which, I think your juvenile C.I. back there gave you the double cross." That earned me a raised eyebrow, so I told him about the kid who'd sent a text just before Victor attempted his getaway.

"Ain't that some shit? What's the world coming to when a couple twenties can't buy a kid's loyalty? I wonder how much Victor gave him."

I shrugged. "More?"

His laugh was husky and made his cheeks dimple, the left one a little bigger than the right. It was hard to imagine him as the same guy who stalked prison escapees to pay the bills. One thing was certain: after watching him in action, I didn't want him hunting me down.

The server brought his omelet and made sure I didn't want anything besides coffee before greeting the guy who'd arrived at the next table.

"No wonder you stay so skinny," Darius said.

"That and trying to stay out of jail. Worrying about getting my dog back isn't helping my appetite either."

As he buttered his toast, he said, "You ever consider keeping the necklace and forgetting about the dog?"

My mouth fell open and my eyes nearly popped out of my head. "No!"

He dug into his omelet. "Must be some dog."

I took my phone out and showed him the picture of Whimsy on my home screen.

He squinted at it. "What is that? A labradoodle?"

"Oh my G—no. She's a smooth fox terrier. You're not much of a dog person, are you?"

He pursed his lips. "I like puppies. They're good for picking up women at the park."

"I'm going to pretend I didn't hear that, because otherwise, I'll leave here thinking you're a humongous pig, and I don't need any more negativity in my life right now." I took another look at Whim's picture; she was sitting there with her ears alert, staring straight into the camera, draped in her miniature red cape. She really was a super dog. "You know, there's something that's been bugging me."

"Given your situation, I'd think there'd be a helluva lot more than one."

"Right? But seriously ... foxies are barkers. They bark at everything. So how come Whim didn't bark when Trammell snuck into my apartment?"

Darius quit eating long enough to give me a blank stare. "Don't ask me. Not much of a dog person, remember?"

I waved him off. "Rhetorical. Though you were going to answer some other questions, right?"

He scanned the restaurant. Being after breakfast but not quite lunch, the place was half full at best.

"Robin Castro?" he asked, and I nodded. "Like you said, she was a small-town girl but had it all going for her: 3.85 GPA, star at the university paper, and of the people who would talk, none of them had anything bad to say about her. She was working on a story about some new rush-week regulations the school had put in place; that was how she met the guys from Delta Rho Sigma. I guess they took a liking to her because they started inviting her to parties or just to hang out."

"They were probably trying to influence her story."

"Maybe. I'll tell you this much, it would've worked on me. Taking off for Vail or Maui at the drop of a hat? It was like they only went to class when they needed a break. Those kids lived fast and partied hard, and Robin was along for the ride."

"Sounds like pretty heady stuff, especially for a girl from humble means."

"Right. But her parents weren't crazy about her new friends and the way they threw money around. They wanted their daughter away from that whole scene, but she was down here and they were up north ..."

And she probably thought she didn't need Mom and Dad telling her what to do. What girl hasn't gone through that phase, especially while she's at college and her parents are hundreds of miles away? For me, it was an origami swan tattooed on the back of my shoulder. Painful and a little stupid, but hardly fatal.

"Twenty-year-old girls don't just drop dead. There should have been more of an investigation. Somehow the word must've come down to squash it. After that, Robin's family reached out to me—"

"Why you?"

He did a double take as though I'd interrupted his train of thought.

"Why did Robin's parents call you, a one-man operation they'd probably never heard of? I'm guessing you don't have an office in Fresno."

"It wasn't her parents. It was her brother, Gilbert. We served in the same unit and did a tour in Iraq together." He paused, I guess to see whether that had answered my question. I gestured for him to keep going. "We were tight, me and Gil. That happens when a guy takes a bullet for you in a firefight. We stayed in touch after I got out, and when the madness with his sister happened, he called. His parents had already lost their daughter, and Gil was afraid the grief might kill one of them too. He asked if there was anything I could do. The case was officially closed, but I poked around. I got a few people to talk to me, but most wouldn't, especially the Briarwood set ..." He shook his head. "Those folks really circled the wagons."

"Briarwood set?"

"The country club they all belong to."

Their stonewalling shouldn't have come as a surprise, what with their sons being friends with Robin. If Darius had turned up even a smidgen of foul play, one of the Delta boys could've been a prime suspect. But last night when I was digging up information about the case, the news coverage had come to an abrupt halt. There were no follow-up stories, no headlines screaming that justice had indeed been done, and from the looks of things, Robin's killer was still out there.

"Do you think they were hiding something?"

"Could be. Or maybe since the investigation was closed, they didn't feel the need to answer any questions, especially from somebody who looked like the help." Darius stared at his half-eaten omelet before tossing his knife and fork on the plate with a clank and shoving the whole thing aside. "Don't ask me to figure out rich folks."

"No kidding." Trammell was acting unhinged, and Ellington had bought a necklace he'd known was stolen. I hadn't met Richard Spencer yet, but if he ran in the same circles, chances were good he was pretty far out there too.

"I hate that I couldn't get answers for Gil. I let him down."

"It was the police who let him down, not you. I'm sure he knows that."

"Yeah." He didn't sound convinced.

The server cleared his plate, tore the top ticket from her order pad. "I'll take care of that whenever you're ready."

I reached into my purse for my wallet but Darius stopped me. "I got it. All you had was coffee."

"Thanks."

"I don't know if I helped you any," he said.

"I don't either."

"Look. I don't plan to go volunteering that I spoke to you, but if I get asked ... I ain't interested in doing more time. Hear what I'm saying?"

More? Now wasn't the time to ask. "Got it."

"And sooner or later, you're probably gonna have to talk to the police."

"Later. Thank you."

He paid the bill and left a seventeen percent tip (I notice these things; my parents ran a restaurant). The ride back to his office was quiet except for the sound of traffic — he didn't even have the radio on — but as we arrived at the strip center, I asked if he could think of anything else that might be useful to me. I doubted the people he'd tried to interview would be any more likely to open up to me, but if someone had murdered Robin Castro, could they have been so adept as to have left no trace behind at all?

"There's a notepad in there," Darius said, pointing to the glove box. I handed it to him. He jotted something down, ripped off the sheet, and gave it to me. "He works at Briarwood and probably knows this crowd as well as anybody. Maybe you can get something out of him."

I looked up from the sheet. "Really?"

"Really."

"Did you ever talk to any of Robin's friends?"

Shaking his head, Darius said, "Not really. All those frat kids she'd been hanging with dummied up just like the adults. Her classmates liked her but couldn't shed much light on anything. There was another girl she was supposedly close to, but I never could run her down. What was her name?" He stood there, racking his memory before snapping his fingers. "Shawna. Shawna ... Larson. For whatever that's worth."

"Who knows? But right now, I'll take anything I can get. Thanks."

"Not a problem. And tell Jimmy Spyder says hi."

"What's up with the whole arachnid fascination, anyway?"

"I've never heard it put quite that way." He laughed, bringing back the mismatched dimples. "When I was in the desert, things got pretty boring when the Iraqis weren't shooting at us, or vice versa, so we killed time by racing camel spiders. I was damn good at it. Made an extra forty or fifty bucks a week sometimes."

"You're totally making that up."

He shrugged. "Google it."

I opened the car door. "Whatever. I'm still not calling you that."

"Well, only my mother calls me Darius, and I'd protest that shit if I thought I could."

"What about D? Can I call you D?"

He tossed his hands up. "I guess."

"Cool. See you around, D."

13

I wasted no time jetting back across town. Maybe my luck was turning. Not only had D given me a lead, but Sterling-Ross, a jewelry store just outside of Beverly Hills, was on the way to Briarwood. I decided to make a pit stop to get started on that favor I owed Mel. As compensation for leading me to the necklace, he wanted a certain diamond ring of the eighteen-carat variety. I wasn't planning on waltzing in and picking one up today, but I could at least see what I was dealing with.

D seemed like a good guy, if a little rough around the edges. That had its uses, though, as I'd witnessed firsthand when he'd taken down Victor Stanton. The disappointment of failing a good friend must've been one of the worst feelings in the world, although it didn't sound like there was much he could've done about it; the game had been rigged and not in his favor. Still, from the look on D's face as he'd told me the story, Robin's ghost had been keeping him awake at night for over three years.

On the way to the jewelry store, my phone rang. Again, the

number was blocked, but hoping it was Trammell, I answered before the second ring.

"Hello, Miss Albertson. I trust you're well?"

"Save it, Trammell. What was that about yesterday, setting me up for the cops to grab me?"

He chuckled as if he thought I was slow on the uptake. "Well, you are wanted for questioning. I was just doing my civic duty."

"This is all a big mistake. You and I both know I didn't do anything to hurt Denise Ladd."

"I don't know that, but what I do know is that you're untrustworthy."

"Me? We had a deal, and I kept my end of it."

"Was it time for your six-month checkup?" he asked. "Or were you sticking your nose where it didn't belong?"

"What?"

"Why did you go see the dentist, Kate?"

I swerved, drawing a blast from the car next to me. I gave her an apologetic wave and shifted back into my lane. Had Ellington said something about a visit from a phony cop who fit my description? Why would he do that? And why would Trammell care?

"Is everything all right, Miss Albertson?"

"Peachy. Listen, when do you want to meet to do this exchange? Sans police this time if you don't mind."

"I'll be in touch. In the meantime, I suggest you keep to the business at hand. Remember: I know where you live."

He hung up before I could ask what that meant. Was he planning to pay me another surprise visit? As long as he got his necklace back, why would he care if I did a little investigating? Maybe it was his way of reminding me who was calling the shots. Men like him always had to be in control. I didn't like it, but for now, I'd play it his way.

Sterling-Ross was located on the ground floor of a shiny high-rise that was filled with attorneys, agents, and other professionals who supported the entertainment business in one way or another. I parked in a lot down the block and walked to the store, pulling my hair back and donning a pair of shades on the way. Being wanted for questioning was only one reason for the camouflage. Heaven forbid someone I knew should see me decked out in Hotel Westcott gear like the worst kind of tourist.

A gentle electronic chime announced my arrival. My shoes scrunched against the polished floor, and mirrors along the walls gave the store the illusion that the space was bigger than it was. An older blonde woman in a turquoise suit sniffed at me from behind a glass counter before returning to the customer she was helping.

Her much younger co-worker, a man in a suit, approached me. "How can I help you today?"

I adjusted my shades and summoned my long-lost central Texas accent. "Hey there! I was passing by and saw your precious little store here. I thought I might see a celebrity like Jennifer Lawrence or that Angelina Jolie."

I really emphasized the Joe in Jolie. Out of the corner of my eye, I was fairly certain I saw the woman at the counter roll her eyes.

The salesman stammered, and I placed a hand on his arm. "Hon, I'm just kidding you. Can you show me something in an emerald cut?"

The blush faded from his cheeks and he gathered his composure. "Of course, ma'am. Right this way."

For the next five minutes, I oohed and aahed over a selection of extremely fine, high-priced jewelry while getting a good look at a mind-blowing eternity ring featuring no fewer than a dozen perfectly matching diamonds in a platinum setting. Mel had awfully good taste. After I'd cataloged the details, I thanked the salesman for his time and left. The door hadn't fully closed behind me when the saleswoman, her voice loaded with sarcasm, muttered, "Oh, do hurry back."

Back in my car, I sketched the ring and made a few notes. I took a picture of everything and texted it to Shrevie, asking, *How long?*

He replied: *How good?*

Me: *Immaculate.*

He said three days, but he always asked for more time than he really needed, and we agreed on two.

It would be such a pleasure doing business with Sterling-Ross.

BRIARWOOD WAS ANOTHER TWENTY MINUTES OR SO AWAY, AND I spent the last few weaving back and forth along Sunset until I reached a small drive with an arch made of weathered, gray stone. The drive wound past several trees before taking a sharp right and heading uphill. As I climbed, the trees yielded to acres of lush, green grass that made up part of the golf course, which stretched out on either side of the narrow roadway and eventually disappeared behind gentle, sweeping hills.

The road ended in a circular drive in front of a sprawling white, two-story clubhouse. The valet — a teenage kid with black slacks, a red jacket, and acne — stepped up to my car and proudly held the door open for me, even though the Chevy was probably worth less than the little golf carts the members drove around in.

As I stepped out, I asked, "Do you know where I can find Jimmy?"

"Oh, sure. He's in the pro shop." He handed me a claim ticket and pointed to a brick pathway laid in a crisscross pattern. "Just follow the cart path. You can't miss it."

The trail took me around the clubhouse and past the practice green where three men, all wearing grim expressions, were practicing their putting. As I passed by, they stopped what they were doing — which was missing putts, for the most part — to stare, as if those polyester shirts and knobby-knee-revealing shorts looked any better than my sweats.

From the outside, the pro shop looked like a glorified hut, but the inside was pure heaven ... for those into golf-themed clutter. I was immediately assaulted by racks of shirts, sweaters, belts, shorts, socks—you name it. Beyond the apparel were golf clubs. Some were grouped in sets while others, like putters and drivers, were displayed separately. Also on display were golf bags in a multitude of colors. I guessed they'd run out of floor space for the bags, because some were hanging from the ceiling. Lining the opposite wall were shoes, mostly hideous things that resembled the demon spawn of a reptile and Air Jordans. At the front of the store was a counter with a display case containing balls, books, and sunglasses. Mounted on the wall behind the case was a large, framed print of a golf course along the coastline. The photographer had caught the waves breaking against the rocks. The photo was actually pretty.

Behind the counter, presiding over all of this, was a heavyset man in his late thirties or early forties. He had a ruddy face, reddish-brown hair, and a matching mustache. Unless I missed my guess, the word *jolly* was often used to describe him. He was watching golf on a small television that occupied the counter, while absentmindedly tossing a golf ball into the air and catching it with the same hand.

The lighting wasn't great, and with my shades on, I didn't notice a stray golf ball on the floor until I'd already stepped on it. The ball skittered across the shop, and I nearly did the same. If I'd been wearing heels, the end result probably would've involved ankle surgery, but in this case, the only thing broken was the guy's concentration on the TV.

"Hi," I said, after regaining my balance. "I'm looking for Jimmy."

He took me in and said, "Well, that makes this my lucky day."

"You're Jimmy?"

He adjusted his pants, which only served to accentuate his belly. Flatter him, they didn't. "Jimmy One-Ball. What can I do for you?"

First D and now this guy. I almost told him that what he could do for me was explain why men insisted on these nicknames. It was probably the same gene that made them laugh at farts and treat fantasy football like life or death.

"Let me guess: A psycho ex with a sharp instrument?"

He grunted a one-syllable laugh. "That's cute, but no. I've still got the factory-installed equipment, and if you ever need verification —"

I put my hand up. "Eww."

"TMI?" he asked.

"Way."

"Sorry. Here's the deal: damn near everybody who plays this course loses a ball at one point or another — in one of the lakes, in the trees, somewhere — but when I was fifteen, I played here three straight times with the same ball."

"Hence the name. Got it."

Jimmy tapped his nose with his meaty index finger. "So what's your story? You need a lesson? Something more stylish to wear maybe?"

"Not hardly. A mutual acquaintance thought you could help me out."

His eyes widened. "Oh? And who might that be?"

"Darius James ... private investigator."

"Darius J—" The fog around his memory lifted, bringing a smile to his face. "Oh! You mean Spyder. Great guy. Can't swing a golf club for shit, but a great guy. What reason could he possibly have for sending you to me?"

Before I could answer, the door opened and two men in golf attire entered. They perused the clearance rack for a few minutes, murmured to each other, then left.

"These bastards," Jimmy muttered. "They think nothing of dropping two hundred grand on a membership but then they come in here looking to bargain hunt."

My mouth dropped open. "Two hundred thousand dollars?"

"Yep. Annually. Hand to God." He leaned forward, resting his considerable weight on the counter. "But anyhoo, you were about to say?"

"I'm working on a little something and I wanted to know what you could tell me about Trammell Preston, Tad Ellington, or Richard Spencer, and if there's any reason to think they were involved in the death of Robin Castro or Denise Ladd, the girl who died a couple days ago."

He had the look of someone undergoing serious contemplation. "I can tell you they're all esteemed members here."

Esteemed. Right. The party line if there was ever one.

"But as for them being involved in any homicides, why would you want to know about a thing like that?"

Talking about this to D had been one thing. He didn't have a particular interest in who killed Denise Ladd, but if the case were at all connected to the death of Robin Castro, he'd want the person responsible locked up, even if he wasn't the one applying the cuffs. Jimmy, though, was another matter. Surely those six-figure-paying members wouldn't hesitate to have him canned if they found out he'd been dishing dirt behind their backs. Could I really trust his info? Or him? D had joked about handing me over to the cops. Jimmy might actually do it.

He reached up and carefully lifted the sunglasses from my face. "Mmm hmm. I thought I saw those wheels turning. Didn't you just hear me say I think the world of Spyder? If he sent you here, he must've had a reason, so let's have the truth and not some nonsense about the little 'something' you're working on. Or I could call up Spyder and ask him." He opened a drawer beneath his computer and rummaged through it. "I think I still got his card around here somewhere."

"Fine," I said. "Have you heard about Denise Ladd?"

"Oh yeah. She's been a hot topic of conversation around here."

My guess was that she'd been a hot topic pretty much everywhere. My exploits hadn't helped that either. I gave Jimmy the quickest version of my story possible. For one thing, I was getting tired of telling it. I also didn't trust him one hundred percent yet.

When I was done, he said, "And you're thinking whoever killed Denise also killed Robin?"

"You have to admit, the cases are pretty similar, and they knew some of the same people, so yeah."

The roar of the crowd burst from the television as a golfer made a long putt. The guys outside on the practice green should've been watching and taking notes. Jimmy picked up a remote and muted the set. "Like I said, lots of folks have been talking about Denise since she died. The only members who didn't know she was having an affair with Ellington were the zombies."

"Zombies?"

"Yeah, the ones who are like ninety years old — the walking dead. And ever since Mrs. Ellington filed for divorce, there's been a bunch of speculation over who'd get the membership, him or her. Ellington brought Denise here for lunch one day not too long ago — I guess he figured there wasn't much to hide at that point — and when Mrs. Ellington found out? Whoo, boy. She was playing tennis with some other members and said she'd choke Denise with her own extensions before seeing her become a member here. Allegedly."

"Right ... allegedly. I wonder if the cops have bothered looking into that alleged angle?"

Jimmy shrugged.

"I can't believe she'd say something like that ... even around friends."

"She might've been ..." He fashioned his hand into a bottle and knocked back a swig from his thumb. "Besides, people are pretty comfortable with each other around here. A lot of 'em are second-, even third-generation members, like Ellington and Spencer. They grew up together and were in the same class at the Stinson Academy and then at USC. That's where they met Trammell Preston. Those must've been some times."

"Sounds interesting."

"That's one way to put it." He scanned the shop for eaves-droppers. We had the place to ourselves. "It's a very ... circular relationship that group has with one another. Spencer's wife? Celeste? He met her in college and they started dating, but she dumped him and started seeing Ellington."

"Wow."

"But wait," Jimmy said. "Then Ellington dumped *her*—"

"And she went back to Spencer?"

He shook his head. "Quit interrupting, will you? After Ellington, Celeste hooked up with Trammell. They got married after college, but it didn't last long. The divorce was nasty. Celeste comes from money and Trammell had signed a prenup, but he got it invalidated. He ended up with a pretty cushy settlement from what I understand. After all the dust settled, *then* Celeste went back to Spencer." He frowned. "That's a little too ... I don't know. I mean, if Celeste slept with Ellington *and* Trammell *and* Spencer, then basically it's kinda like Spencer slept with—"

"O-kay, Jimmy. I don't need a picture."

My head was reeling. He'd called the relationship circular, but twisted was more like it. When these people died, it was going to take a corkscrew to dig their graves.

"And the Spencers still associate with Ellington and Trammell after all that?" I asked. "How in the world does that work?"

"Like I said, Spencer and Ellington have known each other since they were kids. I guess they found a way to get past it."

I shook my head. There was no way I'd be able to let go of something like that. "If I were Celeste, I would've left town."

Jimmy laughed. "And give up being a Spencer? You obviously don't know the woman."

"I know they're kind of a big deal in this town."

"Yeah, they take themselves seriously. Too seriously, considering they got rich off some real estate scams after the Civil War."

"Really?"

"Yeah, but now they're all respectable and shit, and that Celeste is especially sanctimonious. Her son brought Robin here once." Jimmy held up an index finger. "Once. Celeste didn't want him hanging out with some dark-skinned girl from the San Joaquin Valley."

Already I didn't like this Celeste. Robin Castro could've been the most awesome girl in the world, but because of circumstances she had no control over, she'd never be welcome at the Spencers' dinner table. I got the feeling none of them had shed many tears when Robin died.

"So what if the police came around and started asking questions about Denise Ladd's death?"

Jimmy chuckled. "They'd do what they always do: watch each other's backs. Besides, I don't think they're too worried about the police. Shit, they own the police."

14

After collecting my car from the valet, I took a ride, heading for the address Jimmy had given me.

As his story played through my head, Celeste Spencer began to make sense as a suspect. She certainly had motive.

She'd left her boyfriend for one of his friends, only for him to dump her. So she ended up marrying another one of his friends, who had not only dumped her as well, but had also gotten a fat settlement in the process. Now, decades later, she'd been presented with the perfect opportunity to get back at both of them by killing Ellington's mistress, who also happened to be starring in Trammell's movie. Two birds, one stone. It was hard to imagine a more perfect scenario.

But how could I prove it? Like Jimmy had said, a police interrogation would likely result in radio silence from the Briarwood crew, same as it had with D.

Jimmy had looked up the Spencers' home address on his computer, then tried to trade it for my phone number. Needless to say, that didn't happen.

The weird part was that the Spencers had recently moved.

He'd been certain they lived in Pacific Palisades, but the address in the members database was in West L.A.

The Spencer home turned out to be a cozy-looking ranch-style house south of Olympic. Don't get me wrong, the house was nice: high, sloping roof, columned front entry, at least four bedrooms, and an impeccable flower garden. Plenty of people would've killed for a house like that. But compared to the Palisades? This was a comedown no matter how you looked at it.

I sat parked in front of the house with my windows down. A warm breeze flowed in, as did the sounds of kids laughing and splashing about in a nearby pool. I stared at the shiny red Mercedes and black Range Rover in the driveway until an idea hit me, but I couldn't call on Celeste while rocking my Hotel Westcott gear.

I cut back across town and drove by my apartment, only to find it still under police scrutiny. Now what? I had no clothes, no place to stay, and not enough money to resolve either dilemma. The credit cards in my purse were in my real name, so I couldn't use those, and I didn't dare try the escort ring ruse at another hotel. Sleeping in my car was starting to look like more of a possibility.

I headed for the library to use one of the computers. Every machine was taken, mostly by kids who looked as though they should've been in school, resulting in a half-hour wait before a slot opened up.

Starting with the license plate number of the red Mercedes, I worked backward, combing through public records until I found the background I needed on the Spencers. I also turned up a LinkedIn page for a Shawna Larson that matched the description of the girl D never found; she'd graduated from USC two years ago, with a degree in journalism, the same major as Robin. Now she was working as an account assistant at a local public relations firm. Her profile picture showed a fresh-faced woman in her early twenties with short blonde hair. I was in the middle of making notes when I felt a presence looming.

Broussard.

"Hey there, girlfriend." Again, she was wearing jeans and a t-shirt, but her cap was red with a white Nike swoosh. In her arms was a copy of *A Tale of Two Cities*. Give me a break. Broussard didn't read anything with more pages than a passport.

She paused as she took in my outfit. "That's an … interesting look. I always thought you were more of a fashionista."

Ouch. A wardrobe critique from a woman whose attitude was: it's casual Friday somewhere. "And I thought the word 'fashionista' went out with that Gangnam Style guy."

She laughed, no doubt meant to butter me up.

"I'm not even going to ask what you're doing here," I said, to which she held up her book. "Good. I thought you were about to bug me to work with you again."

"The thought crossed my mind, but I'm more interested in knowing what you're doing here." Broussard jutted her chin in the direction of my notes. "What's up with that?"

I slid my elbow over the sheet of paper. "It's nothing."

A sly grin crept over her face. "Uh huh. Don't forget who you're talking to. You're researching a job, aren't you? I'll bet it's huge, right?"

"Yeah, you could say it's huge, but it's not what you think, and I'm not going to discuss it with you. Not even a little bit."

"Well, that's pretty crappy of you, Kate."

"I can live with that."

She stormed off, leaving me to finish writing my notes. The second I was done, I returned to my car and crawled around it — muttering the entire time — until I found the tracking device Broussard had concealed inside the front fender. I promptly tossed it into the nearest trash can. Too bad I wouldn't be around to see the look on Broussard's face as she trekked out to the landfill to keep tabs on me.

When I turned on the ignition, I noticed that the gas gauge's yellow needle was hovering dangerously close to the letter "E." I sighed. Another expense. Maybe I should've taken that reward money Denise's sister had wanted to give me for finding Yoda.

I cut the engine to save the little gas I had left and sat in the library parking lot, watching the late afternoon sun prepare to call it another day. Aside from not making the evening news, I wasn't sure I'd accomplished much. I had a hunch about Denise's murder, but it was nothing more than that until I could meet Celeste Spencer face-to-face. I wasn't any closer to getting Whim back either. Why hadn't I heard from Trammell? And when he did call, what if he wanted to meet in Lake Elsinore or some other place I couldn't reach on the fumes left in my gas tank? That wouldn't have made much sense, but neither did his behavior.

Of course, my stomach picked that moment to growl. "Oh, shut up."

As dusk took hold, I kept arriving at the same conclusion: the only way to solve my immediate problem — my lack of both money and clean clothes — was to slip past the cop outside my apartment.

Using my phone, I located a hardware store a few sips of gas away. It wasn't one of the mammoth stores with endless aisles, but I wasn't in the market for new flooring or a ceiling fan, just a few basics. A cashier pointed me toward the tool section, and I set about the business of choosing a screwdriver. The store carried the Arsenal line—a personal favorite—and it was on sale to boot. The only thing left for me to do now was wait.

The security at my apartment building was pretty good — that was the reason Terry and I had picked it in the first place — with an alarm for each apartment, but with the right equipment, gaining access wasn't beyond me. Still, I would've been lying had I said the irony of having to break into my own place wasn't messing with my head.

I returned to my neighborhood after midnight and parked one street over to avoid the black-and-white loitering outside my complex. The rear of the apartments backed up to the rear of the ones on my street, so my plan was to jump the fence separating the two, but that was where I encountered a problem, which is never good when you're not even two minutes into a job.

A gate barred the entrance to the building directly behind mine, same with the one next to it and the one after that, but not the fourth. Wearing my backpack, I followed a narrow walkway down the side of the complex to the parking area in the back. The lot was half-full and quiet — good.

The fence in back was eight feet tall, separating the parking lot from the next apartment building. It was also topped intermittently with razor wire. I was pretty sure I could avoid the latter, but first I had to get on top of the wall. I crouched and jumped, reaching for the ledge. Not. Even. Close. Plus, when I landed, I lost my balance and executed a gold-medal winning, butt-first pratfall.

I held my breath and waited, listening for signs that I'd disturbed anyone, but the only harm done was to my backside.

In a darkened corner next to an SUV, I spotted a large trash bin, perfect for giving me the boost I needed. I hurried over and nearly gagged as the stench of rotting eggs, fish, and other things I probably didn't want to know about scurried up my nostrils. I held my breath and, using the SUV's front tire, pushed myself onto the hood of the car. From there, I transferred to the top of the garbage bin. With my lungs aching, I stood on my tiptoes and reached for the ledge. It was so close. I leaned out and stretched with everything I had. If I could just grow another inch ... I calmed myself and channeled Helena, my yoga instructor.

"Breathe deep into the muscle," she'd say. *But* ... "Inhale all the way into your toes." *What about the fish?*

My breath gave out and a wicked funk rushed up my nose just as I snagged the ledge with my fingertips. I felt dizzy, and for a split second, I swore I was falling, but my grip was solid.

The trash bin, however, rolled out from under me.

I scrambled for purchase, but that only knocked it farther away, leaving me dangling like a misplaced modifier. My fingers burned as the concrete dug in. I planted a foot against the wall and pushed, boosting myself up a few inches before I slipped.

I tried again, getting a better hold, and lifted my elbows onto the ledge. Now I was able to get a hand on the top of the fence. I pulled and threw a leg onto the ledge. I paused, my heart hammering away while I sucked air into my lungs, not even stopping when I tasted garbage at the back of my throat.

When I tried to bring my other leg up, I and snagged my sweats on the razor wire. The sound of ripping fabric echoed off the apartment buildings, and cool night air bathed my leg. I looked down to see a gash just below the knee of my sweats, but no other damage had been done.

After taking a few seconds to gather myself, I got to my feet and negotiated the wall, working my way toward my apartment building. The wall was flat and just wide enough for me to navigate without much trouble, except for the trio of six-inch black spikes that marked the end of one building's parking lot and the beginning of the next. They looked more decorative than protective, but I took care not to catch my clothes again as I stepped over them.

At the back of my complex, I stopped to survey the area. The pool took up most of the left half of the space, and the courtyard, paved with cobblestone, sat to the right. The courtyard was darkest at the edges, so after lowering myself to the ground, I pressed myself against the fence and tiptoed around the perimeter until I reached the metal box that housed the alarm panel. I gave the door a gentle tug. It didn't budge, but I'd expected that. Feeling around the edges, I found the lock that secured the door, but as I ran my hands over it, I got a sick feeling in my gut. I pictured the door from memory: it was dull grey with a latch held in place by a simple, round padlock. The lock in my hand wasn't round, but square. It also felt more substantial.

Cupping my hand around my phone to contain the light, I confirmed my suspicion: someone had changed the lock. In place of a padlock that I could've popped open with my screwdriver was a Sur-Guard — an upgrade to say the least. Could I have picked it? Sure, with enough time and someone else holding the light. Broussard came to mind, but that was temporary insanity.

I backtracked to the car and contemplated what to do next. Before I knew it, I was driving east, deeper into the city. The streets were mostly empty, and I made good time, arriving at D's office about twenty minutes later. The gas gauge had slipped another notch.

Mine was the only car in the small parking lot, the nail salon and sushi joint both having been closed for hours. Like his neighbors, D's window had a sticker warning would-be intruders that an alarm protected the premises. However, the other stores' stickers were neatly applied, while his was curled at the edges, as though, perhaps, it had been peeled off another window and placed on his as a decoy. Homeowners planted alarm company signs in their front yards to fool burglars all the time. Having been in D's office, that seemed like a shrewd move; the monitoring service probably would've cost more than the contents inside were worth.

Using the tools from my purse, I made quick work of the lock, cracked the door open, and jumped back in my car. From the gas station on the adjacent corner, I watched and waited. If I'd been wrong and D's place was equipped with an alarm, the police would respond. When they didn't, I returned to the office and locked the door behind me.

I rolled his desk chair into a corner where it couldn't be seen from the window and tried to get some sleep, but between my tidal wave of thoughts and the less-than-ideal arrangements, I napped for only a couple hours before my phone's alarm woke me at six. I crawled out of the chair and headed for the small washroom in the back. With the complimentary toiletries I'd taken from the hotel, I freshened up as best as I could, though I still felt gross. And my neck had a kink thanks to a night spent huddled in an office chair.

Outside, the nighttime blackness was giving way to daybreak, and the air was warm and dry, courtesy of a Santa Ana wind that carried the scent of donuts from the shop across the street. It was pointless trying to ignore my stomach's rumble, so I ventured over and spent my last two dollars on coffee and an old-fashioned with maple icing.

Booths lined the windows, and opposite them was a row of small tables. I chose a table where someone had left a rumpled copy of the Times and fanned through it over breakfast: wildfire in the Angeles Forest; a Hollywood power couple announced their divorce; the Lakers won; nothing new about the case.

It was shortly before eight, and D didn't strike me as a morning person, but parked right in front of the door was his Mustang. He looked up from *Variety* as soon as I pushed through the door.

"Morning," he said.

"Hey." I sat across from him. There were five twenties spread out in front of me on his desk. "Do you always leave money sitting around?"

"Are you saying you can't use it?"

"I didn't say that. I just—"

"And next time you need a place to crash? Ask first."

"How—"

Motioning toward the door, he said, "When I leave at night, I put an old popsicle stick against the door. If it's not there in the morning, I know somebody's been in here."

I shook my head. So low-tech, yet so effective. "But how'd you know it was me?"

He shook his head and smiled. "A girl like you don't wear the same shit two days in a row. Especially anything that ugly."

"Hey! They're not that ..." I looked down at my sweats and sighed. Knowing this was all the gift shop had had was little consolation. "Even Broussard said they were ugly."

D folded his magazine and set it aside. "And Broussard is?"

"An acquaintance; one without much fashion sense." I told him about how I'd cut ties with Broussard a few years earlier, only to have her turn up wanting to reconcile.

"What's up with calling her Broussard?"

"Because her friends call her Patrice."

"So you think she's got an ulterior motive?"

"I think she's full of it. Broussard's a liar and a backstabber. I don't know what her game is, but trust me. The last thing she wants to do is make up for the past."

"Damn, you always so cynical?"

I waved him off. "D, people don't change, and it's better not to put too much trust in them; they'll just let you down. We are who we are; leopards, spots, and all that."

"Not always." He rested his chin in his hand and got this distant look in his eyes. "Sometimes a kid's father dies way too young, and it pisses the kid off. He goes through life mad at the whole world, constantly getting into fights, getting sent home from school, shit like that. Kid ends up joining the army and gets sent to the Middle East. Sounds perfect, right? Let him take out that anger on the enemy. Only he never really understands what he's fighting for, especially when he's with his unit on a support mission and his C.O. decides to take advantage of one of the girls in this little village. She looks like she's still in high school. She has no idea what's going on either and is scared out of her mind."

I put a hand to my mouth. "Oh my God, D. What happened?"

"The kid ... I broke his nose. Got tossed in the stockade while command figured out what to do with me. Can't have soldiers going around punching their C.O.'s lights out, but they didn't want the whole story to come out either. So I got dishonorably discharged. No medal, no letter from my Congressman, just a ticket back home ..." He looked around his barren office. "... to this."

"D, I'm sorry."

"Hey, I learned ... the hard way. Sometimes that's what it takes. Didn't you say Broussard did some time? When you're locked up, even for a little while, you got plenty of time to think about how you want to live your life."

15

From D's office, I went directly to the gas station across the street and bought ten dollars' worth of unleaded, giving me three-eighths of a tank. Woohoo, I was free to roam! At Target, I hit the clearance rack, looking for something to replace those hideous sweats. Sifting through the clothes, I spotted a nice little t-shirt dress that would've only set me back twelve dollars, but then I remembered that night's mission. The jeans and top I picked out cost almost twice as much, but they were more suitable for climbing walls and sneaking between hedges.

I changed in the fitting room, paid, and left the store in my new outfit, happily tossing the Hotel Westscott garb onto the backseat of my car.

Next, I made another trip to the hardware store for a pair of bolt cutters and a Sur-Guard padlock to replace the one I planned to remove so I could access the alarm panel.

That night, I returned to my neighborhood and approached my apartment by scaling the wall that bordered the parking lot the same way I had last night. The Santa Ana winds, mild a few hours earlier, were blowing so hard that the rustling palm trees sounded almost like the ocean. This time when I reached the panel box, I was ready. I took the bolt cutters from my backpack, gripped the shank of the lock in the bolt cutter's jaws, and squeezed the handles as hard as I could. The shank barely gave. I tried again and then a third time before I heard a satisfying click. The lock fell away, allowing the door to drift open, exposing the system wiring. Now came the tricky part.

I closed my eyes and steadied my breathing. My pulse echoed in my ears while I counted down.

"*... three ... two ...*"

On one, I cut the wire to one of the fourth-floor apartments, which sent a signal to the monitoring company, informing them that there'd been a security breach. Next I unscrewed the lead for the wire dedicated to my apartment's alarm, enough to break the contact but not enough to be noticed by anything less than a thorough inspection. Then I shut the panel door and clamped the new lock in place to make it look as though no one had tampered with the box. Time elapsed: twelve-point-five seconds. Excellent. But now wasn't the time to flatter myself.

Keeping low, I peeked around the edge of the building. Any second, there'd be a call from police dispatch reporting a break-in at the very address where an officer happened to be stationed.

First came the squelch of the radio through the cop's open window, followed by a male voice. "I have a report of a 459S at the Royal Vista Apartments, 1466 Westchester Court, apartment 412. Available units, please respond."

A code 459 was a burglar alarm and the "S" meant it was silent. All the better to catch a suspect in the act.

The cop grabbed the mic attached to his radio. "Unit 3-Lincoln-14 responding." He sprinted from his car and dashed through the front door, using a key I could only guess he'd gotten from the manager. I edged around the building for a better look through the mostly glass door and saw the cop forego the elevator in favor of the stairs. I gave him what I thought was a three-floor head start and entered the building using my own key.

Rather than go upstairs right away and risk running into him, I sought refuge in the janitor's closet. I turned over an empty bucket, had a seat, and started counting. The closet smelled of bleach, pine, and ammonia, which I didn't mind at first, but by the time I hit two hundred, my nose was itching. At five hundred, my eyes were watering, and when I cracked the door open after reaching a thousand, I swore that smell would be in my head forever.

I located the stairwell and crept up six flights in the dark. D was right: we always returned home. I'd set my alarm connected to my apartment, like I did any time I left home, but since I'd loosened the wire inside the control panel, there'd be no record of my coming and going should anyone bother to check.

The good thing about breaking into my own home was that, even in the dark, I knew where everything was, like the kitchen counter. Without thinking, I ran my hand across it, feeling for Terry's keys. They weren't there, and it was stupid of me to think they might've been. I made a beeline for the kitchen pantry, where, inside a fake bottle of two-liter soda, I kept my go-bag: a super cute molasses-colored leather pouch that contained a fake ID, an accompanying passport and credit card, and twenty-five Benjamins.

Next, I packed. I filled a duffle bag with a few outfits, shoes, and essentials from the bathroom. I ran down my mental checklist and, certain I had everything, set off to make my escape. Halfway to the door, however, a rattling sound stopped me in my tracks.

Thinking someone was trying to get in through the front door, I dropped everything and raced back to the bedroom. I peeked out from the doorway. Nothing. I returned to collect my duffle bag when I heard the rattle again — from above. The skylight. It must've come loose during the windstorm. I'd have to report it to the manager once my life returned to normal. I started for the door, but froze once again, looking up at the skylight.

Of course! That was how he'd done it.

I took the stairwell up to the building's roof, a flat surface covered with clay and gravel. All the top floor apartments had skylights, marked by translucent plastic half-domes poking up from the roof. I located mine just as another gust of wind came up, blowing my hair across my face and creating the rattle I'd heard. I tucked my hair behind my ears and kneeled to examine the skylight. The four bolts that fastened the dome to the roof were missing, and a small nudge moved it easily. This was how Trammell had gotten in — only it couldn't have been Trammell. He was in his fifties with a bit of a spare tire, and the drop from the roof to the floor of my apartment was at least twelve feet. He must've had help; someone he trusted who could also do gymnastics.

Searching the area around the skylight, I saw perfectly formed shoe impressions in the clay, thanks to the other night's rain. They were considerably bigger than mine. That wasn't a whole lot to go on, but it gave me an idea. I went back to the apartment, grabbed my phone, and returned to the roof. After snapping a couple photos of the footprints, I grabbed my stuff and cleared out, back the way I'd come.

I checked into a moderately priced (for L.A.) hotel favored by business travelers in Century City. It was nothing at all like the Westcott, but the room was clean and safe, and it provided me with the best night's sleep I'd had since this nightmare began.

THE NEXT MORNING, THE BOUNCY MELODIES OF MAROON 5 snatched me from deep slumber.

At first, I fumbled for the remote, thinking I'd left the television on, but remembered it was my phone's alarm, which I'd set for six a.m. I groaned and stumbled out of bed. A peek through the drawn curtains confirmed that, for the second day in a row, I really had woken up before the sun. To think there were people who willingly did that five days a week. Ugh.

I slogged through a shower, dressed, and headed for the offices of Briggs & Harper Public Relations in Venice.

The company shared a rectangular duplex with a law firm. The lights inside were off, and the small parking lot in the back was empty. I parked across the street from the building and kept watch on the entrance.

At 7:25, two cars arrived in near succession, followed eight minutes later by Shawna Larson, at the wheel of an older, maroon Honda Civic. I jumped out of my car and hurried across the street, reaching the parking lot behind the building just as she was getting out. She was tall and broad-shouldered. Her dishwater blonde hair was pulled into a simple ponytail.

"Shawna?"

She looked up, startled.

"I'm sorry," I said. "My name is Kate. Can I have a moment of your time?"

Let's add this up: a strange woman called her by name and approached her in the parking lot of her workplace first thing in the morning. I deserved the guarded look she was giving me.

I tried again. "I'm conducting an investigation into the death of Denise Ladd, and I was hoping you could give me some information."

She furrowed her brow. "I don't think I know a Denise L—"

"Actually, my questions are about Robin Castro. I believe there's a connection."

When she heard Robin's name, she swallowed and shrank back. "I really don't think—"

"It'll just take a moment. I promise. I was curious how the two of you met."

"What does that have to do with anything?"

"Honestly? Maybe nothing, but if you'll humor me for just a moment, I promise I'll get out of your hair."

She sighed and then paused, recalling the memory. "We were both journalism majors and had a couple classes together. She was always friendly and easy to talk to. At first, I just saw her around campus, but then we started hanging out, going to parties, stuff like that."

"So you guys got to be pretty close?"

"Uh huh. For a while anyway."

"Then what happened?"

On the street, the sound of a car racing by briefly drew Shawna's attention, but she turned back to me once the engine's roar faded down the block. "She met the rich guy."

The conversation lapsed as I waited for Shawna to elaborate. She must've thought "the rich guy" said it all.

Spurring her on, I asked, "Do you mean Trey Spencer?"

"Yeah, Trey. She started spending a lot of time with him and his friends. First it was parties and clubs. Next thing I know, I'm on Facebook and there's pictures of Robin with him in Chicago or Napa or some other place."

"You two didn't hang out as much after that?"

"I still saw her sometimes, just not like before. She invited me to a couple parties, but it was mainly a Greek scene — not really my thing. I don't think I was their kinda girl either — you know, the cutesy type."

Her words were nonchalant without a hint of bitterness, which surprised me at first, but then again, this had happened three years ago. Now working a job that required her presence at the crack of dawn, perhaps she didn't have the bandwidth to worry about what a bunch of guys from college thought of her.

"But Robin? She and Trey were happy?"

"I guess so. She didn't really talk to me about him, and I didn't ask, but I saw lots of happy-looking Instagram pictures."

All that jet-setting around was nothing to people like the Ellingtons or the Spencers, but I couldn't believe it didn't have an impact on someone like Robin, a girl from a working class background with no means to speak of. "So everything was okay, as far as you know?"

Shawna nodded but seemed distracted. She kept looking past me toward the street.

"Really?" I asked.

"I gotta go. I have to be at my desk before the partners get in. Besides, that's ... that's everything I know."

"Shawna, wait."

"I'm sorry. I can't."

She turned away and hurried to the safety of the building, the door banging shut on any further questions.

For whatever good it would do, when I was back in my car, I looked up her LinkedIn profile and sent her a message. I gave her my phone number and asked her to call me if she remembered anything. Next I put in a call to Aubrey's office.

"Hey. I see you're still out there making trouble," she said, referencing my Hollywood and Highland escapade.

"Yeah, well, that's me. Listen, I need a favor."

She sighed. "What is it now, Kate?"

"This movie of Trammell's," I said. "Any chance there's a stuntman on the payroll?"

16

I t was trash day in Lucas Blaisdale's neighborhood, one of the older sections of Burbank. Bins and cans sat along the curb in front of houses that looked as though they'd been built around the same time as the Karmabile.

From the moment I pulled up to Lucas's house, I had trouble believing he was associated with Trammell Preston. Far from a sprawling mansion, Lucas's place wasn't much bigger than a house for an American Girl doll, albeit one considerably down on her luck. Patchy grass surrounded a small square house with a paint job that had faded to a pale shade of green, and the left edge of the roof was sagging. But if he had Whim, or knew anything that could help me find her, none of that mattered.

Things could've gone differently for Lucas. A decade earlier, he was a rising star as a stuntman. He jumped off bridges, stood atop the roofs of speeding cars, even dangled from the skids of a helicopter in some of Hollywood's biggest blockbusters. Then meth happened. He churned through his money, and when that was gone, he held up a dry cleaner at gunpoint. To make matters worse, he carjacked someone in the parking lot during his attempted getaway. Three minutes, two felonies—not bad. The cops caught him without further incident, and he did three years in Lompoc, but when he got out, he discovered that the movie business no longer had any use for him. Until Trammell Preston came along.

Walking up to the house, I noticed a pair of boots and some old sneakers outside the door. I held one of the dusty boots up to the light. A crusty layer that was the same color as the clay on the roof of my apartment caked the sole. Then I compared them to the pictures I'd taken near my skylight. I couldn't be certain, but Lucas's boots sure did look like the ones that had made those footprints. I walked the boots back to the curb and dumped them in the trash bin as the growl of a garbage truck's diesel engine came from down the block. Two guys riding on the back of the truck hopped off, darted to opposite sides of the street, and began emptying trash bins into the back of the truck.

I returned to the house, knocked, and endured several quiet seconds before I heard footsteps pounding against a bare floor. When the front door swung open, an unshaven Lucas stood before me without a shirt or shoes. He was wearing jeans that had long since given up trying to be blue. In his mid-thirties, he was the kind of thin that didn't make people jealous; it made them want to buy him a hamburger. There was something familiar about him.

"Yeah?" he said.

"Lucas Blaisdale?"

His eyes narrowed as he tried to place me. I did the same.

"Who's asking?"

"The woman whose apartment you broke into a few nights ago."

His eyebrows lifted briefly before he recovered his tough-guy stance. "I don't know what you're talking about … either do you."

"That's *neither* do you, and of course you know what I'm talking about. You came in through the skylight while I was sleeping, you creeper, and you made off with my dog. Is this ringing any bells?"

He rubbed the back of his neck and smiled, revealing a missing upper cuspid. Drape a hoodie over his head and — *Whoa!* He was the same guy who'd let me into Denise's apartment building.

Looking at the approaching garbage truck, he raised his voice so I could hear him over it. "Like I said, I dunno what you're talking about. Besides, you gotta pin it on me first, sweet cheeks."

He turned, poised the slam the door in my face.

"Yeah, forensics is really good for that."

He hesitated.

"You know, footprints on the roof that match yours, dirt or fibers from your boots that you left on my carpet when you jumped down from the skylight, a stray hair with your DNA on it ... Does a guy with your history want to have to explain that to the district attorney?"

I could practically hear the thoughts ping-ponging in his head as he debated whether to call my bluff.

"Here's the deal, Lucas. My dog is a purebred, valued at over a thousand dollars. That's grand theft, and you know what that means for someone in the state of California who already has two felony convictions? You go away for a while, with none of that suspended sentence stuff this time."

His face went blank while his knuckles whitened around the doorframe. I guessed he was having a not-so-pleasant flashback of his prison stint.

"Your boots are just a text message away from going to LAPD's crime lab," I said, nodding to the empty spot on the porch. "They're already in the hands of a good friend of mine who's a PI. All I have to do is say the word."

When Lucas saw that his boots were indeed gone, he licked his lips and shifted his weight to the other foot. "What? You ... you took my boots?"

"That's nothing compared to you taking my dog. I just don't know how you managed to not get bitten."

"Well ..." He gave me a sheepish smile. "He mighta been sleeping."

"Excuse me?"

His smile evaporated. "Your dog, he—"

"She."

"Oh. She mighta had a little something to help her sleep ... before I came in."

My eyes flew wide open. "You slipped my dog a Mickey?"

"Umm ..."

"You slipped. My dog. A Mickey?" A tattered, rolled-up issue of the community paper was lying on the porch. I picked it up and threw it at him.

He ducked and it smacked the front door like a dead fish before hitting the ground.

"Hey! Come on."

"Where is she?"

My question bounced off him as he was once again preoccupied with the doorstep. "Those were my favorite boots ..."

"Lucas!" I snapped my fingers to get his attention. "If you don't start talking, the only boots in your future are the ones you'll be knocking in San Quentin."

The garbage truck pulled up to Lucas's curb. One of the men seized his garbage bin, emptied its contents into the back, and tossed the bin in the general direction of the yard before moving on to the next house.

"Where's my dog?"

"I-I-I don't know. I gave hi—her to Preston. You're not gonna tell him I told you this, are you? I really need this gig."

That was obvious. While I had no interest in ratting him out to Trammell or seeing him go back to prison, Lucas Blaisdale was a dognapper, and not a particularly bright one either. So he wasn't getting off Scot-free.

"Cross my palm with silver, dude."

He did a double take. "Huh?"

"You want me to keep quiet? I want twenty-five hundred dollars, and I better not hear you say you don't have it. A little bird at Cash4U told me you're in there every two weeks like clockwork, cashing a tidy paycheck, and guess what yesterday was?"

Actually, the little bird was Aubrey, but I'd given her my word that I wouldn't let any of this blow back on her. She'd said most of the others on the payroll received their money by direct deposit, but Lucas insisted on getting a check that he took to the check-cashing service near his house.

He looked at me squinty-eyed again. "Who are you?"

Rather than answer, I crossed my arms and waited, until finally he dug a wallet out of his back pocket. It was thick, like one holding plenty of cash. He counted off several bills, got confused, and started over.

"How 'bout fifteen hundred?" he finally said. "I gotta pay bills ... and I got alimony."

While digging into Lucas's background, I'd learned that he was indeed divorced, but I doubted his ex-wife was seeing any of that money. More than likely, Lucas's cash was finding its way into his friendly neighborhood meth dealer's pocket.

"Consider this a goodwill offering to the universe for someone being willing to marry you in the first place." I pocketed the money and then, just to mess with him, added, "I'll be back for the rest."

Lucas stood watch from his doorway as I walked back to my car. He and Aubrey made two industry outcasts who'd been hired to work on Trammell's movie, and I knew enough about him to safely say he wasn't rehabilitating lost souls.

I looked back at Lucas before getting into the car. "What kind of stunts are you doing for this movie anyway?"

SHREVIE'S PLACE, THE CLAY POT, OCCUPIED A WEST HOLLYWOOD side street next to a chiropractor. A mammoth billboard featuring lingerie models loomed above. I parked down the block from the doctor's office and checked out a quintet of parking violation signs attached to a nearby light pole: the top one said no parking from seven to seven; the second one upped the ante — no parking at all on weekends; however, that was trumped by the third sign, which allowed you to park where you wanted if you had a city permit; except, according to a sign beneath it, on Thursdays because of street sweeping; and the bottom sign advised drivers to curb their wheels or risk a citation. Outlaw that I am, I tempted fate and left my tires parallel.

Inside the shop, three middle-aged women and a guy who looked around thirty stood over pottery wheels powered by whiny little motors. With heavily stained smocks and slickened hands the color of mud, the group did its best to coax mounds of wet clay into bowls. Or were they vases? Or, in one woman's case, something strongly resembling the Leaning Tower of Pisa.

An older, thick-bellied man with tousled salt-and-pepper hair on his head and chin walked back and forth among the group, nodding and musing and offering a suggestion here or a compliment there. He wore those round glasses that I always thought were more appropriately described as spectacles. When he noticed me standing inside his doorway, he displayed his version of a smile, which was more like a lopsided twist of his lips.

"Good day, Miss," he said as though I were a total stranger. No sense in risking raising his students' suspicions. "Can I help you?"

"I placed a special order. The, um, diamond-shaped platter?"

He pondered, looking for all the world as if he couldn't remember. "Oh, yes! Right this way, please."

I followed him across the dusty floor to a door in the back that led to a small work area. A bench with a scarred tabletop was covered with tools, and a magnifying lamp clamped to the edge.

No sooner had he shut the door behind us than he reeled me into a bear hug. "Kate, how are you?"

He smelled of clay and ham, the latter probably came from a bit of his lunch that had gotten stuck in his beard, but it didn't matter.

"I've been so worried about you," he said.

"Oh, Shrevie. Don't believe everything you hear on the news."

I assured him that I was fine, I'd had nothing to do with Denise's murder, and the whole thing would clear up before either of us knew it. One of us might have even believed the last part, though I couldn't tell which.

He nodded and changed the subject to my outfit, a white eyelet overlaying a white dress cinched at the waist. It was complimented by a whiskey-colored shoulder bag. "Not that you don't normally look smashing, but you especially look so today. Would your outfit have anything to do with this?"

He took a key from his pocket and opened a drawer underneath the workbench. Inside was a small, black jewel box that he handed to me.

"You know I can't tell you that. Plausible deniability and whatnot." The ring inside the box was a nearly perfect replica of the one at Sterling-Ross. "But I can tell you that you are a true artist."

He shrugged. "It pays the bills. Heaven knows these classes don't."

Years ago, Shrevie opened up a shop downtown, where he sold these beautiful vases that he made by hand. The business was hardly thriving, but he was doing something he loved. One day, he got a visit from two guys calling themselves "insurance salesmen." Long story short, Shrevie wouldn't pay, and a couple weeks later, his shop was torched. He had insurance, but because the fire looked like a case of arson meant to bail out a struggling business, the insurance company rejected his claim. He was about to start over, but then his wife had a stroke, maybe because of all the worry and stress. He racked up some serious debt to get her the care she needed. The energy, not to mention the money, to try again just wasn't there, so he did whatever it took to make ends meet, including doing me the occasional favor.

I handed him an envelope with cash inside. He took the money out and counted it. Not because he thought I'd shorted him, but just the opposite. I used to slip him an extra Benjamin or two as if I'd miscounted, but he got wise and insisted on taking only what we'd agreed upon, not a penny more, even though he could've used it.

"Be careful out there, hear me? And let me know if there's anything else I can do to help."

"You got it, Shrevie." I gave him another hug and quickly left, as usual. He was the closest thing I had to a father in L.A., and that tiny studio on that tiny street made me sad. Shrevie wasn't like Lucas. His misfortune hadn't been self-inflicted.

The trip to Sterling-Ross was quick and, even better, the salesperson who greeted me was the same woman I'd encountered during my first visit. From the moment I walked in today, though, it was, "Good afternoon, ma'am!" "How are you today, ma'am?" "Is there anything I can show you today, ma'am?" No doubt it had everything to do with my outfit. She had no clue she was talking to the same person she'd treated like used toilet paper two days earlier.

I perused the display for a few minutes, barely acknowledging her suggestions, when I wasn't ignoring them altogether. When I reached the ring, I showed a hint of interest, hoping she'd smell a sale.

"Ooh!" she gushed, not disappointing me. "The Criswell. That's an exquisite piece!"

She prattled on about its cut and color and a half dozen other things, some of which she got wrong, proving the old adage: if you can't dazzle them with brilliance, baffle them with you-know-what.

"When one wears a ring like this, you can feel your inner superstar bursting out!"

Did people actually talk like that? Did other people actually fall for it?

"*One* can just feel," I said.

Barbara knitted her brow and quit rambling. "How's that?"

I continued admiring the ring's fit and addressed her as though we were discussing the weather or toothbrushes. "You said, 'When *one* wears a ring like this, *you* can just feel *your* inner rock star' or something like that. It should've been 'one can feel one's inner rock star' blah blah blah. I mean, unless you want people to think you're an idiot who doesn't recognize an improper shift in pronouns."

From the corner of my eye, I noticed her cheeks redden. She ahemmed and glanced across the showroom at her smirking co-worker. Nice to know someone else was enjoying the moment as much as I was.

A reflection in the showroom mirror caught my eye. A man in a suit was approaching the store. He reached for the door handle while propping his phone against his ear with his other hand. The chime sounded, announcing his arrival, and Barbara, probably grateful for a reason to get away from me, looked toward the door.

In the time it took her to welcome him to Sterling-Ross and

assure him someone would be right with him, I reached behind my neck and pretended to adjust my hair. What I was really doing was a little sleight of hand: I slipped the ring off my finger while removing Shrevie's copy, which was hanging from a hairpin threaded through my hair. Then it was a simple matter of switching the two, and Babs would never be the wiser.

Holding my hand up to the light, I admired the ring once more before thanking Barbara for her time. "I need to think this over."

I slipped the fake ring off and placed it back on the felt-covered display stand. With a forced smile, she said she understood and put the ring back in the case. That was my cue to vanish.

I was nearly out the door when I was yanked back by the shoulder. Panic raced through me before I realized it was just my purse strap getting caught on the door handle. I freed myself and, with a more graceful exit, was on the way back to my car.

Halfway down the block, I'd just slowed to a normal pace when someone behind me called out, "Miss?"

17

I turned and came face to face with the man in the suit who'd entered the store moments earlier.

There was a handful of other pedestrians around, about half of them women. I hoped whoever had called out was talking to one of them and quickened my strides without bothering to look back, but the footsteps behind me picked up pace as well, matching mine.

"Miss? Can I have a word with you, please?"

The voice belonged to a man, one who wanted to catch me bad enough that he'd all but broken into a sprint. Great. My second foot chase in three days. But this time I was rocking cutout leather Louboutins (they *so* set off that dress), and I couldn't have outrun five o'clock traffic on the Hollywood Freeway. I was certain I'd gotten away clean, but maybe I had to give Babs credit. I'd figured she wouldn't spot the fake for a couple of days, if that.

I turned, expecting to see the salesman from Sterling-Ross as my pursuer, but instead came face to face with the man who'd entered the store while I was making the switch. Talk about a surprise, and a nice-looking one at that.

He stood somewhere around six feet tall, with a slender but athletic build, light gray eyes that caught the sunlight, and dark hair that he wore in a short, low-maintenance cut. His suit was charcoal gray herringbone, paired with a white shirt and a soft blue tie. Men's footwear wasn't really my thing, but I could tell his black Oxfords hadn't come cheap.

I waited for him to say something, but he didn't. He swallowed. He had a nice Adam's apple, as far as those things go.

"Yes?" I finally asked.

"Uh ... hi." He shifted his weight to the right and stuffed his hands in his pockets.

No. Way. In the middle of a heist? Once, during a job, I was treed by a Rottweiler. I'd also gotten a flat tire, lost my keys, and had to change an infant's diaper. But getting hit on? Never.

"I ... noticed you back there in the jewelry store."

"Oh. Yeah. Look, I swear it's nothing personal, but I'm kind of in the middle of someth—"

"That's okay," he said. "You don't have to explain. It was stupid of me."

He stuffed his hands in his pockets and, with a forced smile, started back the way he'd come. He was taking no for answer? Just like that? So not what I'd come to expect from an L.A. guy. Was it possible he was ... different? From Terry or, heaven forbid, Niles? Just then, I wasn't sure about dating anybody, but yet I found myself blurting out, "Wait." He turned, and I lifted my shades and smiled. "Hi."

Still with his hands in his pockets, he smiled in return before dropping his gaze to the pavement. It's not like I'm some smoking hot supermodel who leaves guys speechless (if my hair feels like behaving, I might achieve cute), so why was such a cute guy having trouble using his words? Was there a hunk of food stuck in my teeth that was giving him second thoughts?

"I'm Connor."

Whew. Nothing edible on display. "Theresa."

Shoot! Where had that come from? Having just walked off with an eighteen thousand dollar piece of jewelry, my guard must have been up. I started to correct myself, even though it made me look like a total ditz. Who confused Theresa with Kate? Maybe, though, my subconscious had just done me a favor by getting me to use my alias. Kate Albertson was wanted for questioning. I wouldn't have told him my last name, but if he'd been paying any attention to the news at all, just knowing my first name plus my description might have been enough for him to put two and two together. Then, instead of calling me up for a date, he'd be calling the cops.

"Theresa," he repeated, probably committing it to memory. *Awesome.* He had a bashful smile that was charming in its own way. "It's very nice to meet you."

"It's nice to meet you too."

He shifted his weight back to the left. "Uh, you looked like you were in a pretty big hurry, so I don't want to hold you up—"

Interesting choice of words. Indeed, I was in a hurry, and yes, because of a hold-up.

"—but I was wondering if you'd like to get together sometime?"

I smiled again. "Um ... sure. I mean, I'd like that."

I gave him my number and apologized for making him run after me. When I was safely back in my car, I couldn't stop laughing over the absurdity of getting hit on while making my exit. I reached back and freed the ring. The stones glinted in the afternoon sunlight. Babs's nonsense about my inner super-star aside, the ring was perfect.

THE RED MERCEDES — WHICH, AS I'D LEARNED BACK AT THE library, was registered to Celeste — had the the Spencers' driveway to itself. With any luck, that meant Mr. Spencer was still at work. I parked in front. As I approached the door and pushed the doorbell, I tried to calm my butterflies. The bell hesitated before responding with two long chimes, the second one a little lower in pitch.

While I waited, I surveyed the neighboring houses. Most of them were large, but on small lots. In a few cases, neighbors could have shaken hands through their kitchen windows. The Spencers lived next door to a two-story hunk of stone that probably left their house in shadows when the sun was just right. They must have spent a small fortune on their gardener though. Starting on either side of the walkway and fanning out was a floral rainbow consisting of roses, lilies, daisies, and a slew of other flowers I couldn't hope to recognize.

A fifty-ish woman answered the door. She had shoulder-length, light-brown hair and chiseled cheekbones. Her eyes were a deep shade of brown, and she looked at me like I was there to rob the place, but I'd already pulled my heist for the day.

"Can I help you?"

I smiled, trying my best to put her at ease. "I hope so. I'm looking for Celeste Spencer."

She gave me a once-over, the wariness of her expression deepening. "I'm Celeste Spencer."

"Hi, I'm Theresa McDermott." Proper use of the alias that time. I extended my hand. "Would it be possible for us to talk for a moment?"

We shook, although she broke it off quickly. "About what?"

"Can we talk inside? It's ... sensitive."

She glanced back over her shoulder and then held the door aside, inviting me in. I followed her across a ceramic tile floor to a sitting area that would be nice once all the moving boxes were out of the way. As it stood, the room was furnished with an olive-green sofa and a glass coffee table. The area was small, but with the sunlight bouncing off the light-colored floor, it seemed larger. The walls were bare, and a handful of moving boxes were sitting just inside the hallway.

Celeste motioned to the sofa. I sat, and she followed suit, with an erect posture and crossed arms.

"I apologize for the clutter. We're still getting settled."

"Oh, no apologies necessary." I took in the sitting area and the family room across the hall. "It's lovely. How long have you been here?"

"Just a couple weeks. My husband wanted to be closer to his work."

I nodded, even though I knew she was spinning fiction.

Sitting in traffic is part of life in L.A. People don't move to be closer to work, and that goes double for people in Pacific Palisades. They just buy nicer cars.

"But what can I do for you, Ms. McDermott?"

I took a long, deep breath and gave what was meant to look like a nervous smile. "Well, as I mentioned, I find myself in a very delicate situation. Quite frankly, I'm not sure how to handle it, and since it involves a friend of yours, I thought you might be able to give me some guidance."

"What friend?"

After inhaling again, I said, "Virginia Ellington."

Celeste tried to play it cool, but the gentle lift of her eyebrow at the mention of Virginia's name suggested I had her attention.

"I'm ... I'm her daughter."

The sound of her clearing her throat echoed through the mostly vacant room.

"She was young ... in high school," I continued. "She put me up for adoption and ..."

I stopped to compose myself, giving Celeste a chance to say something, but she sat silently. Only now, she'd unfolded her arms and was leaning forward a bit.

"I found out the truth from my ... my other parents. It's taken me a while to find her, and I'd like to meet her, but ..."

Celeste shifted closer to me and lowered her voice. "But what?"

"I'm not sure if now is the best time, with her divorce and everything. I mean ... I heard she can be sort of ... ruthless?"

I couldn't quite put my finger on her reaction. Her lips hinted at a smile that matched a brief flicker in her eyes. If Virginia Ellington had skeletons, I sensed Celeste knew exactly which door they were hiding behind.

"Who told you a thing like that?" she asked.

"I'm not sure I should say, but ... that actress who was having an affair with Dr. Ellington? The one who died the other day? I heard Virginia threatened to kill her."

Celeste threw her head back and gave a hearty, almost boisterous laugh. Frankly it was out of character for someone who, according to Jimmy, was obsessed with maintaining a prim and proper image. The idea of Virginia committing murder must've sounded that ridiculous to her.

"I see you've tapped into the Briarwood gossip mill." She laughed a little more before composing herself. "Well, yes, Virginia may have said such a thing. However, it shouldn't be taken any more literally than when someone says, 'I'm so hungry I could eat a horse.'"

The phone rang, and a check of the caller ID prompted a groan from Celeste. I expected her to let the call go to voicemail, but she answered it. "Hi, Mom."

That explained her reaction.

"Yes, we're still unpacking." Celeste rolled her eyes and reclined in her chair, which I took to mean that the call might take a while. The conversation excited me even less, so I signaled for her attention and mouthed for directions to the restroom. She pointed over my shoulder, and I left her to carry on.

Getting to the bathroom required stepping around a handful of boxes littering the hardwood floor leading from the den, past the kitchen, and down a short hallway. The bathroom was the first door on the left. I'd assumed it was the powder room for guests, but lining the counter were a razor, shaving cream, a bottle of prescription medication, and some body spray that, according to the commercials, would inspire women to eat off a man's naked torso.

I finished up and had every intention of returning to the den, really, but farther down the hall were open doorways and, doggone it, to someone like me, that might as well have been a written invitation.

The first door led to a bedroom, sparsely furnished like much of the rest of the house, with just a bed and a dresser. Though there wasn't much to see, the mirror atop the dresser caught my eye, or rather, the photo tucked into the corner did. In it were five college kids — three boys and two girls — standing in front of the It's A Small World ride at Disneyland. They were sporting Mickey Mouse ears and mile-wide grins as they posed for the camera, arms draped over one another's shoulders. The boys wore blue t-shirts with white fraternity letters — Delta Rho Sigma.

Immediately, I saw Celeste in the boy occupying the middle of the photo. They had the same eyes and smile. That must've been his stuff in the bathroom. I would've expected him to be sharing a place with roommates closer to his age, but if I had access to a house as nice as this one, I might've still been living at home too.

The girl on the end was a cute blonde, but the girl huddled next to Celeste's son, holding his hand, had thick, dark hair down to her shoulders and a face that belonged on the cover of a magazine. I flipped the photo over. Written on the back in delicate print was: *To Trey, My favorite Spencer man ... as if. LOL Love, Robin*

The late Robin Castro. Sorrow flooded through me just as it had when I'd spoken to Denise's sister. It was so unfair that there hadn't been any justice for them. And yes, I'm entirely aware of how that sounds coming from a professional law-breaker.

A sigh escaped me as I turned the photo back over. Hanging onto it, seeing it every time he looked in the mirror, must have been devastating Trey. Then again, like Michelle hanging on tightly to her sister's dog, what else did he have left of her?

As I put the photo back in its place, another one caught my eye. This one was hanging from the wall and was made up of a series of black-and-white, oval-shaped portraits, with "Decades of Distinction" printed across the top. Each portrait was of a man in a dark suit, white shirt, and tie, with each man's name and a date — the year the picture was taken — at the bottom. Arthur Spencer's portrait, on the far left, was the oldest, taken in 1886. Trey's, from 2009, was the most recent addition. Six other men, all with the last name Spencer, were in between, but it came across as more of a club photo than a family picture. Written at the very bottom of the picture was, "No generation gaps in our excellence," but that wasn't true. Between two of the portraits was a blank space that had been smoothed over, but upon closer inspection, the outline of an oval was still visible. Someone had been taken out of the picture. Was that how the Spencers dealt with their proverbial black sheep? Erasing them from existence?

I needed to get back to Celeste but couldn't resist peeking inside one more room. The master was at the end of the hall and in a similar state as the rest of the house — livable but hardly what anyone would call decorated. A mammoth bed with a walnut panel headboard took up a big portion of the room. Celeste would probably be mortified if she knew I'd seen the mound of disheveled sheets atop the mattress.

Through the open closet door, I spotted a pair of scarlet

cutout sandals and knew I couldn't leave without seeing them up close. I held one up and — between the snakeskin print zipper closure on the back and the four-inch heel — decided that prim and proper Celeste must have a wild side she kept hidden, except for when she and her hubby ventured out to a swingers' club.

Smiling at the thought, I put the shoe down next to its mate, turned, and then whipped back to face the closet. It was one of the few places that had been fully unpacked. An upper and lower row of Celeste's dresses, skirts, slacks, and gowns lined the left side, while her husband's things were on the right. About halfway down the top row on his side, between a tuxedo and a navy pinstriped suit, was a black-and-white tartan jacket, just like the one I'd seen a guest wearing at Trammell's party. And not just any guest, but the one who'd nearly caught me coming out of the host's bedroom with a certain diamond necklace in my possession.

Was it possible? Sure, L.A. was a big place, but two guys in the same social circle with the same poor taste in sports jackets? Plus, the guy who'd been wearing that jacket that night at the party had been a zipper or two away from hooking up with Thor. Was *that* Celeste's husband? Did she have any clue?

I ran my hand along the jacket. Near the pocket, something rattled. I pulled out a bottle of pills — something called risperidone — prescribed to Richard Spencer, III. My mind raced back to the night of the party. When Niles had walked in on the two guys in the bedroom, he'd called one of them R.J. ... as in Richard Spencer, *Junior?* So why did he have Richard III's pills? I returned to the bathroom. The medication on the counter was also prescribed to Richard Spencer, III, or to Trey, the guy in the picture, and it was the same medication as what I'd found in the jacket pocket. Was Dad mooching his son's pills?

What other information could I have unearthed with a little more time to poke around? Probably something that would've made my head explode, but the hourglass was out of sand. After giving the toilet a courtesy flush and running some water, I returned to the den, where Celeste was poking through one of the boxes.

"Everything okay with your mom?" I asked.

"Yes. I just had to endure the latest drama involving my sister in San Francisco." She shook her head. "Anyhow, where were we?"

"You were saying you think it was simple exaggeration? I mean, for Virg — my mom to say something that sounded like a threat toward that girl who died. You have to admit the timing sure is strange."

"Yes, simple exaggeration." Celeste sat back in the loveseat, regaining her perfect posture. "Well, that and ..." She pantomimed sipping from a glass, making her the second person to allude to Mrs. Ellington's drinking problem.

I did my best to act surprised. "Alcohol? Really?"

Celeste placed a finger to her lips. How much of that Briar-wood gossip mill originated with her, and what else might she spill? Before I got the chance to ask, a large, gunmetal grey SUV motored up to the house, and through the window I saw two men climb out from the vehicle, laughing so hard I expected Jimmy Fallon to step out as well. When they burst through the door a moment later, the laughter had barely subsided. Perhaps Virginia Ellington wasn't the only one who enjoyed knocking back a few.

A man who looked around Celeste's age entered the house first, followed by Trey, a few years older than he was in the photo I'd seen in his bedroom. Both were dressed in casual slacks and polo shirts that showed off their tanned arms. They took note of me, bringing an end to the hilarity, and crossed over to where Celeste and I were sitting.

"I wasn't expecting my two favorite Spencer men back this soon," she said.

The younger man, draping an arm around the other man seemingly for support, said, "And yet back we are ... by pop'lar demand!"

His remark prompted more laughter. Even Celeste joined in. The joke passed me by, but I never found drunks funny.

The older man leaned toward Celeste and kissed the cheek she offered.

"We called it a day after nine holes," he said.

Golf. That would explain the tans and also the drinking. When I was a kid, my dad dragged me out to the golf course with him a few times, and he always insisted on drinking beer while he played.

Celeste nodded before turning back to me. "This is my husband, Richard, and our son, Trey.

"This lovely young woman is Theresa McDermott," Celeste said, indicating me. "She's with the homeowners' association and stopped by to welcome us to the neighborhood."

I was impressed by how easily she fabricated a story. In fact, I made a mental note to remember the homeowners' association bit.

The elder Spencer stepped forward and took my hand. "Pleasure to meet you, Theresa. I'm sure we're going to love it here."

"I'm sure you will too," I said. "It's a great neighborhood."

Following his father's lead, Trey shook my hand. Golf wasn't the only thing they had in common. They shared the same height as well, practically standing shoulder to shoulder.

"It was a pleasure," the younger Spencer said and excused himself to clean up.

Having gotten what I'd come for — more than that, really — it was time to make myself scarce. Celeste walked me to my car, where I complimented her on her quick thinking with the homeowners' association bit.

"It was nothing," she said. "Besides, we girls have to stick together, don't we?"

"Absolutely." We exchanged an embrace. "So you think it would be okay for me to talk to Virginia?"

"I think she'd love to hear from her daughter after all these years. She'd probably be thrilled to see what a beautiful young woman you've turned out to be. And if you're worried about her violent tendencies," Celeste said, laughing, "just meet her in public. She has lunch at the club on Tuesdays and Thursdays."

I didn't have any allegiance to Virginia one way or another — I just wanted to know if she could've committed murder — but Celeste seemed awfully invested in our supposed reunion, maybe because she stood to benefit from Virginia Ellington's out-of-wedlock child emerging from the shadows. No doubt, moving out of the Pacific Palisades had kicked her down a peg in the eyes of her friends at the club. She probably wouldn't mind taking someone else down with her.

18

Evening was fast approaching by the time I left the Spencer home, with a head full of information but nothing that pointed to Celeste as the killer. She'd lied to her family about me easily enough, but that alone didn't make her a murderer. They seemed like a close-knit group — sharing inside jokes, father and son hanging out on the golf course — although something in the dynamic felt a little off, but I couldn't put my finger on it. And judging by the portrait in Trey's bedroom, being a member of the Spencer family was serious business.

I was heading down Sunset for a pass by my apartment, planning to then grab some dinner and call it a night, when I got a phone call. The number was blocked, but I answered, correctly guessing it was Trammell.

"You're not doing as I asked, Kate."

"What? You're the one who won't live up to the deal."

"Do you still want Whimsy back?"

"Of course."

"The price has just gone up."

"Gone up?"

"Are you familiar with the ACA's? The Artistry in Cinema Awards?"

"I can't say that I am."

"Last year, I collaborated on a project that won an award, but my partner saw fit to exclude my name from the nomination."

"Why would anybody do that?"

"Probably to take all the credit for himself."

"What does this have to do with me?"

"The winners receive a beautiful crystal statue in the shape of a movie camera. You're going to retrieve mine from Dynasty Filmworks."

"No way, Trammell. That wasn't part of our deal."

"We have a new deal now. And Ms. Albertson? Tick tock."

He laughed and hung up. It was all I could do not to hurl my phone out the window.

I was in the right lane on Wilshire, signaling for a right turn, when I decided to hit this little tapas bar a couple of blocks straight ahead.

Back when I was first getting my license, my driving instructor preached how important it was to check your rearview mirror any time you slowed down. I guess that was in the case of an impending rear-end collision, you'd have a millisecond to freak out before impact. Anyway, it became a habit, and just then I could've sworn the car behind me had signaled for a right turn too, but as I kept going straight through the intersection, the car was still behind me.

Suddenly, dinner became an afterthought. I passed the restaurant's entrance and kept straight on Wilshire, moving one lane to the left and then once more. In the mirror, I saw a pair of headlights two cars back, take the same path.

I'd never been followed before, but suddenly red flags were flapping like crazy. Farther down the street, I looked in the mirror again — still there. As I neared the heart of Beverly Hills, I turned left and took off. Just a block off Wilshire, the area transitioned from commercial to residential, and I flew down an empty neighborhood. I looked in the mirror again and saw only darkness. I was about to exhale, thinking I'd been pranked by my own imagination, when a car turned down the street after me. My grip on the wheel tightened. I gave the car more gas, rounded the next corner, and then made another left and a right, putting me back on Wilshire, heading in the opposite direction.

Looking in the mirror again, I saw that I still had company. At the next intersection, I got into the left turn lane. My stalker did the same, with a car in between us. There was a break in the oncoming traffic, and when I didn't make the turn, the driver behind me blasted his horn, but I waited, which only made him honk again. I inched forward and, as another cluster of cars approached, I shot through the intersection. The cars bearing down on me sounded their horns, while the traffic behind me was left waiting.

I twisted back and forth through the neighborhood, not even paying attention to where I was going, just making random turns. By the time whoever was following me made the left turn, they'd have no clue which way I'd gone.

I paused for a moment in front of an Italian restaurant on Little Santa Monica Boulevard. Even with my windows rolled up, the smell of garlic filled the car. My stomach raged in protest at having been neglected for the better part of the day. So that was it: I'd go back to the hotel, change into something comfortable, then treat myself to a nice dinner. I pulled away from the curb, took the next left, and headed toward Century City.

A shiver worked its way down my back as I checked the mirror. Call me crazy, but there was something familiar about the headlights behind me. At the first opportunity, I turned right and right again. When the car mimicked my every move, I gunned the engine and flew down the street.

Trammell's was the first name that came to mind. Had he been right behind me when he'd called? I didn't know why he'd be following me, but if he was, it only added to the list of things he'd done that didn't make sense. Or what about the cops? Was watching my apartment not enough? No. If L.A.'s finest knew where to find me, they wouldn't have wasted time with a tail. They would've pulled me over, snatched me from my car, and stuffed me into the back of theirs.

I managed to dig my phone out of my purse, dial, and put the call on speaker. It rang three times, then a fourth. "Come on. Pick up, pick up."

"Hello?" D said. In the background, I heard the unmistakable sizzle of a frying pan. I had him pegged as more of a to-go kind of guy.

"D? It's Kate."

His end of the line went silent, save for whatever was on the stove. "How's the fugitive life?"

"Not so good. I think I'm in trouble."

He snorted. "And you just now figured that out?"

"I'm serious. I'm having a religious experience."

"What?"

"I'm driving down Wilshire, and I've got someone following me like a disciple."

The cooking sound drifted off. He must've changed rooms. "And you wanted to know if it was me?"

"No, I ... I need help. I thought you might have experience with this sort of thing."

I heard him settle into a chair and laugh. He was laughing at me. "Are you sure you're being followed?"

I gave him a quick recap.

"Okay, yeah, that's a tail," he said.

I took a corner, wheels squealing.

"Kate? Are you speeding?"

"Well, duh. How else am I supposed to get rid of this—"

"Girl, you need to slow down."

"But—"

"Kate." D's voice was firm. "Slow. Down. You're supposed to be *avoiding* the police, remember?"

He had a point. Not only would the cops take great joy in busting a street racer, but this particular one had been evading them for days. By driving like a maniac, I risked dropping right into their laps.

"You up for a little game of chicken?" he asked.

"I'm up for anything that'll get whoever this is off my backside."

I listened carefully to his directions, which led me away from Beverly Hills. I headed east and then south through the Fairfax district. I kept a close eye on the rearview mirror. My stalker maintained a distance of two or three cars the whole time.

When I reached the 10, the freeway connecting L.A.'s west side to downtown and beyond, I passed underneath and kept going straight. Almost immediately, on the other side, the area underwent a demographic shift: still plenty of kids and couples getting gas or pulling into drive-thrus, but they tended to be brown or black. All of the businesses at the strip mall across the street had called it a day, except for a doughnut shop with a red neon sign in its window that read *abierto* — open.

A smile came to me as I passed what looked, at first, like some kids hanging out on a street corner but turned out to be a couple of Mickey D employees waiting on a bus. I got what D was up to, and a few blocks later, my friend had given up the ghost as D had predicted. Whoever was back there took advantage of a break in the median and made a U-turn, doubling back the way he'd come. He didn't want to tail me badly enough to venture into what he thought was "the 'hood," even though it really was just a basic blue-collar neighborhood.

D was already sitting in his car with the door open in the parking lot of a place called Koffee 'n Krepes — according to the yellow neon sign — when I pulled up. I parked on the opposite side and got out to see him standing there, focused on the street.

"Where's your shadow?"

"Headed back to the Valley or wherever, I guess. Sorry to interrupt your dinner," I said. Now that I wasn't preoccupied with creepers, another thought hit me. "Was it your dinner, or yours and someone else's?"

He smiled. "Someone has a high opinion of herself."

"What?"

"Do you really think I would've gone off and left someone I was willing to cook for just to bail you out?"

I was so disappointed in myself for not thinking of a good comeback until I was on my way home. (*Maybe you left a shiny object in front of her and she didn't realize you were gone.*) *Whatever* was the only thing I had handy — that and a change in subject.

"By the way," I said as he held the restaurant door open for me. "Thanks *so* much for telling me to Google camel spiders. Now I don't know if I'll ever get that image out of my brain."

"They're cute, huh?"

"Yeah, like the Elephant Man."

19

With its clean but well-worn floor, plus the vintage sofa and bookcases, Koffee 'n Krepes gave off an inviting, familiar vibe. The warm, earthy scent of dark roast, with hints of vanilla and pumpkin, filled the air, and the earnest pleas of Nina Simone played lightly over the sound system, briefly interrupted by the hiss of the espresso machine. A girl with braids and a tattoo of an octopus crawling up her arm took our order, and we found a table along the window, where the only other person close by was a kid with the latest designer headphones plugged into his ears, oblivious to everything except his laptop.

"What did you do to rate a tail, even if it was carried out by an amateur?" D asked.

First, I rattled off my theories about Trammell, including his latest request. There was also my just-concluded visit with Celeste Spencer, although I couldn't imagine her giving chase down darkened streets.

The barista shouted D's nickname that shall not be mentioned. He got up and returned with a pair of beige beverage cups with black lids. He slid the taller one over to me.

"What about a crazy ex-boyfriend?" He asked. "Is that who could've been following you? It's a very crazy ex-boyfriend thing to do."

"I have to admit, I hadn't considered that, but I don't think so. Maybe if I'd been the one to dump the last guy I was seeing, but ..."

"Get outta here. You got kicked to the curb?"

"Yup."

"I wouldn't have figured you for the dumpee."

"That makes two of us. 'Dumpee' isn't a real word, by the way."

"Now you sound like an English teacher."

"I almost was," I said.

D had been half-slouched in his chair, but now he was sitting upright, giving me his full attention.

"I was an English major in college. My plan was to teach in high school. I wanted to be the teacher who could discuss the classics but wasn't afraid to bust out some anime. You know, the cool teacher. The one who was up on the latest music or fashion, went to football games, that sort of thing. Somebody who could relate to them on their level."

"So how'd you get from that to ..."

"Acquisitions?"

"Yeah. Acquisitions."

I sighed. "My parents owned a restaurant back in Texas. They worked their butts off in that place, and it was pretty successful. They'd put away a decent amount of money for retirement or whatever — they both loved working so much I doubt they were actually planning to retire. Then my dad had a stroke and my mom had to run the place by herself, plus take care of my dad."

D's face was blank as he focused on the cup wrapped in his hands. "That sucks."

"Tell me about it. And as if that weren't enough, my mom got caught up in an investment scam and—"

"Don't say it."

I didn't, but that didn't undo the fact that my mom had lost almost all the money she and Dad had saved.

"Eventually, I ran into somebody who helped me find the guy and I got a lot of the money back, but by then I'd embarked on another career path. I sort of stumbled across it in college, but not in the classroom."

"Now that sounds interesting."

I waved it off. "Digression."

One of the guys from behind the counter approached our table, carrying a pair of plates. "Who has the carbonara?"

D lifted a hand. The server put one plate in front of D, and the one with a heavenly smelling prosciutto crepe before me, asked if we needed anything else, and left us to our meal.

"So you have to go and get your drink, but they deliver your food?" I asked.

He shrugged. "It's a system, I guess."

I didn't know if it was because the crepe tasted that good or because I simply hadn't eaten in a while, but my reaction to the first bite was audible. The cheese was warm and gooey, and its tartness offered a perfect complement to the sweetness of the grapes. "D, this is incredible!"

He broke into a smile. "Hey, you call me for help getting rid of unwanted attention and you get dinner too. Package deal."

"Awesome." I took another bite, which was as good as the first. "Now if you could just do something about the unwanted attention staking out my apartment."

And help me get my dog back. And make the whole thing with Denise go away.

"So what's going on out there?" he asked. "I haven't seen you on the news lately."

"You were right about these people. They *are* weird." I told him about my trip to the Spencer household and my subsequent meeting with the family. "Celeste said they'd moved to a new house because Richard wanted to be closer to work."

"Please. Nobody in this town does that, especially at the expense of an ocean view."

"Right? And you know what else I found out?"

D spread his hands out, telling me to continue.

"The house they're in is owned by Celeste's parents."

"What?"

"It's in the property records. Paul and Chelsea Benson are the registered owners, not Richard and Celeste Spencer. Celeste totally lied to me about that."

"Maybe they bought it from her parents."

"There's no record of a sale or a transfer in ownership. Besides, why would the proud Spencers voluntarily give up their Pacific Palisades zip code?"

"What are you thinking?"

"I think they had to move for some reason. I just don't know what it is yet."

D sat back in his chair, thinking. I fell into the shop's rhythm — the music, the customers' chatter, the street noise rising and falling with the opening and closing of the door — but the barista brought that to a whiplash-inducing halt when she called out, "Patrice!"

My hand tensed around my fork. Even with my back to the register, I knew.

"Hey, girlfriend!"

I turned and there she was in her typical jeans, t-shirt, and cap — black with FBI on the front — sipping from her beverage as she sauntered over and took the spot next to me. Of course.

"Imagine running into you here," she said.

"Let me guess: you're a regular."

"Absolutely. I love this pl—"

"Knock it off, Broussard. Was that you following me up and down the streets just now?"

She put a hand to her chest. "What, you mean like a stalker? Kate, of course not. I would never—"

"Whatever."

"This is Broussard?" D asked.

"Oh. Yeah. D, Broussard. Broussard, D."

Smiling, she leaned forward and gave him her hand. "Patrice."

"Spyder."

Oh, shoot me. Two names that would never pass from my lips, and if I didn't know better, I would've said they'd make a perfect couple.

"You were just leaving, right?" I said to Broussard.

She looked between D and I, probably getting the wrong idea, but at that moment, I didn't care. "Right. I didn't mean to interrupt. But before I go, I just wanted to apologize for that thing on the Whittaker job and beg you to reconsider ... what we talked about?"

"Not that," I said. "Not now."

"Not what?" D asked. "You two being partners again?"

Broussard looked at me and I shrugged.

"Come on, Kate. Help her out."

I glared at D, trying my telepathic best to shut him up, but it didn't take.

"She knows she messed up before; she just wants to make up for it, that's all."

Was he being serious? Was he that naïve or just messing with me? Or worse, was he trying to get in good with her? The thought made me shudder.

D kept going. "We just met, but I like to think I'm a pretty good judge of character. Kate, I think—"

"All right!" I said. "I don't know what's gotten into me, but let's talk ... later, okay?"

Broussard pulled me into a hug. "Oh, thank you, Kate! This is going to be so awesome, just you wait." She stood and collected her cup. "D ... Spyder, it was nice meeting you. I'll leave you two alone."

As she left, D checked her out.

"D? Stop. She's awful."

He smiled. "Doesn't look that bad from here."

"Remember when I told you I stumbled into my current career?"

"Yeah, in college."

"That's where I met Broussard. We lived in the same dorm, across the hall from each other. We got to be pretty good friends, and one day she tells me she thinks her boyfriend is cheating on her. She wanted to snoop around his room for evidence. I felt bad for her, so I said I'd help."

"Help how?"

"At my parents' restaurant, sometimes kids would leave the bathroom doors locked even when no one was inside—a joke, I guess. Calling the locksmith every time that happened would've gotten expensive, so my parents learned how to pick the lock themselves."

"And you learned too?"

"Right. Anyway, we got into this guy's room and sure enough, we found phone numbers for not one other girl, but two. One was written on the back of a coaster with a lipstick imprint. Then there was the underwear that belonged to someone other than Broussard."

D shrugged. "Maybe it was his."

"That's not better. Anyway, somehow we got ratted out, and university administrators take a dim view of students letting themselves into another student's dorm room, so we were bounced out of school. Broussard came here to L.A. and

I didn't hear from her until a couple years later when she called to tell me about a business opportunity I'd be perfect for."

"Acquisitions?"

"Exactly. It took her a while to convince me, but finally I agreed, and we actually made a good team for a while. That is, until she sabotaged a job we were working on and then ditched me just as the cops showed up. I found a place to hide and didn't get arrested, but I swore never to work with her again."

"Come on, Kate. Doesn't it feel good to give her a second chance?"

"It feels like I'm about to ruin my reputation."

"Uh, it might be a little late for that. I mean ... you *are* wanted for questioning."

I buried my head in my hands. "Yeah, that minor detail."

"Sorry. You were saying the Spencers must've had a reason for moving out of Pacific Palisades. Did you find out anything else?"

"Did Jimmy ever tell you the story about ..."

"About what?" he asked.

I hesitated. Jimmy might have relished the sleazy details, but I found the whole thing disgusting. "Celeste ... and her history."

"That one never came up. Why don't you fill me in?"

I did, and when I'd finished, D asked, "So you got Celeste on your list of suspects?"

If I'd been Celeste, I would've been mad, even after all these years. Mad enough to kill? No, but I'm rational. Maybe she was unhinged and it manifested itself in her thirst for status, but was it also possible that, in Denise, she'd seen an opportunity to double up on her revenge?

"It makes sense, doesn't it? Take out Trammell's leading lady and Ellington's mistress all at once."

"Yeah, maybe ..." He'd barely touched his crepe. Sitting

with his chin resting atop one of his fists, he looked like someone taking a math test.

"What are you thinking?"

"I like your theory, except for one thing: If the murders are connected, what was Celeste's beef with Robin Castro?"

"Jimmy said Celeste didn't think Robin was WASP-y enough to be hanging out with her son."

D whistled and shook his head, a sentiment I couldn't argue with.

"And get this," I said. "Richard is helping himself to Trey's pills."

"He what?"

"I found meds prescribed to Trey in the pocket of one of Richard's jackets."

"Hmm. Doesn't necessarily mean anything devious. He could've been picking up Trey's refill."

"Yeah, maybe. I guess I'm inclined to think the worst right now."

The shop had grown emptier since our arrival, although Nina was still wailing on the stereo.

"It's probably safe for me to hit the road now," I said.

He nodded, but as I was getting out of my chair, he said, "Hang on. Can you drive a stick?"

That was an odd question, and I wasn't even certain I'd heard him right. "Well, my other car is a Karmann Ghia, so yeah. Why?"

"Karmann Ghia? You serious? That thing's older than you are." He laughed while taking a keychain from his pocket. He unclipped a key and handed it to me. "Take mine. I'll drive" — he looked toward the parking lot — "whatever that is out there."

"Really?"

"Yeah. It'll throw off your boy or whoever's trying to follow you."

There was little doubt about that. It would come as a real shock to anyone who thought they were tailing me to discover D at the wheel of the Chevy.

"For someone all opposed to aiding and abetting, you sure have been helpful lately."

"Yeah, well, if these murders really are connected, I've got a vested interest in your well-being. Matter of fact, I think I'll retrace some of your footsteps and see who pokes their head up at the sight of your car."

A server brought D a container for his leftover crepe. I was carrying mine out in my stomach. I looked at my empty Styrofoam cup, noting the shop's yellow logo. I'd definitely be back.

"I can't believe you're trusting me," I said. "I mean, what if this situation gets out of hand and I skip town in your car?"

He looked up from the container with the sort of glare that could've stopped a herd of buffalo.

I put my hands up. "Kidding, D. You knew that, right?"

We left the restaurant and I gave him my key. He sighed and took another look at his car before climbing into the Chevy and driving off.

On the way back to the hotel, I pulled over and searched my purse. The tracking device was tucked into a seam on the bottom. Broussard had hidden it well. I thought back to the day I'd found her waiting for me outside of Ellington's townhouse. She'd put one of the locators on my car while I was inside. Then she hopped inside my car, uninvited, and held my purse on her lap. That must've been when she attached the second one. And with the right app, all she had to do was check her phone to know where I was at any given moment. Hence her ability to show up, seemingly out of the blue.

The police cruiser was still parked in front of my building, so I had to take the back way to the complex, where I stashed the tracker in the bushes near the security alarm panel. Now, if Broussard checked the tracking device, it would look like I was just hanging out at home. Despite her recent propensity for showing up wherever I was, I doubted that she had any interest in my being a couch potato. And if she did swing by to check on me, maybe she'd manage to get herself arrested by the cop out front. Score!

20

W hen I returned to Briarwood, the reactions to me were completely different. My navy crepe sheath dress and perforated pumps went over a lot better than those gaudy sweats. And while it wasn't in the same league as some of the other cars, D's Mustang was a step up from my generic sedan. The valet had been professional and businesslike before, but he was a lot friendlier, and maybe even flirty, today. There was no mistaking him sneaking a glance or two while I stood waiting for him to retrieve a claim ticket, and when I passed the putting green, the golfers all smiled instead of staring at me as if I'd just stepped out of some bad reality TV show.

Jimmy seemed especially impressed as I entered the pro shop, but honestly, I didn't know how much of an accomplishment that was.

"Damn!" he said. "Please tell me you're here to take me to one of the cabanas by the pool and have your way with me."

"Afraid not, Jimmy."

He sighed. "Ain't that the story of my life. What brings you by then?"

"I need to talk to Virginia Ellington. She's supposed to be having lunch here, but I don't know what she looks like."

"So ask the hostess at the restaurant. Name's LeeAnn. Tell her I said hi."

"I don't want to look like an outsider who doesn't know her way around the club."

"But you are."

"I know, but I don't have to broadcast it. Come point her out to me."

Jimmy shrunk back from that suggestion — or tried his best to. The spare tire around his midsection only allowed for so much shrinking. "I don't know, Kate. I got a feeling you're up to something here."

"Please?"

"What are you gonna do for me?"

"Excuse me?"

"I said, what are *you*" — he jabbed an index finger at me — "gonna do for *me*?" He poked a thumb at his chest. "I'm a man, and a man has needs, you know?"

"First — like I said last time — eww. Second, I'm not asking you for a kidney. Just show me who Virginia Ellington is."

Jimmy huffed, scrunched his eyebrows, and tried on a look that was probably meant to come across as formidable. Unfortunately for him, he looked more like a muppet.

He hung a "back in five minutes" sign on the door of the pro shop (I always hated those signs because they don't say five minutes from when) and led the way to the main clubhouse. The sun was shining brighter than it had in days and glittered across the ripples in the pool. Sitting on an elevated deck were the cabanas — small white huts with tan curtains waving in the breeze. Passing an afternoon or three in one of those sounded fantastic, although Jimmy's wasn't the company I had in mind. As we walked, I stole a moment to see whether I'd missed a call from Connor. Nope.

Inside the clubhouse, the August Spencer ballroom — according to the bronze placard on the wall — was empty, but all the tables were set as though waiting for members to arrive. The room even had a piano in the corner. We continued past, following the sound of chatter and the clink of silverware to another dining room that was casual only by comparison. The area was spacious, with walls almost completely made up of full-length windows looking out across the golf course.

From the hallway, Jimmy scanned the room before nodding toward a table on the right. "See those three women at the table under the chandelier?"

I nodded.

"The one with the dark hair and glasses? That's Virginia Ellington."

Virginia was sitting at the nine o'clock position, with her companions at three and six. She wore a white chiffon dress with a cobalt blue floral print. Her hair was pulled back, highlighting a slender pair of petal tortoise shell frames. She was, by just about anyone's measure, beautiful, and her style was elegant. Too bad the thick glass tumbler, half full with a golden liquid and ice cubes, ruined the effect; it was barely lunchtime. Both Jimmy and Celeste had mentioned that Virginia enjoyed downing a few, and by the looks of things that was no exaggeration.

"Need anything else?" Jimmy asked.

"No, thanks. I owe you ... just not what you're thinking."

With an "oh darn" snap of his fingers, he turned back toward the pro shop. I didn't want to engage Virginia in front of her friends, but I didn't know how long her lunch would take.

I stepped into the dining room, where an adorable young blonde in a black dress met me by the host stand. Her name tag read, "LeeAnn." Jimmy probably had a better shot with me than with her. I told her I was meeting someone and asked if I could wait at the bar. Her answer was an animated, "Of course!"

The bartender appeared as soon as I sat down. Had he known I was just having a mineral water with lemon, he wouldn't have been so Johnny-on-the-spot. I turned so it looked as if I was enjoying the view while keeping an eye on Virginia. She appeared to be holding court, as she did most of the talking while the other two women mostly laughed or nodded, and when she wasn't talking, she was downing a sip of her drink. I made note of where the bathroom was located. At the rate she was going, it wouldn't take long for nature to call. I watched the soon-to-be ex-Mrs. Ellington and smiled when I realized her name could be rearranged to: "tell gin no." Okay, it wasn't my best effort, especially since she wasn't drinking gin, but the sentiment was on point. She really needed to slow down—or maybe not. Perhaps she was a chatty drunk, and that suited me just fine.

A monitor attached to the wall opposite the bar displayed a montage of photos taken at Briarwood events. There were golf tournaments, weddings, dances, dinners, and parties. It was a monotonous succession of images, right up until one of Denise whispering in the ear of Trey Spencer. Tiny type beneath the picture claimed it was from a party the club had thrown the night before Denise had died—she was wearing the same dress as the one I'd seen on her Twitter feed. She was also holding one of those aquamarine drinks she seemed to enjoy so much. So she and Trey were friends? Two minutes later, when the picture reappeared, I wondered whether they weren't something more. It was just a single moment in time, but they looked enamored. I couldn't imagine Dr. Ellington would've been too happy about that. And jealousy made people do crazy things.

Unfortunately, my chance to speak with Mrs. Ellington wouldn't be coming any time soon. Despite a three-cocktail lunch (plus whatever she'd had before I'd gotten here), she didn't once get up to use the restroom. I would've needed a catheter to still that long. At one point, her friends made a visit to the facilities, but Virginia remained tableside, talking on her phone. I considered approaching her but didn't think there'd be enough time for us to really talk before the others returned.

I picked up my water and gave it a swirl but didn't actually drink anything; at nine-fifty a pop, I was in no hurry to finish it. While I was falling under the spell of the swaying palm tree leaves outside, my phone rang. It was D.

"Hello?" I said.

"Hey, it's Spyder."

"I don't know anyone by that name."

"Ha ha," he said. "How 'bout Lucas Blaisdale? Know anyone by that name?"

"Lucas ...? He's Trammell's errand boy. What about him?"

"He's also your shadow."

"No way," I said, even though there was very much a way. The little weasel must've started following me after I'd paid him a visit, probably wanting to get his money back. "How'd you find him? Or how did he find you?"

"I took a drive through Trammell Preston's neighborhood and a little while later there he was, following me toward Beverly Hills."

"Did you talk to him?"

"I did one better: I got his license plate number. After that, finding him was simple."

"Yeah?" There was an uptick in my voice. I was glad to hear that something—anything—had gone simply.

"When he's not following you, he's hanging out at a construction site in Van Nuys. Looks like he's some kind of foreman."

A foreman was the guy in charge, which didn't fit my idea of Lucas at all, but I grabbed a cocktail napkin and jotted down the address D gave me. "Thanks a bunch, D."

An hour and eighteen minutes later, lunch started breaking

up. The ladies rose from the table and exchanged the kind of hugs that looked as if they were trying not to touch each other. They proceeded toward the exit as a group, but Virginia broke off from the others and stepped into the ladies' room. Finally!

I left a generous tip — nursing a single, non-alcoholic beverage for more than an hour doesn't endear you to bartenders — and stepped into the hall, where I waited for Virginia to emerge. I took out my phone and used the waiting time to get into character.

While talking into the phone, I strode back and forth, gesturing with my free hand.

"She what?" I said, trying to sound incredulous. "Points? She's asking for ..."

Two members passed by, each giving me a "Do you mind?" glare. I lowered my voice.

"She's asking for points? Larry, you're killing me. Nobody's getting points on this one ... No, for real. It's one of those trendy little art house flicks that get released just in time for Oscar nominations ... Does she know Charlize is begging to do this? *For scale*?"

Behind me, the door creaked. I pivoted to see Virginia emerge from the restroom. I paused my faux conversation, letting her see the recognition on my face.

"Let me call you back," I said and stuffed my phone in my purse. "Virginia? Virginia Ellington?"

She stopped and stared at me with an unsteady look, probably from a combination of the alcohol and having a total stranger recognize her. That aside, she was pretty in the same way as Celeste: a well-maintained woman in that phase between soccer mom and grandmom.

She adjusted her glasses. "Have we met?"

"Well, we haven't been introduced." I put a hand out. "Theresa McDermott. I'm a producer with Gold Coast Media."

She had the firmest grip of any woman I'd ever shaken

hands with, her forearm sporting some serious muscle tone. Strangling Denise probably wouldn't have been too hard for her.

"Wow." I flexed my hand. "I think I want the name of your trainer."

She laughed and apologized. "It's from tennis. Years of swinging a racquet will do that to you."

"Yeah, that figures. Hey, do you have a minute? I'm working on something that I think might interest you."

"Oh? And what might that be?"

I motioned back toward the dining area and she followed. We took up a couple spots at the bar. The bartender nodded at me but was considerably happier to see Virginia, probably because he knew he had a live one.

"Good afternoon, Mrs. E. What can I get you ladies?"

I asked for another mineral water while Virginia ordered bourbon. Talk about hardcore. The moment our bartender turned his back, she said, "This project of yours, tell me about it."

Swiveling in my seat, I faced her and put on an earnest expression. I was going for trustworthy, but then again, I was supposed to be a Hollywood producer, so how trustworthy could I really be? Hopefully, that thought wouldn't occur to her.

"There's a new unscripted show in the works called *Hollywood Wives Uncensored*. Right now, we're just casting, and I've come across a few maybes, but no real winners. No one I can build a show around. That's where I think you'd come in."

The bartender set our drinks in front of us, and Virginia wasted no time reaching for hers. After a gulp, she asked what I meant.

"I'm looking for someone prominent, but interesting. To be honest, so many of the women I've met are downright boring. Nobody wants to watch a show about someone who doesn't do anything more exciting than complain about her thread count, you know what I mean?"

She meant to laugh, but my comment had caught her mid-sip, causing her to cough instead. She recovered and used a cocktail napkin to dab the corners of her mouth. So refined for a lush.

"I know the type all too well," she said. "Just now, I was having lunch with a woman whose idea of fun is watching dog videos on YouTube."

While I saw nothing wrong with dog videos, I ignored the comment and pressed on.

"Virginia, that's too funny. And that sort of personality is exactly what the show needs. Plus, you have a great story. I hope you don't mind my bringing this up, but the divorce angle will play really well with viewers everywhere." I paused to gauge her reaction. I thought she'd at least raise an eyebrow at the mention of her divorce, but all I got was a simple nod, so I pressed on. "And the thing with your husband's mistress, it's awful, but — and I'm just being honest again — great for ratings. You must've hated her."

Virginia waved the thought away with the hand that wasn't hoisting her beverage as she knocked back more of a gulp this time. "She was a silly girl with fake hair and an inflated chest. He would've cheated on her too, if he wasn't already."

Her comment landed like a right cross as I thought about Terry. How long had he been seeing someone else before deciding to take off with her?

A divorce was probably the best thing for Virginia, and I wondered why she hadn't gotten one before now. If she was that certain of his ways, he must have cheated on her before meeting Denise. I could only guess that Virginia had finally grown tired of looking the other way.

"You know, I have to say, I'm a little surprised the cops haven't taken an interest in you."

"Oh, they have. I received a visit from some detectives just this morning."

"Really?"

"They asked all kinds of tedious questions, intimating I had something to do with that girl's death. I suppose I would make an excellent suspect — you know, the jealous spouse who publicly threatened her husband's mistress, even though I might've been a little tipsy at the time."

Might have been? I was beginning to think that Virginia spent a great many of her waking hours more than just a little tipsy.

"There's just one tiny problem with that theory," she said.

"Which is?"

"I've been in Seattle for the past week, visiting my parents. I have plane tickets, receipts, not to mention numerous eye witnesses who can put me there."

She finished off her drink, and with it, my suspicions of her. Seattle wasn't so far away that she couldn't have caught a flight down to L.A., done the deed, and flown right back, but that would've required someone far less prone to getting plastered.

She gazed at the ice cubes in her glass. "I suggested they have a chat with my dear husband."

I perked up. Did she know something that might blow a hole in his alibi? "Why is that?"

"Maybe the little gold digger was having better luck than I was ..."

Virginia was hypnotized by the lonely pieces of ice swirling around the bottom of her glass, but this wasn't the time for her to lose her train of thought. Something good was about to come out of her mouth.

I flagged down the bartender. "Another one here, please."

"Oh, thank you!" Virginia said.

"No problem. Now what was that you were saying? Your husband's mistress was having better luck ... with what?"

"Just ..." She inched her glasses up the bridge of her nose and focused on me as though she just realized someone was sitting beside her. I wanted her to get back to the topic at hand, but didn't want to press for fear of raising her suspicions.

When the bartender delivered a fresh drink to her, I picked up my glass and offered a toast. "To TV shows that'll make the network rich ... and us too, hopefully."

She held her glass aloft. "Is that ... possible?"

"Oh, sure. There's first-run, home video, and licensing. A cut of all that goes to the stars. Plus, if the show does well enough in the ratings, the network will re-up for at least another year, maybe more, so the whole thing starts all over again."

Virginia smiled, either from her buzz or from what she was hearing. I found it odd that the possibility of appearing on some tacky television show appealed to her. Would that really go down well with the members? Then again, maybe those who walked around in a drunken haze, threatening homicide, weren't as concerned with what others thought.

"The money is probably no big deal to you, though," I said. "I'd guess you're about to become one very rich woman, what with this being a community property state and all."

"You have to find the property first," she muttered.

"What?"

"Nothing." Virginia took a long draw from her glass, watching me all the while. Great. She'd decided to clam up.

She finished her drink and stood. "This television show of yours, what happens next?"

The bartender delivered me the bill. Thirty-eight dollars for two bourbons and a water. And people called me a thief? I settled up and led the way back to the valet stand.

I pretend-searched through my purse. "Wouldn't you know it? I don't have any cards. Let me get your number, and I'll be in touch." She dictated and I entered her information into my contacts. Who knew? I might actually have a reason to call her one day.

At the valet stand, she swore up and down she was fine to drive, but the valet wouldn't surrender her keys. "Come on, Mrs. E. I'll call you a cab as soon as I get back with her car. I can't let anything happen to the queen." He winked and jogged off to retrieve D's Mustang.

"I didn't know you were royalty," I said teasingly to Virginia.

"That silly nickname," she said under her breath.

"What nickname?"

Virginia shook her head. "Several years ago, Tad suggested we purchase a couple of those Wick-ed Ways franchises. The candle store? He thought it would, in his words, 'give me something to do.' As if I'd asked for anything to do. In any case, I wound up with the nickname Candle Queen." She sighed. "Oh well, I guess there's one thing to come out of it: even Tad can't hide an asset that sits in the middle of a shopping mall."

Virginia asked more questions about the show, making me wish I'd chosen a different cover story. I didn't know how much longer I could pull off the Hollywood player bit.

An emerald-green convertible Jaguar pulled up, and behind the wheel was a guy who rung a bell, but his shades kept me from pinning down his identity, although judging by the way he was staring at me, I was familiar to him, too. He hopped out of his car and, as recognition dawned, Richard Spencer's goofy grin gave him away. "Don't tell me ... Don't tell me ..." Finally he snapped his fingers. "Ms. McDermott! Right?"

Perfect. Of all the people to show up. I just hoped Celeste hadn't told him I was Virginia's long lost, illegitimate daughter, otherwise this was about to get sticky.

"Um, yes. Good to see you again, Mr. Spencer."

"You two know each other?" Virginia asked.

Richard gave her a quick embrace and removed his shades.

"We just met. I didn't know the homeowners' association had a membership, though."

Virginia turned to me, puzzled. "Homeowners' association? I thought—"

"Just a side gig," I said, trying to short-circuit that conversation.

"I'm glad I ran into you," Richard said. "Celeste mentioned having you back over to the house."

She did? "She did?"

"Yes, she thinks you're absolutely adorable. She kept meaning to look you up through the homeowners' association, but now I can tell her she doesn't have to. That is, if you wouldn't mind giving me your number."

"Oh, um, sure," I said and rattled it off.

The valet returned with D's Mustang, and I drove off, following Sunset Boulevard's snaking curves back into the city. While my encounter with Virginia Ellington had been interesting, and she had motive for wanting Denise dead, her alibi meant I'd have to take her off the suspect list.

There was still her husband, though. I called up the app linked to the bug in his office, hoping to catch a break and overhear something meaningful for a change. I'd tuned in a couple times before, but the office was either completely silent, which I took to mean he was tending to patients, or I heard something mundane, like Ellington telling his assistant he was going out for lunch. It was more of the same today, which sucked all the fun out of eavesdropping. Not just because it was boring, but I had the feeling I was missing something.

He didn't have a clear motive — not that I'd found anyway — but his behavior was suspicious. First, there was the purchase of Trammell's necklace. And then there was his reaction after my visit to his office.

On the phone — I still had no idea who he was talking to — he'd been freaking out. If my phone hadn't kept dropping the signal, I might've had a better idea what that had been all about, but Ellington had said one thing that had come through clearly: *Just like Delta house.* What he meant, I had no clue, but there seemed to be a Delta component to both Denise's and Robin's deaths.

Having Ellington perform a root canal sounded better to me than visiting his old fraternity, but I couldn't avoid it any longer. It was time to go back to school.

21

I hadn't been on a college campus in almost a decade, but that evening, as Aubrey and I traversed the streets in search of parking, it seemed as though time had stood still, especially on fraternity row — one large, unspectacular house after another. The only distinguishing characteristics were the Greek letters prominently displayed on the facades. Otherwise, the structures were largely interchangeable.

"A frat party?" Aubrey said. "Please tell me you didn't call me up to invite me to a frat party."

"I didn't call you up to invite you to a frat party."

"Then what are we doing here?"

"Going to a frat party."

"Kate! You just said—"

"I told you what you wanted to hear."

Aubrey crossed her arms. "I'm not getting out."

"I need you. I can't go in there by myself. Please?"

"This is ridiculous. We're obviously not college students."

"Come on, we can pass for grad students. Besides, we won't stay that long, I promise. It's really important."

"This is part of your investigation, isn't it?"

I nodded.

"You could've just told me."

"Sorry."

I knew I shouldn't have withheld information from her, all she'd done up to this point was help me, but the minute you trust people is right when they turn on you. Like Terry. Or Broussard.

Ahead was an open space along the curb. I swerved into it, turned off the engine, and stepped out, but Aubrey hesitated, looking as if she was about to reconsider. I walked around the car and knocked on the window to draw her attention. She looked deflated, but she opened her door and left the sanctuary of the car.

My only experience with fraternities came during freshman rush, when some Kappa Phi pledges stood outside the cafeteria, holding the door open for girls on their way in. That is, if the girl was an "eight" or better. One of them looked at me as I approached and said, "Ooh! So close!" He let the door shut in my face and then laughed and high-fived his fellow nitwits. Fast forward to now and honestly, I wasn't any happier to be at this party than Aubrey was.

As we approached the Delta house, a handful of guys were gathered on the front lawn, trying to impress a pair of cute blondes, but everyone else stood in a line that spilled out of the front door and down the sidewalk. I fell in step, joining the creep toward the door as music blared from inside. The volume was so loud that the brass doorknocker bounced with every beat like some invisible ghost of frat parties past was announcing his arrival.

There was a tap on my shoulder. When I turned, the guy who towered over me grinned.

"Hello," he said over the music. "My name is Steven."

Steven had thick, dark hair and a full day's growth on his

face. His long-sleeved plaid shirt was untucked. A junior, I guessed. Maybe a senior.

In return, I gave him enough of a smile to be cordial but not encouraging. Aubrey turned away, pretending to hunt for something in her purse. "Theresa," I said, knowing I was now committed to making small talk at least until I got through the door, but Steven frowned as though he'd rather not be associated with me. He couldn't have seen through my makeup job that quickly, could he?

"They'll send you to the back of the line for that," was what I thought I'd heard him say.

"What?"

He leaned closer to my ear. "Those two up there?" He cut a glance toward the doorway, where two guys in identical navy blue t-shirts with the fraternity's letters were greeting every guest, then writing something on a sticker and applying it to their chest. "When you introduce yourself, if you don't say, 'Hello. My name is Theresa,' you get sent to the back of the line."

"Why?"

The disbelief on Steven's face was unmistakable. "You really don't know what the deal is?"

All I'd bothered to find out was that the Deltas were having a party. It sounded like a great opportunity to blend into the crowd and examine the house without attracting attention. It hadn't occurred to me that there might be any sort of "deal."

"It's an AA party," he said. "So you have to introduce yourself like you're at a meeting."

Of all the ... It wasn't enough to simply serve up free alcohol? They had to come up with a dorky theme, too? Frat boys. Besides, it didn't even make sense. The point of AA meetings was to *stop* drinking. Certainly, the idea here was anything but.

I didn't want to believe it was true, but closer to the entrance, I received confirmation.

"Hello. My name is Tammy," said the girl in front of us, giggling while one of the Deltas got a little too friendly for my taste as he plastered a nametag on her chest. Right then and there, I decided to apply my own.

As our turn came up, Aubrey said, "You first."

Following the others' lead, I properly introduced myself. The nametags were the kind with "Hello. My name is" already printed on them. One of the Deltas dutifully scribbled down my alias, but I relieved him of the tag when he reached for me. He scowled, and I thought that might be grounds for being sent to the back of the line, but I was allowed to enter. A blow for common sense, if not womanhood.

Aubrey followed suit, with Steven right behind her. "Can I get you guys a drink?"

Even though the music was blasting, I'd heard him just fine. Still, I cupped a hand to my ear and shouted, "What?"

"Do you guys want something to drink?" he said with more volume.

"I can't hear you," I said, leading him to try again. I turned to Aubrey and shrugged. She did likewise. "Okay, nice talking to you. We'll see you later."

I took her by the hand, and we vanished into the crowd, leaving Steven to find another female alcoholic to enable.

The house was swarming with people, and even with doors and windows open, the air was thick and dank. We threaded our way between people dancing, congregating around furniture, and three guys who seemed to be wrestling.

Aubrey bent over to my ear. "It's like a rainforest in here."

"I know."

"What are we looking for?"

"That I don't know, but I overheard part of a phone call. Tad Ellington said something about Denise's murder being 'just like Delta house.' In college, he belonged to this fraternity. So did Trammell Preston and Richard Spencer."

"No kidding?"

"Yeah. Their kids, too."

"Okay, but why do you care?"

Aubrey only knew about Denise's murder, so I filled her in on what had happened to Robin. During the story, her mouth dropped open more than once.

"There's a connection?"

"I think so. I just haven't figured out what it is."

Framed portraits of past Delta Rho classes lined just about every available bit of wall space. Some dated back to the late 1800s, the earliest days of the university itself. The faded black-and-white images of clean-cut, bespoke young men were in direct contrast to the herd of casually dressed guys and girls hoisting drinks from blue plastic cups and gyrating against one another in time to the music.

As I was studying the pictures, I felt a push from behind. A split-second later, something cold and wet splashed against my neck and slid down my back.

It was a young couple trying to balance drinks during a full-on tonsil inspection.

"Oh, hey, I'm really sorry about that. Are you okay?" the guy said when he noticed what had to be a spreading stain on the back of my shirt.

"I'm fine. Just wet."

His date — or perhaps, sticking with the party's theme, his sponsor — up-and-downed me before taking him by the hand and leading him across the room.

"Oh please," I muttered before going in search of a bathroom.

There were two on the main floor, both occupied with five or six more people in line. Fabulous. With Aubrey in tow, I opted for the kitchen. It was surprisingly modern, with granite countertops and brushed aluminum appliances. Plus, the noise level had tapered off considerably. Every party has its kitchen dwellers, and this one was no exception; maybe a dozen people had gathered here, probably looking for someplace relatively quiet to talk. Sitting on the counter was an open package of napkins. I grabbed a handful to blot the stain, but what caught my attention was the set of nearby canisters: four scuffed and scarred pale blue metal rectangles with copper tops, each one progressively smaller. They were labeled sugar, flour, coffee and tea, but they could've just as easily been used as hiding places. I imagined that the tins had been passed down over generations' worth of Deltas, which might explain why they'd survived the kitchen's renovation.

No one was paying me much attention, so I peeked inside one of the containers: sugar, just like it said. Same with the one marked flour. In fact, the contents of all four canisters were exactly as advertised.

Watching me, Aubrey asked, "No luck?"

"None."

The kitchen had a door that led to the backyard, but I ruled that out as a hiding place; too easy for a random person to stumble across it. There were the upstairs rooms, which brought back bad memories of Trammell's party. I'd save those for last.

Down the hall from the kitchen, near the rear of the house, was a room marked by an arched doorway. The lights were dim, but it appeared to be a den. It was furnished with a leather sofa along one wall and, across from it, a matching chair and ottoman. At the far end of the room, a bookcase was nestled into the corner and beside it was a fireplace. The floor was made of wood, though a large, blue carpet marked with the fraternity's letters in white covered much of it. I crossed the room, feeling the wall for a light switch, but I couldn't find it. The only light came from triangular sconces on either wall.

More pictures celebrating the Deltas' heritage decorated the room. Painted above the fireplace were the fraternity letters and an inscription: *A good reputation is more valuable than money. Publilius Syrus, 100 BC.* As I touched them, I realized the Greek letters hadn't been just applied with paint; they'd also been carved into the wall.

"Hello again."

Aubrey and I both jumped. Behind us stood the couple that had spilled the drink down my back. The guy, nice looking in that collegiate way, had a smile on his face but his date, girl-friend, or whatever she was, regarded us with scorn. She wore a cream-colored top and a tight, black skirt, with a pair of heels high enough to be dangerous given her apparent blood-alcohol level. She took the guy's hand and pulled him to her.

He kissed her head before turning back to us. "How do you like my room?"

"Your room?" Aubrey asked.

"It's the estate room. Off limits to everyone but the chapter president and those he invites in."

"Oh," I said. "Oh! We're sorry. We didn't know—"

He put up a hand. "It's cool. I'm Ben. This is Stephanie."

"Hello. My name is Theresa."

That got a laugh from Ben, but Stephanie's expression said she wanted to take me out behind the frat house. After Aubrey introduced herself, Stephanie said, "I don't think I've seen either of you around. Which house are you guys with?"

Aubrey and I exchanged a look. "House?" I asked.

"You know, sorority."

"Oh," Aubrey said. "We're just—"

"Crashers?" Stephanie said.

Ben slipped his arm around her. "Come on, babe. Be nice."

Stephanie snorted and rolled her eyes.

"Do me a favor," he said to Stephanie. "Grab me a fresh cocktail, would you?" When she gave him the evil eye, he added, "Please?"

She turned to leave, but not without an exaggerated exhale.

I hadn't even spent two minutes with Stephanie, but it was clear the drama was strong with that one. "I hope we're not making trouble for you."

The suggestion made him laugh, as though trouble was the furthest thing from his mind. And why not? He was Ben, Lord of the Deltas. He could've strolled out into the midst of the party, announced his availability, and replaced Stephanie in five minutes. And she thought the whole static-cling bit made her special. Poor, foolish Stephanie.

"I didn't want to say anything, but you're not the typical Delta party guests," Ben said. "Which I mean as a compliment."

"We were sort of passing by ..." I started.

"And I bet her that she wouldn't go in," Aubrey said. "Sorry for dropping in uninvited."

"It's cool. Never let it be said that a Delta stood in the way of a bet."

On one of the walls, inside an antique silver frame, was a collection of head and shoulder portraits. Among them were Trammell and Ellington, and just beneath their pictures were two guys I recognized from the Disneyland photo in Trey Spencer's bedroom. Delta Legacies was printed across the very top.

Pointing out the picture, I asked, "What does that mean?"

"Legacies are fraternity brothers with relatives who were also members. The people in that picture are multiple generation members of this chapter."

"I recognize some of the people, but shouldn't the Spencers be up there? Aren't Richard Spencer and his son members?"

Our previously gregarious host became solemn, turning away from the picture. "Um, that's sorta ..."

Before I could question him, Stephanie returned with a drink in each hand. She was holding a glass out to Ben when she tripped on the edge of the carpet and stumbled forward, dousing me with the glass's ice-cold contents.

"Oh my God!" she shrieked. "I'm so sorry."

With a better job of hiding her smirk, her act might have been believable, though I wasn't even sure she was trying.

"You have got to be kidding me!" I said.

Ben looked at her with disappointment. "Aw, babe. What was that?"

"It's called an accident! That's why I apologized. Can I get you a towel or something?"

A towel wouldn't cut it. I was soaked clean through, and once it dried, the syrupy drink covering me from one arm to the other would be an icky, sticky layer caked onto my skin.

"No. Aubrey, let's just go." We were nearly out of the estate room when I doubled back to address Stephanie. "You know what? One day you'll realize it's not a good idea to go through life with heels higher than your GPA."

22

I seethed all the way back to the hotel. I reeked of vodka and fruit juice — Aubrey was fairly certain that the drink I was wearing was Sex on the Beach — one of my favorite tops was ruined, and it had all been for nothing. Ben knew something that would've explained the Spencers' exclusion from the legacy photo, but he'd gone into shutdown mode.

After a shower, I collapsed on the bed and turned on the television. With no new details on Denise's murder investigation to report, the local media had resorted to the human-interest angle — interviewing Denise's agent, her friends, even random people at the beach — to prolong the story. I nearly changed the channel when a familiar face appeared onscreen.

I'd come to know Richard Spencer's blond beauty as Thor, but the name at the bottom of the screen was Lance Waltrip. He gave the predictable speech, describing Denise as a sweet, gentle person who didn't deserve what had happened to her. However, the picture shown during the interview reduced his commentary to white noise. It was a magazine ad that showed Lance and Denise in bed gazing at each other while covered by a strategically placed, flowing white sheet. *Seraphina*, a brand of perfume, was printed at the bottom. So they hadn't been just friends; they'd been co-workers.

A quick search turned up Lance's website, which was brimming with glamour shots from his modeling gigs. Several photos featured him pressed against another woman, often in various stages of undress. Comparing that to my recollection of him locking lips with Richard Spencer made for an odd juxtaposition.

Lance's Twitter feed was embedded in the right side of the page. His most recent post was two hours old and informed his followers that he'd be on that night's newscast, but earlier in the day, he'd written: *Shooting at Innovations tomorrow in* (where else?) *the Valley. Wish me luck!*

First thing the next morning, I looked up the studio's location and then headed for the Sherman Oaks address, making a stop along the way. On his website, Lance professed a weakness for blueberry scones, so I brought a few to use as icebreakers.

The studio was in a nondescript, single-story, square, grey building on a street too narrow for the amount of traffic passing by. Whoever had put the number on the front had done me no favors by using paint barely a shade or two darker than the rest of the structure, and I nearly overshot my mark. Instead, I made a sharp left into a gated area, found parking in the middle of the lot, and took stock of my surroundings. A white parcel truck was parked near the building, and some guys were taking lighting equipment out of the back. A security guard stood near the entrance, not far from a man with a clipboard. He stopped the guys from the truck as they approached the door and engaged in a brief exchange. Then he consulted his clipboard before waving them through.

I got out of the car and, on my way to the door, I reached in my bag for my badge. I smiled at the guard, and as soon as I was past him, I pulled my badge out of my purse just enough to show the guy with the clipboard, hoping he was the lesser trained of the two when it came to spotting a fake. Sure enough, he couldn't open the door for me fast enough.

The majority of the studio was covered in darkness, save for the set — made up to look like the first class section of an airplane — and the far edge. There, three beautiful women and three equally beautiful men sat in chairs with white bibs draped over the front of their clothes, being worked on by makeup artists. Lance occupied one of the chairs and alternated between chatting with the woman doing his makeup and looking at his phone.

The studio's air conditioner must have been set on "arctic." My arms had goose bumps before the door shut behind me, but no one else seemed bothered.

I stood along the darkened wall, watching the guys from the truck tinker with the lights until Lance got up from his chair. Adjacent to the makeup chairs was an impromptu break area that included a pair of tables and some folding chairs, as well as coffee and other refreshments. With his makeup bib still attached, Lance engaged in a conversation with one of the other models, a tall black guy whose build was more svelte than Lance's. They each wore suits that fit them impeccably, and I guessed they were playing the role of businessmen. They chatted for a minute or two before Lance turned to inspect the refreshments. I probably wasn't going to get a better opportunity, so I hurried over.

"Good morning!" I said.

He offered a curt smile and went back to looking over his snack options.

I held out a paper bag. "Scone? They're blueberry."

That got me a much more engaging expression — the kind he gave to the camera. He peeked inside the bag. "Ooh. Don't mind if I do." Helping himself to a scone, he drew in the freshly baked pastry's aroma before taking a bite. "*That* is bliss. Where did you get these? And please don't tell me it's some place out here in the Valley."

"Nah. Acadia Bakery on Olympic near Sepulveda."

"Excellent." He found a napkin on one of the tables, brushed some crumbs off his hand, and then extended it to me. "I'm Lance."

"Nice to meet you. I'm Theresa, one of the assistants. Actually, I saw you on the news last night. That's so horrible." I waited, hoping he'd say something, but he gave only the slightest nod of his head. "She was a good friend?"

"Yes. Very good. We worked together several times and got to know each other well. In fact, when she booked the *Seraphina* gig, she recommended me. We've been the feature couple in their print campaign for the past two years. We spent so much time together on shoots we were almost like a married couple. We talked about everything."

"I'm so sorry, Lance. If California still had the death penalty, whoever did this would totally deserve it."

"Yeah. Twice."

"Who would do a thing like this?"

He dropped his head into his hand, shielding those baby blue eyes. "I don't know. I don't know."

"I heard she was dating that dentist. What's his name? Ellington? Do you think it's possible he—"

"I don't know."

This wasn't going well. How was I supposed to get a read if Lance was just going to stand there with his head down, echoing the same three words? "I heard she was poisoned. Do you think that's true?"

Lance's back stiffened, but he kept his hand against his face. "I don't know."

Maybe he didn't know about the poison, but between his refusal to make eye contact and that involuntary reaction, he knew something. "I just thought because dentists use chemicals, he might—"

Lance snapped toward me, his eyes red. "Look. I don't want to talk about this, okay?"

"Sure. I'm sorry. I didn't mean to—"

"Where's your credential?"

"My what?"

"Everyone with access to the set is supposed to be wearing a credential." He pulled his makeup bib aside. Dangling from his neck was a plastic badge attached to a lanyard. "Like this."

Oops.

"I must have lost it. It probably got caught on something while I was straightening up earlier."

"Yeah, that's probably it. Thanks for the scone." He walked away, not toward the set but to the studio entrance, looking back at me shortly before he reached the door. I hurried toward the door and turned down a hall just off the entrance. Through a window, I saw Lance talking to the security guard. I couldn't hear what Lance was saying, but he was holding his hand near his shoulder, likely indicating my height.

A handful of doorways stood along either side of the hall, but the only unlocked one was to a supply room. I slipped inside as I heard the front door open and footsteps thunder past into the studio. I stepped out of the closet and peeked out the window. Lance and the guard were gone, but the guy with the clipboard was still there. I chose a door on the opposite side of the hall, took my toolkit out of my purse, and went to work. The footsteps were on their way back when I got the door open, and I ducked into an office cluttered with paperwork and photography magazines. Across from the door was a window. I opened it and scrambled outside, then ran along the side of the building until I reached the parking lot. I weaved my way through the other cars and piled into the Chevy just in time to see the guard exit the studio with Lance on his heels. They ran after me as I backed out of my parking space. I gunned the engine and shot through the gate. A speed bump rattled my spine, but otherwise, I was safely away from the scene. The same couldn't be said for the security guard. In my rearview mirror, I saw Lance giving him an earful.

Not wanting to talk about Denise was understandable, but why was a guy whose job it was to sit back and look pretty instead ruining a fifty-dollar-an-hour makeup job trying to chase me down?

MY BREATH WAS SHORT AS I ARRIVED AT THE COFFEE SHOP. Broussard was already there, sitting comfortably in a red, crushed velvet armchair, nose-deep in Twitter or whatever was on her phone. She'd just reached for a sip of her beverage when I took the seat next to her.

"Hey," she said. "I was beginning to think you'd no-showed."

For effect, I added a couple more huffs and puffs. "Sorry. Traffic."

She nodded, and why not? It was L.A. after all, and getting stuck in traffic was as common as spotting a celebrity. In truth, I'd been parked across the street when Broussard arrived, and as soon as she'd left her Fiat unattended, I returned the favor she'd paid me, attaching a tracking device to her car's rear bumper. D's very touching story aside, I still wasn't ready to trust this woman.

"You want a drink?" Broussard asked.

I shook my head. "I'm pressed for time. There's something I have to take care of."

"Something to do with Denise Ladd?"

My chin dropped at the mention of Denise's name.

"Sorry, I didn't mean to catch you off guard. It's just that I heard you mentioned on the news," she said, quickly adding, "But don't worry. I'm not going to sell my partner out. I never figured you for a murderer anyway."

"Thanks," I mumbled. "So, tell me about this job."

"Like I said, I've always felt bad about the Greg Whittaker job going south and wished I could make it up to you. Well, now I can. I've got it on very good authority that he's added a trio of superb blue diamonds to his private collection."

"And you're proposing that we make *another* run at his place?"

"I know it sounds crazy, but we can totally do it. He's added some new security, but it's nothing you can't get around. Seriously, I've never met anyone who gets past systems like you do."

"Thanks for that, but returning to the scene of a crime? It's not just a cliché, it's a terrible idea."

"But look at these, Kate."

She called up a picture on her phone and showed it to me. It was a shot of three oval-shaped stones with a greenish-blue tint. Their symmetry was perfect and, even in a picture, their brilliance was unmistakable. Assuming the picture hadn't been retouched, each diamond could bring a half million, easily.

"Nice," I said, playing it cool. I asked her some questions about the jewels and also about Whittaker's new security that she'd mentioned. "Wow, Broussard. You really came through. I still want to gather some more information, but I have to say this has potential."

23

Fourteen. That's how many steps it took to cross my hotel room, and I'd done enough pacing to be certain.

Something had really set Lance Waltrip off, and with each step I took, I became more convinced that it wasn't just the loss of a close friend. I'd introduced myself using my alias, so the possibility that he'd figured out that I was the "person of interest" mentioned on the news seemed pretty slim. So what then? Could he have had something to do with the murder? That might explain his reaction to my questions — evasive at first and then panicked. And if he'd been honest about how much time he'd spent with Denise, he would've had plenty of opportunities, but what about motive?

My problem was that every person I ran into did more to muddy the water than clear things up. I stopped pacing and sat at the little desk in the corner of the room. Such a simple act and yet it felt good. Lately, I'd done so much running, sometimes literally, that I'd forgotten what it was like to relax and think.

What clues did I have to work with? A necklace. Snippets of

a conversation. A second, similar murder. A movie that was taking longer to make than the pyramids. And a boatload of total wackos.

Wait.

Dismissing them as crazy was too easy. What if there was a reason for their behavior?

The hotel room had a safe in the closet. I opened it and took out the necklace. I was certain now: it was a mundane piece of jewelry, and I couldn't see why anyone would kill for it. I put it away and looked up Denise's Twitter feed. I'd hoped that another look at the various pictures would shed new light, but except for some RIP tweets that had come in since she'd died, it was the same as I remembered it.

There was another clue I'd forgotten about: Denise's journal. I ransacked my purse and every drawer in the room before remembering it was in the Chevy's glove box. Great. I called D but had to leave a message.

After hanging up, I went back to pacing and thinking about my suspects when, just past the bed but not quite to the bathroom doorway, I stopped in my tracks. The Candle Queen. Virginia Ellington said she was out of town when Denise died, making her innocent, but what if she'd found a way to carry out the murder despite being over a thousand miles away?

Just minutes before she died, Denise had walked out of a Wick-ed Ways scented candle store. The Ellingtons owned some of their franchises. The thought hadn't crossed my mind before, but with a little research, I quickly discovered that certain aromas were fatal. I'm not talking about something like secondhand cigarette smoke or toxic waste, but perfumes, colognes, and other fragrances — like those found in candles.

As a storeowner, Virginia probably had access to customer records. If Denise had been in the habit of ordering candles with a custom scent, Virginia could've found out about it easily.

She also could've monkeyed with the order and had the candles laced with something toxic. Then all she would have had to do was sit back and wait — or better yet, leave town — while Denise inhaled the toxic fumes.

That approach also came with risks though. What if Denise had had a roommate? An innocent person — or a pet, like Yoda — could've been the victim. Or maybe that was what Virginia had wanted; knowing that her husband and Denise were seeing each other, maybe she'd figured to take them both out at the same time. With him dead, maybe Virginia would stand to get her hands on a lot more than she'd otherwise get in a divorce settlement.

Using my phone, I navigated the Wick-ed Ways website. At the bottom of the home page, next to the "become a franchisee" link, was text that read "customize your candles." I followed it to a page that contained an order form with options like sizes, colors, and—drum roll, please—scents.

I typed in an order, and when I got to the scent option, I entered a synthetic musk sometimes used in perfume. The site returned a message that read, "We're sorry, but the scent you requested is known to have harmful effects. Please consider one of the many selections from our fragrance catalog." The same thing happened when I plugged in some other scents my search had turned up.

The folks at the Wick-ed Ways corporate office were a step ahead of me — there'd be no toxic candles on their watch — making it all the more likely that the lush had told me the truth; she wasn't Denise's killer. Shoot.

Trying to determine where the investigation should go next brought Trammell to mind. Not because he was high on my list of murder suspects, but because he wasn't, yet no one's behavior had been more erratic than his. He'd set me up to be arrested at Hollywood and Highland, and when that had failed, he'd not only threatened me, he almost certainly was the one who'd given my identity to the police.

The thing was — aside from the B&E of my apartment, which I didn't like but at least understood — his outrageousness hadn't started until after I'd questioned Ellington about the murder. Even this latest errand Trammell had given me, supposedly to right some imagined wrong, seemed like more of a distraction. If he wasn't Denise Ladd's killer, why was it so important to him that I not find out who did?

D's call interrupted my rumination. "Hey. Got your voicemail."

Behind him, I heard what sounded like a band, one that was heavy on guitars.

"Where are you?" I asked.

"Just taking care of a little business. What's up?"

"Are you near your — my car? There's a journal in the glove compartment that belonged to Denise. I was wondering if you could take a look at it."

"Hang on." A door closed and the sounds of the jam session fell away, replaced by traffic. After a short walk, he opened a car door. "Okay, what am I looking for?"

"Thumb through it and tell me what you see."

"Lots of T.E.'s ... with hearts and smiley faces ..."

"Those are dates she met with Tad Ellington."

"Looks like she got paid every two weeks, or are those also dates with Ellington?"

"Don't be crude."

"Okay, okay ... I see codes: dashes, letters, numbers, some plus signs ... Uh oh, here's a T.E. with a frowny face next to it."

"When was that?"

"Two weeks ago."

I repeated after him. I had no idea what had happened two weeks ago, but it had been just over a week since I'd stolen the necklace. The first time. A day or so later, Denise took it from

Ellington's desk, leaving a note telling him all was forgiven. "You said codes. What kind of codes?"

"There's the dashes ... M-slash-SIN ... with a heart."

As he spoke, I could practically see the letters forming before my eyes. "Okay, that was the trip to Vegas with her sister, Michelle."

"Vegas?"

"Sin City."

"Oh. How 'bout M-dash-P? Another trip with Michelle?"

"Hmm, I'm thinking mani pedi."

"How did I not guess that? L-dash-8. Got anything for that?"

I turned it over in my head. "Are you reading that right?"

He clicked the roof of his mouth. "Yeah, I'm reading it right: L-dash ... Oh hell. Late. She meant late." There was a pause before he whispered, "Damn."

Late. He was right. Those dashes and plus signs were the results of pregnancy tests. What was it Lance had said when I'd mentioned Denise's murderer should get the death penalty?

Twice.

The killer should die twice, which I'd thought was Lance simply expressing his hatred for the person who'd taken away his friend, but it was more than that. Like he'd said, he and Denise told each other everything. He knew she'd been pregnant, hence the cryptic reference: one death sentence for killing Denise, and one for killing her baby.

I had D recap the dates for me to confirm the timeline worked out: Denise found out she was pregnant and told Ellington; for some reason — maybe he didn't want to be a father — they fought over it and made up shortly thereafter. But maybe Ellington had been having second thoughts about fathering a child. Or, thinking back to the picture of Denise and Trey Spencer I'd seen at Briarwood, maybe Ellington learned that the baby was someone else's; someone like Trey. Either way, did Ellington feel strongly enough about things to commit murder?

I checked the clock on the nightstand and saw it was nearing lunchtime. "Thanks a million, D. I'm going to see Ellington."

With my phone on speaker, I listened to the bug in Ellington's office on the drive to Brentwood, hoping he'd stick to his routine. It would've been just my luck that he'd pick today to break the monotony, but shortly after noon, he told his assistant, "I'm going to run downstairs for a bite."

I hurried to his office building and parked, just in time to see Ellington approach the counter at the sandwich shop on the first floor. I watched through the glass as he placed his order, took his receipt from the cashier, and found a table along the window. Once he was seated, I went inside and joined him.

"Is this seat taken?"

He snapped out of his daydream and fixed his eyes on me, searching his memory. Finally, it clicked. "You. What the hell are you doing—"

"Nice to see you again, too."

"I don't know who you are, but I suggest you get going before I call a cop. A real one."

"There's no need for that. I come in peace, and to prove it, I'm going to provide you with some helpful information."

With a scoff, he asked, "What would that be?"

"I don't know how it got there, but there's a listening device in your office."

Creases appeared on his handsome forehead. "You mean like a bug?"

"Exactly. It's plugged into the back of your computer." I took my phone out and showed him the picture I'd taken. "I noticed it when I was in your office the other day."

"And you saw it fit to keep that information to yourself until now. How convenient."

"Yeah well, better late than never."

"Who—" Ellington had drawn the attention of two older women sitting nearby, so he lowered his voice. "Who are you?"

"I'm someone trying to find out who killed Denise."

He chuckled. "Right. You seem to enjoy playing police officer. Is that what the little girl wants to be when she grows up?"

Over the years, I've gotten better about handling short jokes, but that still isn't the best route to my good side. "Yeah and you wouldn't believe what an awesome investigator I already am. For instance, when you told me you and Denise had been getting along great? Lie. You'd just had a nasty fight." Other than a cold stare, Ellington had no response. "Was she pressuring you to get married as soon as your divorce was final?" He smirked and opened his mouth to speak, but I cut him off. "Or was it about the baby?"

Just like that, the smirk was gone. He began grinding his teeth, nostrils flaring. The look in his eye was anything but dispassionate now.

"You don't know what you're talking about," he said. While he spoke, his fist was clenched so tight that the color was draining from his fingers. "She wasn't pregnant."

I decided to take a flyer. "That's not what she told Trey Spencer the night of the party at Briarwood."

The words were barely out of my mouth when he lunged forward, bumping the table as he snatched my wrist. "Now *look*."

Across the restaurant, witnesses stopped eating and directed their attention to our table. Seeing this, Ellington let go of my arm but was still only inches away from me. "You have no idea who you're messing with, so I strongly suggest you butt the hell out."

He got up from his seat and marched out of the restaurant, nearly colliding with the server about to deliver his lunch.

One of the older women at the next table looked on in concern as I massaged my wrist. "Are you all right?"

"Yes, I'm fine. Thank you." I collected my purse and prepared to make my exit as well. "Usually, it's the dentist who hits a nerve."

THE EXCHANGE WITH ELLINGTON WAS A REAL EYE-OPENER. HE liked to come across as cool and in control — it was an act that probably served him well when approaching a patient with a drill — but twice now I'd caused him to come unglued. And since I wasn't prone to self-flattery, I was less inclined to believe it was me specifically who had freaked him out, but rather what he thought I represented. Whatever that was. The point was that the doctor had a violent streak, and boy had the topic of the baby set him off. Was that how he'd tried to handle Denise? And when that didn't work? Space was getting awfully crowded at the top of my suspect list.

I'd only been back at the hotel for a few minutes when I got a call from Trammell.

"I'll get right to the point," he said. "Dr. Ellington seems to think I'm responsible for the listening device he found in his office. Where might he have gotten an idea like that?"

The bug was Trammell's doing? Even with everything I'd learned about this Briarwood crowd, I wouldn't have made that connection, but one thing was clear now: Trammell knew about my first visit to Ellington's office because he'd been listening in at the time. "I don't know."

Instead of responding — because we both knew Ellington had sold me out — he said, "Have you made any progress on the job we discussed?"

"Not exactly."

"Not exactly or not at all? Ms. Albertson, I want that statue in my hands in my hands tomorrow, or I'll deliver Whimsy to her new home. I know a family in Montana that would love to adopt her."

He hung up before I could tell him he wouldn't dare, which was just as well because he would dare. Trammell Preston absolutely would.

24

Coronado Plaza was the fancy name given to what had, for the longest time, been a forsaken part of the old warehouse district east of downtown. Then, cheap rent attracted lots of young, creative types, which in turn drew in some hip coffee houses and small galleries. All of that got the attention of real estate developers, and there went the eclectic neighborhood. The four buildings that made up the plaza had all been renovated and now served as the home to ad agencies, high tech start-ups, and other businesses that were typically at home in office spaces with exposed ceiling beams and open floor plans.

In the midst of the buildings was a courtyard dotted with round, glass-topped tables, each one shaded by a red- and white-striped umbrella. I sat at the one closest to the street, waiting for Aubrey and her silver Mini Cooper to arrive, which she did right on cue. She also found a parking spot along the street right in front of the building. Hated her.

As she approached the table, I got up to give her a hug. Not one of those pretend hugs either, like Virginia and her friends. I genuinely liked Aubrey, even though I'd only known her for a few days.

We sat across from each other, with Aubrey facing what was left of the afternoon sun. Her pink cat-eye sunglasses had a retro look that worked for her. "So we really are going to happy hour this time and not another frat party or something else lame?"

"Sorry about that. But yes, happy hour. Absolutely ... as soon as we do one other thing."

"Kate! I knew you had me drive all the way across town for something besides drinks."

I wasn't getting anything by her, especially after the frat party incident. Even though, for the record, she hadn't come that far. It wasn't like I'd asked her to drive to Orange County. "Fine, you're right. I want a second opinion."

"Why? Are you contemplating surgery?"

"Cute. Let me show you something."

A multicolored stone path threaded its way between the buildings, leading to one at the rear of the small complex. A line of palm trees bordered the area, while a few feet in front of the entrance, a three-tiered fountain splashed and gurgled, the only sound in what could easily have been a little oasis.

"What do you see?"

Aubrey shrugged. "An office building?"

"Yep. An older one ... off the street ... with lots of privacy so you won't be disturbed ..."

"Oh ... kay."

I led the way inside, where a perfectly tanned and bleached security guard was stationed behind a console, grinning at his phone. He looked up. I smiled and waved but didn't break stride on my way to the elevator with Aubrey close behind. He nodded and smiled back before returning to his game or the text from his bro.

We rode up to the top floor and stepped out into a quiet

hallway. The floor had eight offices, half of which were empty. Dynasty Filmworks, a production company that used Trammell's camera thing, was the last office on the left. According to him, the award was prominently displayed in a trophy case inside the office.

"Kate?" Aubrey said. "This is all very nice, but I already have an office."

We rode back downstairs, and this time, I stopped at the security desk. The guard looked up again as I leaned over to peek at what was on the other side of his desk — a monitor that currently displayed a grainy view of the street. I guessed it alternated between multiple views of the complex.

I pointed to an array of red and black buttons. "So what does all this stuff do?"

He leaned forward to shoo my hand away. "Hey, like, don't touch that."

"Sorry, I was just curious. I wasn't trying to make trouble or anything."

"No big."

Back outside, the walkway took us around the side of the building and eventually to the rear exit. The plain white door had a decent lock, but one I could probably pick in less than a minute. Of course, having an access badge allowed me to bypass the lock altogether. I swiped the badge across the black card reader mounted on the wall next to the door. A tiny green light on the reader flashed and the door clicked open.

Aubrey's eyes flew open. "Oh my God! Where did—Did you just take that off the guard?"

"In a matter of speaking."

A stairwell provided access to each floor, and there weren't any cameras on either side of the door; probably a corner the developers cut while renovating the property. We took the walkway back to the front of the building, where I left the badge on one of the tables in the courtyard, and started down

the block toward the Sonora Bar and Grill, which had a
hibiscus margarita to die for. I hadn't taken four steps before
Aubrey snagged my arm.

"Kate! What was all that just now?"

"Conducting a survey."

She stared me down the same way Mrs. Nathan, my fourth-
grade teacher, had when she'd caught me eyeing Erin Boyle's
paper during a math test. "A survey? As in a casing-the-joint
survey?"

My laugh came out as a snort. "Casing the joint? Did you
really just say that?"

"I'm not joking. Am I some kind of accessory now?"

She still had her shades on, but I didn't need to see the look
in her eyes to know she was serious — unnecessarily
concerned, perhaps, but serious. Putting myself in her flats, I
couldn't blame her. She'd been caught fixing records and had
paid a steep price. In a way, she was still paying it. She wouldn't
ever get that CPA license back. I, on the other hand, had never
gotten as much as a jaywalking ticket, although I was on some
pretty thin ice at the moment.

"Aubrey, of course not. I mean, maybe ... if I were planning
on letting myself in."

"Letting yourself...?" She shook her head at me. "I swear,
you have more euphemisms!"

I sensed she was waiting for me to offer some sort of explanation, but what could I say? I was colorful.

"So you're not going to break into that building?" she asked
as we approached Sonora's entrance.

Music flowed from the premises while people shuttled
through the door, most of them on their way in. Just ahead of
us were three guys wearing jeans and untucked shirts. When
they noticed us, two of them held the doors open for us.

"Thanks, guys," Aubrey said.

"Oh, any time," said the one closest to me.

We had to wait for a table, so we camped out at the bar, wedging in next to a couple with matching rat tattoos on their forearms, the respective rodents leaning in for a kiss.

Aubrey nudged me with her elbow and said, "I think that guy liked you. He was totally trying to make eye contact."

"There's eye contact and then there's staring. He falls into the second category. Besides, he looks like the kind of guy who uses *prahhhduct* in his hair."

Aubrey's throaty voice allowed her to do a bang-on impression of my dudespeak and we laughed until the bartender stopped by to take our orders: a pair of margaritas. "How about Connor's hair?" Aubrey asked as the bartender went to work mixing our drinks.

I'd mentioned him to Aubrey on our way to the Delta house, leaving out the part about heisting the ring. She was happy for me, saying I needed to find someone better than Terry, but I wasn't sure.

"I wouldn't know," I said. "About his hair or anything else."

"Still no word from him?"

I shook my head. "Either he lost my number or he's having second thoughts. I'm betting on the latter. I don't even know if I want him to call. He's probably just looking for some action on the side ... like Terry."

"Kate, stop. You just met him. Give him a chance." I didn't say anything, but my body language must have made it clear I didn't want to talk about it because Aubrey changed the topic. "So you're not gonna ... let yourself into that building over there?"

Moments earlier, my euphemism had frustrated her, but now she was using it. "I don't think so."

"Why not?"

"Because Trammell wants me to."

"Really?" she said, her eyes a mile wide.

I told her about him upping the price on me for getting

Whim back, the arrival of our drinks briefly interrupting my story. The bartender set our drinks down and Aubrey took a sip. Out of nowhere, a smile appeared.

"So why not just do it?"

I've picked up many skills over the years — I can tell by touch which pick to use on which lock — but nothing has been more valuable than my instincts. When it came to Trammell's request, my intuition was telling me not to try walking out of the office with that statue in my possession.

"It's too easy," I said. "You saw it. The building is all but hidden from view. That surfer dude isn't fit to guard a tree house, much less anything of value. And the floor was virtually free of any potential witnesses. *You* could pull that job off. No offense."

"Gee, none taken."

"My point is this feels like some kind of setup. If Trammell really wants that award, he doesn't need someone like me to take it. That's like asking Bobby Flay to whip up a peanut butter and jelly sandwich. Why not have Lucas Blaisdale get it for him?"

Aubrey looked confused. "Why would he do that?"

"I didn't tell you? Lucas is the one who broke into my apartment and stole Whimsy."

"What?" Aubrey shrieked. The tattooed couple next to her halted their discussion and eyed us as though we might be mental.

To be honest, mental was starting to sound pretty good. I could have had a nervous breakdown and no one would've blamed me. The cops sitting on my apartment, Trammell holding my dog hostage, Lucas following me, insecure sorority girls dumping drinks on me, and Ellington trying to break my arm — not to mention that I was getting nowhere in finding Denise's killer — would be enough to push anyone over the edge.

I lowered my head to the counter and hid beneath my arms. The bar was sticky and smelled like the Delta house. So what?

"None of this makes any sense," I groaned.

Aubrey rubbed my shoulders. "Kate? Sweetie, you need to sit up before you suck down some E. coli. Besides, I can't understand a word you're saying."

She was right. That was pretty gross. Even Whimsy wouldn't have kissed my face after that.

"I said none of this makes any sense." I counted on my fingers. "Trammell. Why's he trying to rake me over the coals? Why won't he just take his stupid necklace and give Whim back? The Spencers. Why did they move out of their house and into one owned by her parents?"

"They did?"

"Yeah. And get this. They can't afford their house, but they have money for a fancy club membership *and* to invest in Trammell's movie? Really? Talk about having your priorities out of whack. Lance Waltrip, a model friend of Denise's, went all action hero and started chasing after me when I asked one too many questions. Oh, and Denise was pregnant, by the way."

Aubrey's face registered open-mouthed shock.

"Then there's the soon-to-be divorced Mr. and Mrs. Ellington. She drinks like a fish, so I got a little alcohol in her and she let something slip about some joint assets that have gone missing."

"So Mr. Ellington is stashing things to keep from losing them in the divorce?"

"I guess, or ..." The thought was still forming in my head even as the words were coming out of my mouth. I could barely believe it when I said it. "Are the Ellingtons having money trouble too?"

"But, like you said, he's an investor in the movie," Aubrey said.

The bartender appeared and posed a question, but neither

of us heard her over the shouting and laughter, which had at least doubled in volume since we'd sat down.

"Can I get you guys another round?" she said, but louder.

Both our glasses were nearly empty, though I barely remembered taking a sip from mine. I declined the refill. I doubted the staff here was as diligent about calling cabs as the valet had been at Briarwood. Besides, I needed to keep my head clear.

"Aubrey, what's the story with this movie?"

"What do you mean?"

"Like everything else, it doesn't make sense. The alleged lead actress takes off for Vegas on days she's supposed to be on set. The head stunt coordinator hasn't coordinated a single stunt, unless you count dropping into my apartment from the skylight. Why are Richard Spencer and Tad Ellington investing perfectly good money into a movie that isn't going anywhere?"

She lifted her shoulders. "I dunno. I just make sure everything balances."

And that was the problem. There were all these dangling threads that I was certain were tied together — they had to be — but I couldn't figure out how. "Maybe I should just give up."

"What?"

"Give up. Turn myself in. At first, it seemed like ... I thought I could find a way out of this insanity — but I'm starting to think I can't."

Aubrey reached over and squeezed my hand. "Kate, if you give up, how are you going to get Whimsy back?"

"I don't know. Maybe a judge can order Trammell to give her up."

"You'd have to prove he has her first."

She was right. Trammell had gotten the best of me. He wanted me to stop investigating Denise's death, and I saw no other choice. If I went through with stealing the crystal statue, it wouldn't end well, and I knew it. If I turned myself in, I might not ever get Whimsy back. Either way, the cops would likely look to me as suspect numero uno in the death of Denise Ladd. Checkmate.

I sighed and signaled to the bartender. "On second thought ..."

ubrey talked me out of another margarita and had the bartender bring us coffee instead. By the time I'd reached the bottom of my second cup, I knew I wouldn't sleep, but at least I felt up to the drive back to the hotel. As we walked back to our cars, Aubrey even made me pass a field test before allowing me behind the wheel.

No sooner had the hotel room door closed behind me than I collapsed on the bed. Questions lingered about Denise's murder — Robin's too for that matter — but I couldn't bring myself to care. I wasn't getting Whimsy back.

When we were together, Terry had a strict no-pets-on-the-bed rule, but the night I came home to his note, Whim spent the night curled up beside me, licking tears from my face and listening to my nonsensical rambling. She wasn't just a dog, she was a friend — one I'd failed when she'd needed me most.

I took my phone out and stared at pictures of her — opening a Christmas present, chasing after some ducks at a pond, playing with friends at the dog park. Like Trey Spencer hung on to that photo of Robin, I knew I'd keep those pictures forever. I'd probably make backups of the backups.

Some time later, a soft chime shook me from my sleep, but with grogginess hanging over me, I needed a moment before I could place the sound: the alarm on my tracking app.

Broussard was on the move.

I hopped off the bed, scooped up my keys and hurried to the car. Enough Angelenos had turned in for the night that I made good time across town, mirroring the blinking green dot on my phone's tracking app until it came to rest on La Cienega in West Hollywood.

Broussard pulled up to a cozy bistro just as I arrived. I stayed a half block back, watching as she handed the valet her keys and headed for the door, where she met a guy in his early forties with dark, slicked back hair. The two of them smiled as they approached each other, and then Broussard took him by the lapels of his black jacket and planted a huge one on him. There was something familiar about him, but I couldn't put my finger on it. Someone from television, maybe?

He took her hand and led her to one of the outside tables, which were placed next to a ledge decorated with flowers. They had the area to themselves, and Broussard's companion wasted no time reaching across the table and stroking her forearm. A server arrived to interrupt that nonsense, which frankly was creeping me out. While the server addressed the two of them, I struggled to place the man, turning over one possibility after another until the fog around my memory lifted.

It wasn't television that I recognized him from, but pictures. He'd aged a bit in the time since I'd picked him out as a target, but I was positive that the man sharing a table with Broussard was Greg Whittaker. Four years earlier, I'd come across pictures of Whittaker as I was researching the job she and I were going to pull — acquiring a few items from his private diamond collection, valued at over a hundred million. It was the same job that ended with me hiding among recyclables.

What I needed right now was to be a fly on that flower-covered wall next to their table.

I hopped out and run-walked to the valet, who furrowed his brow at the sight of someone arriving in his lot on foot. "Hi. Uh ... can I help you?"

I stuck my hand in my purse, hesitated as I nearly backed out, but finally I took out my badge. Flashing it in front of the valet, I said, "A blue Fiat just came in here. The owner's sitting at one of the tables outside Zelko's. I need you to go tell her there's a problem with her car."

The look on his face was quizzical. There was also the undeniable scent of pot in his vicinity. "Really?"

"Yeah."

"What's the problem?"

"I didn't say there was a problem, I said I needed you to *tell* her there's a problem."

"Oh. How come?"

"I'm not at liberty to share that information, but if you're refusing to cooperate, I'm sure your supervisor would love to hear about your recreational drug use while you're on the job."

The valet put his hands up. "Hey, I never said I wouldn't cooperate. But what am I supposed to say if she asks me what kind of problem?"

"That it won't start or something, I don't care. Just get her to come take a look at her car."

Leaving him to his device, I returned to the vantage point of my car. The server had just delivered a pair of drinks to Broussard and Whittaker's table when the valet made his approach. He interrupted their conversation and said something that quickly wiped the smile off her face. He pointed in the direction of the parking lot and nodded, to which Broussard jumped up from the table to see whatever it allegedly was for herself. As I'd hoped, Whittaker, being the concerned boyfriend — or at least wanting to appear that way — accompanied her.

Making a break for the unattended table, I started my phone's voice recorder and stashed it among the flowers on the ledge. Then I returned once more to the car, more on edge at that moment than I'd been in the past week, which was saying a bunch.

∿

BROUSSARD AND WHITTAKER CLEARED UP THE misunderstanding with the valet and returned to their table for more than an hour of handholding and giggling over drinks. Afterward, they made an arm-in-arm walk back to the valet lot, where, after another kiss, they parted company.

I retrieved my phone from its hiding place and listened to the recording during the quiet drive back to the hotel. All I heard at first was the sound of the occasional passing car, but then Broussard and Whittaker retook their seats.

"So. You were saying?" Whittaker said.

"Oh, right. She totally bought it. 'Kate, no one knows alarms like you,'" Broussard mimicked. "Greg, this is going to be easier than it was last time."

Her laughter burned my ears. Last time?

"She's not stupid enough to believe I could accidentally trip the alarm again, but she is so cocky that she'll never suspect that there's a second alarm system behind the one she's deactivating. And when she sets that one off ..."

"The cops are there waiting," Whittaker said. "Your friend goes to jail, and I can claim she was behind the millions in losses I've suffered over the years."

So that's what was going on: Whittaker was committing insurance fraud. Now it all made sense: how, even after weeks of rehearsal, Broussard still managed to trip the alarm and then hang me out to dry, claiming she panicked. She wasn't incompetent; she was in bed with Whittaker. Literally.

More laughter was followed by the clink of their glasses, no doubt a toast to playing me for a patsy. But I was getting other ideas — fool me once and that whole thing — and no way were they going to leave Kate Albertson holding the bag again.

WHEN I SHOWED UP AT D'S OFFICE THE NEXT MORNING, MY CAR wasn't in the lot. I thought he might be out chasing down another bail jumper or something, but when I tried the door, it swung open and there he was at his desk, reading the *Times*. He didn't take his eyes off the Metro section as I made myself comfortable—or as close as I could get to it in that lousy plastic chair.

"You know all that's online, right?" I said, nodding at his fish wrap.

"I spend enough time staring at the computer."

But apparently, he hadn't had enough of staring at the newspaper, because he still hadn't looked up from it, not even after my second sigh. I looked over my shoulder at the parking lot beyond the window. The morning was sunny, with street traffic already humming by.

"D, where's my car?"

"At the shop. I had a little fender bender."

I spun back in my chair and was met by a jaw-breaking grin.

"Kidding. I'm having it detailed. Spilled some Cheetos the night before last." While I wasn't crazy about the Cheetos news, it was better than someone having to pound a dent out of my car. "Is that why you're here? Worried about the sedan?"

Hardly. Of all the things I had to worry about, that eggbeater of a car didn't stand a chance of making the list.

I sighed again. "No, I ... Remember when you said I'd have to talk to the cops sooner or later?"

He nodded.

"You think you could maybe smooth things out a little? You said you had a couple of friends on the force."

"That only works for people of a certain net worth. What you need is ..." He opened his desk drawer and rifled through its contents, eventually pulling out a business card. He slid it over to me. "He's good. If anybody can keep you out of lockup, he can."

I picked up the card. The stock was heavier than a typical business card and felt like cloth, exactly what I would've expected from an uptown lawyer. Then I read it.

"Are you kidding me?" I looked up from the card, fully expecting to see another grin, but his expression was solemn. "D, this is a joke, right?" I read from the card: "Alvin Klein?"

"That's the man's name, and no, he doesn't joke about it."

If D said the guy was good, he probably was, and if I were going to waltz into a police station, I wanted to give myself the best chance of waltzing back out. If that meant hiring the lawyer with the funny name, so be it, but trusting my fate to a man who sounded as if he was more acquainted with Fashion Week than habeas corpus didn't exactly inspire confidence. Truthfully, though, Mr. Klein's name wasn't my real problem; turning myself in was. I felt like a quitter. I'd never quit anything, unless I counted the cello in fourth grade, but learning to play hadn't been my idea to begin with, so I never felt too bad about that one.

"Do you think I'm doing the right thing?"

He folded his hands over his newspaper. "Yeah, I do. How much longer do you really think you can play hide-and-seek with the police while you conduct this investigation of yours?"

I shrugged.

"Kate — and I'm speaking from experience here — most people get caught."

Maybe, but I wasn't most people. The closest I ever came to

getting caught was when a heel got stuck in a grate. I hated leaving that shoe behind.

"I have to admit, though," D said. "I was beginning to think you might pull off some kind of miracle."

"Sorry to let you down," I mumbled.

Clicking the roof of his mouth, D dismissed the idea as if he were swatting a bug out of the air. "You didn't let me down. *I* let me down."

His friend, Gil. Robin Castro's brother. When he loaned me his car, D had told me he had a stake in my little predicament. He'd been holding out hope that Robin's killer and Denise's were one and the same and that the news might bring the Castro family some kind of closure.

A typical guy, D was, bottling everything inside, but just then, I could see that some wind had been sucked out of him. I really had been his last hope. Talk about desperate.

"You two must've been close," I said. "You and Gil."

I took his nod and grunt as a yes.

"One of our convoys had come under fire, and a squadron of us got sent out in half a dozen Humvees to control the situation. Here we are flying across the desert, and as soon as we get to the scene, one of the Humvees in front of ours gets hit by an RPG. The thing went flying, and when it landed, it was like nothing I'd ever seen in my life—just this huge bang and the sound of metal twisting and snapping. Our driver swerved to avoid it, and that's when the Iraqis opened fire. Bullets were flying everywhere. The enemy was in trenches on either side of us and had us caught in a crossfire. Our best chance was to take out at least one of the trenches, so we got out and hit the ground, lying flat. 'Make yourself small.' That's what they tell you in training. What they don't tell you is what a bullet sounds like when it just misses the side of your head. I remember thinking: *There's gotta be an easier way to get money for college than this.*

"Anyway, we started shooting back, taking out some of the bad guys on one side so we could make a run for their ditch. I was so focused on what I was doing that I never saw the Iraqi in the other trench rise up and take aim. Gil dove in front of me, taking one in the shoulder. I'll never forget him screaming, 'I'm hit!' Not ever.

"Once we'd taken out most of the enemy closest to us, the rest gave up and ran off. That's when I grabbed Gil and dragged him into the ditch, where he could stay covered until we secured the area. You know what's funny? Afterward, he thanked *me* for saving *him*."

I didn't know what to say that wouldn't sound trite or patronizing, so the room fell silent, except for some teeth-rattling bass coming from a car on the boulevard as it waited for the light to change. The noise grated on my nerves, but if it bothered D at all, there was no way to tell. He sat there lost in his thoughts, and I could only guess they were the haunting kind. As much as I wished I could've gotten myself out of this mess, I'd wanted to help him too, but it didn't look like I'd be doing either of us much good.

Impulsively, I dug into my purse. "Want to see what started all this trouble?"

I pulled out Trammell's necklace and tossed it on the desk, where it landed with a solid thunk. I'd brought it with me that morning, figuring I should hand it over to the police.

He held the necklace up to the light, turning the diamond over between his fingers. "It's nice."

I responded with a Bronx cheer. "It's mediocre at best. See these?" I pointed out several tiny dots on the stone. "Inclusions ... or flaws. If I walked past it in a jewelry store, I wouldn't even slow down."

D looked closer at the necklace. "Okay, now I see what you're talking about. So what you're saying is that this diamond would've been better off as a drill bit or something."

"Very good, D!"

Diamonds have lots of uses besides looking pretty around a woman's neck or on her finger. You wouldn't think it to look at some of the pieces in a jewelry case, but diamonds are tougher than nails. The word *diamond* even descends from the Greek word for unbreakable. In fact, about eighty percent of the world's diamonds are used for industrial purposes — drilling, cutting, polishing, stuff like that. And while I never heard of a diamond being used as a key, as I looked at that very average, triangular diamond dangling from the end of the necklace, I remembered where else I'd seen that shape.

"Holy crap!" In one smooth motion, I took back D's car keys and relieved him of the necklace before pivoting for the door.

"You're not going to see Alvin, are you?"

"Brilliant deduction, Mr. Detective," I said over my shoulder.

26

T hings were much calmer on fraternity row in broad daylight, and when I knocked on the Delta's front door, the echo carried throughout the house. A pudgy, pale-skinned, red-headed boy in workout clothes opened the door and stared at me as if I were a calculus equation.

"I'm looking for Ben. Is he here?"

The way he looked over his shoulder suggested he needed help with the question. I hoped he wasn't the pride of his pledge class. "Oh. Yeah. Come on in."

The boy vanished down the hall while I waited just inside the entrance, listening to his footsteps as he trudged up the stairs and knocked on a door. He must not have been familiar with the house's acoustics; otherwise, he would've kept his voice down when he spoke.

"Hey bro, there's a total nugget downstairs asking for you."

Nugget. Now that was a new one; on me anyway.

Message delivered, my ginger-haired admirer returned and informed me, "He'll be right down."

Ben rounded the stairs moments later with his phone

pressed to his ear. The conversation had his full attention until he noticed me standing there. "Uh, lemme call you back," he told whoever was on the other end. "Hey ... from the party ... Theresa, right? I'm awesome with names."

I nodded. "I'm sorry to drop in this way."

"Nah, it's cool. What brings you by?" he asked, cocky smile firmly in place. Taking a little air out of his ego wouldn't bother me in the least.

"Unfortunately for you, not what you're thinking. Estate room?" Without an invitation from the chapter president, I barreled down the hall and didn't stop until I'd reached the fireplace in his den.

"What's up with you? Wayne said you look like a woman who's been on the news."

For crying out loud, what was Wayne doing watching the news? Why wasn't he pounding brewskis and chasing co-eds like all good frat boys? I ignored Ben's comment and pointed to the fraternity's letters carved into the wall. "What's that for?"

After a glance toward the doorway, he spoke in a hushed voice. "It ... it's just decoration."

I traced the letters, feeling their impressions beneath my fingertips. "Sorry, Ben, but I think you're lying."

"Hey, come on. Don't mess with that."

"It's a hidden compartment, right? You stick some sort of key ..." I ran my hand over the delta and pressed. There was the slightest bit of give in the wall. "... right here."

Ben hurried over and snatched my hand away. "Don't do that! You're gonna get me in a shitload of trouble. That's, like, major fraternity business."

"Jeez, sorry. I'll leave it alone, okay? Just tell me: did Trey Spencer break the rules by telling someone about this little compartment? Is that why he's not in the picture of Delta legacies? Because he's *persona non grata*?"

"What?"

"He got kicked out."

"Oh. Yeah," he said under his breath. "Why are you so freaking nosey?"

He glared at me, really expecting an answer. He took this fraternity thing seriously; too seriously, if you asked me, but to him, it mattered.

"Fine. Your friend Wayne is right. I'm the girl on the news, but I'm totally innocent. I'm just trying to get proof, and it's connected to that hidden door of yours. There, I know your secret, and you know mine. Are you happy?"

"That is so hot."

I didn't mean to laugh at him, but I couldn't help it.

"Seriously, an outlaw," he said. "We're having a thug life party next month. You should come. You could be my date."

"Gee, thanks, but what about Stephanie?"

"Uh, I haven't seen her since the last party. After you said that thing about her heels and her GPA, I kinda laughed. She didn't like that."

"I see. Well, Ben, I'm not sure I can handle another one of your parties, but I'll make you a deal: if you haven't met the girl of your dreams by the time your twenty-year reunion rolls around, hit me up."

～

THE VALLEY. AGAIN.

If I had to descend one more time into that smog-encrusted bowl of asphyxiation, I'd have to invest in a respirator.

From the Delta house, I caught the 110 and eventually the Hollywood Freeway, where the traffic gods showed a girl some love and I was able to drive at a pace approaching the speed limit.

It took me just under a half hour to reach Van Nuys, a neighborhood that had seen better days. The exit ramp led me to an intersection with dueling pawnshops on three of the four corners, plus an out-of-business donut shop. I traveled north on one of the main drags, passing an assortment of restaurants, dry cleaners, hair and nail salons, and other small businesses. Instead of being marked with flashy neon signs like Mel's restaurant, these establishments were identified by sandwich boards duct-taped together or signs written on the windows with white shoe polish.

I turned right at an elementary school and continued down a narrow street until I reached a lot near the apartment complex D had mentioned was being built. The sun beat down on a crew consisting of about a dozen Hispanic guys wearing tattered jeans and t-shirts soaked through with sweat, putting up framework and pouring concrete. Off to the side and beneath the shade of a sycamore tree, Lucas sat in the front seat of a pickup truck with the windows down. He peered down at his phone while sipping from a to-go cup. I parked on his passenger side, drawing his attention. He stared at the Mustang, but the window tint kept him from seeing who was inside until I rolled down the window and waved. His first reaction was a double take followed by a frown. Good to know I'd made an impression on him.

"Hey, Lucas," I said to him through our open windows. I got out, and when I tugged on the passenger door handle of his truck, it opened, so I hopped in beside him. "What's up? Doing a little moonlighting? Stunt work not paying the bills these days?"

He raised both hands. "Look, I don't know what you're doing here, but it ain't payday. I'm tapped out."

"Oh, relax. This isn't a shakedown — not that you don't deserve it. I want to know why you've been following me."

He tried not to look shocked, but I caught the brief twitch in his upper lip.

"Don't bother denying it. Remember the P.I. friend I

mentioned? I traded cars with him, so he's the one you've been tailing. Only, he flipped the script and followed you. That's how I knew I'd find you here. So I already know you're the one who's been following me around. I just want to know why."

"Do you have to bother me while I'm working?"

At one end of the construction site, two guys were holding boards in an L-shape while a third hammered away, the sound echoing across the lot. Nearby, some other men were putting windows into a frame. The rest were toting tools or ladders back and forth.

"Lucas, I see a lot of people working, but you're not one of them."

A pickup truck carrying more windows lumbered by, and Lucas turned to watch. When the truck came to a stop near the edge of the site, he stuck his thumb and index finger between his lips and produced a whistle that rang deep inside my ears.

"Enrique!" he shouted. The driver of the truck looked out his window at Lucas, who waved toward the distance. "Over there!"

Given Enrique's look of confusion, Lucas's instruction wasn't getting through.

"*Allí*," I told Lucas.

"Really?" Lucas asked. After I nodded, he shouted to Enrique, "*Allí! Allí!*" again waving toward the far end of the other side of the construction site.

This time, a smiling Enrique replied with a hearty "Okay!" before moving his truck.

Lucas had the nerve to face me, looking smug. "See? I'm working."

"Whatever. How come you've been following me? Since he put you up to breaking into my apartment, I'll go out on a limb and guess Trammell had something to do with it." He did a better job of controlling his twitch that time, but a poker player

Lucas was not. "Okay, good. Now that we've got that cleared up—"

"Hey! I didn't say nothing!"

I wanted to explain the concept of implied agreement, but it would've just confused him. I also let that horrendous double negative slide. "What does he want? Are you just giving him my whereabouts, or is there more to it?"

This time, a taco truck interrupted our conversation by announcing its arrival with a trumpet riff blaring from the loudspeaker mounted to its roof. The workers put down their hammers and shovels and gravitated toward the four-wheeled Pied Piper. Lucas pulled some crumpled bills from his pocket and called out to one of the men, waving him over to the truck.

"You hungry?" he asked me. "It's pretty good."

I glanced over at the taco truck. It was pale blue with more rust spots than I could count, and an aroma I couldn't place consumed the air. The words Pepto and Bismol came to mind. "Hard pass."

The guy Lucas had called over wasn't much taller than me, but he had the powerful build of someone who met manual labor with gusto.

Lucas handed him the money and said, "Burrito grande, por favor. With onions. Muy, muy onions. Comprende?"

The worker nodded as he accepted the money, but when he turned for the food truck, he did little to hide the grin on his round face. I shook my head at Lucas.

"What?" he asked.

"You do realize you just told him you wanted your burrito with 'very, very onions,' don't you?"

"Really?"

"Really."

He stared straight ahead for a moment, scratching his chin. "Is that why they sorta laugh at me half the time I say something?"

"It could be. Noun-adjective agreement is kind of a big deal ... in any language. Next time, try *muchas*. *Muchas cebollas*."

Lucas nodded and stared out the front window again, repeating the words in little more than a whisper.

He scratched his chin some more and then said, "The other day? After you showed up at my place, I told Preston you just wanted your dog back, but he swears you're out to make trouble for him. He got real anxious when I told him I lost the tail on you. What's up? You got naked pictures of him with his side piece?"

Not that it came as any shock, but Trammell was having an affair? That information might prove useful, although I preferred the thought of camel spiders to the image of Trammell Preston in his birthday suit. As for making trouble? All I'd wanted was to get my life back to normal with no intention of bothering him — until now.

"No, you're right. I'm just trying to get Whimsy back."

"I'm sorry, you know, for taking her. I think it's the meth. Makes you do stupid shit sometimes."

For the first time, he looked at me with something other than mistrust or distaste, and I could tell he meant what he was saying. Maybe he'd just taken step one: admitting he had a problem.

Time was of the essence, so I skipped over taking personal inventory, accepting shortcomings, and all that other stuff, and went straight to making amends. "I could use your help getting her back. Nothing much, just call Trammell and tell him you think he's right about me being up to no good. You need to talk to him. Tonight."

"Do I want to know how come I'm doing this?"

"Probably not. And have him meet you somewhere ... Mezza Luna."

"Isn't that place kind of expensive?"

I shrugged. "He can afford it. Besides, after all you've done for him, you've earned a better meal than a burrito, right?"

A grin worked its way across his face. "Yeah. I guess I have."

He reached for his phone and placed the call, setting the meeting for seven. And do you know what he did after hanging up? He stuck out a toughened hand and gave me a fist bump.

"Listen," I said as I opened the door. "I'm going to clear out before you start getting down on all those onions, but I appreciate your help."

"You got it. And thanks, you know, for the muchas cebollas thing."

"*De nada*," I said with a wink.

27

T

he day couldn't have gotten off to a worse start, but things had turned around completely and it was just past lunch time.

I still didn't know who'd killed Denise or why, but if Trammell agreed to meet with Lucas tonight, I was certain I'd have some answers by the end of the evening.

On my way back over the hill, I picked up my phone to call D about my car. I'd just found his number in my contacts when screeching rubber broke my concentration.

The driver of the burgundy SUV ahead of me had stomped on the brakes, and a rear-end collision was fast approaching. I dropped my phone, seized the wheel, and did my best to put the brake pedal through the floor. My heart rate spiked, and I braced for the crunch of metal — but there wasn't one. D's Mustang had awesome brakes that stopped the car inches from the SUV's bumper. Every nerve in my body was on fire.

Right in the middle of a deep, cleansing breath meant to settle my churning insides, some jerk in a green muscle car behind me leaned on the horn, and I almost jumped through the roof. So much for calming down. Traffic had started moving again, so I eased off the brakes, although I was careful to leave plenty of space between the SUV and me until I got off the freeway.

At the first intersection I came to, the light was red. I reached down, searching the floorboard for my phone, and no sooner had I found it than a car pulled up next to me and honked. It was the green sports car. The driver rolled down his window — it was a young guy, probably early twenties, wearing a matted Budweiser cap — and started shouting at me. I still had my window up and couldn't hear him, but it didn't take a skilled lip reader to tell that one of his words was an F-bomb and that he was suggesting I do something anatomically impossible. Just in case I hadn't gotten his message, when the light changed, he flipped me the bird as he sped off.

My hands tensed around the wheel. Not only were my hands clenching the steering wheel, they were also shaking. I hoped I could make it back to D's office without further incident. Less than a block later, my phone rang. I grabbed it from the passenger seat. I didn't recognize the number. That immediately brought Trammell to mind.

"What?" I said, making no attempt to hide the edge in my voice.

"Theresa?"

That voice. It was too uncertain ... too unpretentious ... too human to ever be Trammell. Plus, he'd called me the wrong name.

Oh no.

"Connor? Connor, I'm so sorry. I thought you were ... It's this ... Never mind. How are you?"

"Okay. Is this a bad time?"

What were the odds? Then again, considering how the past several days had gone, it was probably even money that Connor would've picked this precise moment to call. And I'd probably sounded like someone who'd slice everything in his underwear drawer to ribbons given half a chance. Good luck coming back from that. "No, not at all."

"Are you sure? Because I could call you back later if—"

It had taken him three days to get this far. Or maybe he was just playing it cool? Either way, if he hung up now, I'd be arrested, tried, and convicted by the time he called me again. "Connor, it's fine, really. I'm glad you called."

"Oh. I mean, good," he said. I heard the smile in his voice and imagined that easygoing smile on his face. "I was wondering ... if you'd like to have dinner tomorrow night?"

Was I on a roll or what? With the luck I was having today, I should've stopped and bought a lottery ticket.

"Absolutely," I said.

"Great. Do you have a favorite place?"

"How about Imeldo's? It's on Sunset."

Connor wasn't familiar with it, so I gave him the address and told him I'd meet him there. I wasn't sure whether my apartment was still off limits to me, and I certainly couldn't exactly have him pick me up at the Century City Inn & Suites.

"Sounds great," he said. "I'm looking forward to it."

I couldn't have agreed more. A quiet dinner with a charming guy was just what I needed after several days' worth of nonstop chaos.

⁓

I swung by D's office and saw that the Chevy was back from the detailer, so I exchanged keys with him, making no mention of my near-miss on the freeway.

My thoughts kept returning to Celeste as the killer. The revenge angle — getting back at two of her exes at once — made sense, and a woman like her wouldn't have used a knife or a gun. Too violent. Poison made sense as her weapon of choice. What I hadn't come up with was a way of finding out if she had an alibi. After all, why would Virginia Ellington's daughter need to know a thing like that? Maybe I could suggest Virginia had implicated her somehow. If nothing else, gauging her reaction would've been interesting.

I arrived at the Spencers' house to find Richard and Trey kneeling in the garden. They were both dressed in shorts and t-shirts and were up to their elbows in potting soil. Golfing was one thing, but I'd looked at gardening as a father-son project. They must have really enjoyed each other's company.

My door thumped shut, gaining their attention. Richard looked over with a smile. "Well, this is a surprise! Were you in the neighborhood?"

"Yes, you could say that. I thought I'd take you up on your offer to stop by."

"Well, it's very nice to see you again. I think Celeste is in the kitchen. Why don't you go on inside?"

I followed the walkway up to the house and let myself in (not like that — I used the doorknob, for a change). Celeste had been busy since my last visit. A baby grand piano, as well as a pair of light green armchairs parked near the fireplace, had joined the sofa and coffee table. Every pleat on the emerald drapes was in perfect alignment, and there wasn't a moving box in sight.

"Hello?" I called out. "Celeste? It's Theresa."

"Back here."

I followed the sound of her voice to the kitchen, where I found her arranging decanters of oil and vinegar on an island with a butcher-block countertop. She'd had her hair trimmed and had added some blonde highlights.

"Wow, your hair looks terrific."

"Thank you! There's a fundraiser tomorrow night at the Getty. I thought I'd go for a little different look."

She hugged me and asked what had brought me by, but

before I could answer, the gardening duo entered the kitchen, Richard leading the way.

"Excellent. You found her," he said to me. He clapped his hands and rubbed them together as a smile broke out on his face. "It's always nice to have a guest, especially one so lovely, to brighten things up a bit. Trey? Man the bar and fix us some refreshments, will you?"

"Sure thing, Dad." Trey washed his hands at the kitchen sink before heading off toward the bar.

"He gardens. He makes drinks," I said. "Tell me he does laundry and I'll propose right here on the spot."

Richard laughed. "Afraid not. But yes, he turned into quite the mixologist when he went off to college. They damn sure didn't teach that while I was in school."

"Oh yes they did," Celeste said. "You were just cooped up in the library."

A sheepish look came over Richard, and he half-heartedly raised a hand. "Guilty as charged. Will you ladies excuse me? I'm going to see if Trey needs a hand and maybe get a pointer or two."

He gave us a wink, and once he was gone, Celeste and I moved to the den. We sat next to each other on one of the sofas, and I leaned in so I could keep my voice low.

"I wanted to let you know I met with Vir ... my mom."

Her eyebrows rose. "Really? How did that go?"

I delivered the story I'd rehearsed: that it was super awkward for both of us, she was a very different person than I'd built her up to be, and I wasn't sure what I would do next.

"I understand completely. I'd probably feel the same way." Celeste gathered up my hands and looked me in the eye. "If you ever need to talk, you can always come to me, okay?"

And give her first crack at the inside gossip, no doubt. I nodded and took a moment to compose myself. "I really appreciate your help. It's great that you two are still such good friends after everything that happened in college." I studied our clasped hands before looking back into her eyes. "Has it been hard for you?"

Her eyes began to well up, and she tightened her grip. She wanted to say something, but the words wouldn't come.

Come on, Celeste. Confession is good for the soul.

"I do hate her sometimes," Celeste whispered. "She could've had any boy she wanted, and she often did. It's no surprise she ended up pregnant ... I'm sorry. That was tacky of me."

I shook my head. "It's okay. Go on."

"Richard was never an exciting man — he really did spend much of his time in the library — but we were happy ... until Virginia decided to bat her eyes in his direction. I don't think she was even interested in him, not really. To her, he was just ... a challenge."

The tears she'd been holding back fell, and she buried her face in her hands.

I put an arm around her. "Celeste, I'm so sorry."

And I really was, which floored me. Celeste was gossipy and self-righteous, yet I felt badly for her. This meeting wasn't going at all like I'd intended. What I wanted was a confession, something that would free me from my predicament. Instead, I'd ripped open an old wound.

Suddenly, I doubted my theory about the case. Even though she had plenty of motive, Celeste as a killer? I couldn't see it.

"Let me get you a tissue. I think I saw some in the bathroom the other day."

I hurried to the bathroom and, on the counter next to Trey's toiletries, found a box of tissues, but it looked nearly empty. The only things in the cabinet under the sink were cleaning supplies, but I remembered seeing a closet in the hall.

"Ha!" I said as I spotted an unopened box. I grabbed for it, but as I was shutting the door, a red nugget along the baseboard caught my eye. I picked it up to examine it more closely. It was a kibble of Perfect Balance. If the Spencers had a dog, I'd yet to see or hear any evidence of it. I poked my nose into Trey's room, where I checked the carpet, his comforter, and some of the pants hanging in his closet for any sign of animal hair. Nada.

At the exact moment I stepped out of Trey's room, farther down the hall, Richard stepped out of his. He'd changed into jeans, a polo shirt, and some old sneakers. His expression was different as well; jovial just moments earlier, a sour look now covered his face.

"Lost?" he asked.

My heart did a tap dance, and I swallowed, thinking of a way to explain myself.

"I, um ... Celeste needed a tissue," I said, holding up the box. "And then, well, you caught me. I was thinking about leaving my number for Trey, but that's kind of gauche, right?"

"Indeed."

He wasn't angry, but he didn't look convinced either, so I switched topics.

I nodded at his shoes. "Nice kicks."

He looked down at himself. "Kicks?"

"Sorry. Shoes."

"These old things?"

"Absolutely. They're vintage. Anyway," I said, waving the box. "I'm going to take these to Celeste."

She'd collected herself by the time I returned to the den, but I offered her a tissue anyway. She dabbed at her eyes and tried to smile. "I'm sorry you had to witness that display."

"You don't have to apologize. Really. I think it's sweet you and Richard overcame those difficulties, and now look. You have a great marriage and a handsome son."

"You're right." Celeste gave a long exhale. "We almost didn't make it, Richard and I. I'm not proud, but part of me was drawn to an exciting man like Trammell Preston. However, I realized it's better to be with a man of character than a man who is one."

She was more right than she could've possibly imagined, though calling Trammel a character was a compliment, and one he didn't deserve.

Trey entered the den carrying a pair of extra large martini glasses filled with blue-green liquid. Richard was behind him with two more.

"Ladies, ladies, ladies," Trey announced. "Refreshments are served."

He handed a glass to his mom while Richard served me.

Trey held a glass aloft. "You can lead a whore to culture ..." he said.

His parents chimed in with, "But you can't make her think."

They all laughed, but I'm sorry to say, their brand of humor was lost on me. Nonetheless, I raised my glass, but as I was about to take a drink, I fumbled it and totally doused my top.

"Oh my God!" I shouted. "I'm such a klutz."

"Trey!" Celeste said. "Get her a towel."

"Yes, of course." He hurried off to the kitchen and returned with a blue-and-white striped bar towel.

Trey looked on with his hands in his pockets as I wiped the sticky mess from my hands and arms. The liquid had soaked into my top.

"Don't just stand there, son," Richard snapped. "Fix her another drink!"

"You know what?" I said. "It looks absolutely fabulous, but I'm going to have to pass."

"Are you sure?" Celeste asked. "It won't take him a minute."

"Yeah, I just noticed the time. I really do have to run, but would you mind if I used the bathroom to change out of this top?"

"Of course, you poor thing," Celeste said.

I hurried out to the car, grabbed the Target bag off the back seat, and dashed back inside. Richard escorted me to the bath-room — likely making sure I didn't go snooping around again. With the door closed behind me, I peeled off my top and dropped it into the Target bag. How many people could say they'd had not one but two drinks intentionally spilled on them in less than a week? Even though this latest one had been my fault, and intentional at that.

No way was I drinking from the glass Richard had handed me. I soaked the towel in hot water and cleaned the drink off my arms and chest, buffing the skin until it was almost raw. I also took one of Troy's pills and stuffed it into my pocket.

On the way out, my Hotel Westcott sweatshirt drew a double take from Celeste, but whatever she was thinking she kept to herself.

"Thanks again," I said. "I'll take a rain check on the drink, okay?"

28

The sight of me walking through his door sporting the same sweatshirt I'd been wearing the day we met gave D a laugh.

"Do they pay you to advertise?" he cracked.

I dropped into the chair across from him, squirming against the hardened plastic. "If they paid me, I'd be dressed better than this."

"Do I want to know?"

There was no point in avoiding it, so I told him about my visit with the Spencers. When I handed him the bag I'd brought with me, he took a good, long look at its contents.

D whistled. "I guess I'm about to find out how good my contacts at the lab are."

"That'd be awesome. Thank you!"

"That's not a promise. You still need to see a lawyer."

"Ugh, again with the lawyer talk. You know who needs lawyers? Guilty people."

I left everything with him and returned to my hotel room until it was time for Trammell's meeting with Lucas. What I really wanted was a nap, but if my head so much as touched a pillow, I might've slept for days.

According to Lucas, Trammell was afraid I'd make trouble, but how could I be a threat to him without knowing what had him so worried? It could've been the affair that Lucas had mentioned, but Trammell didn't strike me as the kind of guy to go into freak-out mode over that sort of indiscretion becoming public. Mrs. Preston probably knew about any fooling around, but was kept quiet by a lavish lifestyle and a well-armored prenup. No, whatever had him on edge involved higher stakes, and I only had a few hours to find out what it was, or I'd be saying goodbye to Whim forever.

At six o'clock that evening, I stationed myself near the entrance to Trammell's tony neighborhood. He only needed fifteen minutes, twenty max, to get from his place to Mezza Luna for his seven o'clock meeting with Lucas, but I wanted nothing left to chance. He'd have to pass this way to get to the restaurant, and as soon as he did, I'd head right up the hill to his place.

Traffic through the area was a nonstop parade of Beemers, Benzes, Porsches, and other high-end vehicles. In a strange twist, my normally nondescript sedan might have stood out *because* of its modesty in this neighborhood, but when Trammell rolled past in a champagne-colored convertible Bentley at ten to seven, I didn't even merit a glance.

I waited until he was out of sight and then took the winding road up to the Preston's home, continuing past the wrought iron gates guarding the house to a side street that bordered the back of his property. Everything up and down the street was calm — Holmby Hills was the kind of neighborhood where residents packed it in early on most nights — but the coast was hardly clear. A pair of security cameras kept watch over an ivy-shrouded brick wall meant to keep riff-raff like me out. A closer look at the ivy revealed what I was pretty sure were motion sensors.

I drove up the street and around a corner, where I parked out of sight and then followed a trail back to the wall, slipping on my gloves along the way. The security cameras swept back and forth, monitoring the perimeter, but I noted two small blind spots at either end of the wall, directly beneath the cameras. The motion sensors were probably meant to compensate for that, but if I stayed tight against the fence, there was a chance I could avoid detection.

Starting from the side, which was partially hidden by a very old, very large oak tree, I focused, hugging the fence as I deliberately slipped past the sensors.

Without waking the sensors, I reached the wall, parted the ivy, gained a foothold, and propelled myself to the top. The light was dim, and I guessed there might be more sensors on this side of the wall. I lowered myself into the backyard and peered through the darkness. A line of shrubs adorned the far wall. I made my way over and, using the hedges as cover, snuck across the sprawling yard, past the pool, and near a window that looked into the house.

A glow coming from inside drew my attention, and upon closer inspection, I saw that Amelia, Trammell's wife, was on the couch, watching television. He'd scurried off to Mezza Luna, leaving her behind. Granted, he probably didn't want to talk to Lucas in front of her, but it was still a jerk move, and it made my job that much harder.

Fortunately, there's one thing that's nearly a given when it comes to people who live behind big, imposing gates: a false sense of security that makes them lazy. The night of the party, I'd come and gone through the front door, but entry into the house was also possible through the library, the patio, and the kitchen.

The latter was the farthest from the family room, where

Amelia was parked, and sure enough, the door was unlocked. I crept through the kitchen and into the hall, and came face to face with a towering security guard. I jumped and then laughed at myself when I realized it was just a suit of armor. Taking a deep breath, I continued down the hall to the staircase that led upstairs.

Without a house full of party guests roaming the grounds, the door to the master bedroom had been left unlocked as well, and I made a beeline for Trammell's side of the closet. I slid his clothing aside, revealing the safe and fraternity letters I'd seen on the night of his party.

I hadn't attached any significance to it at the time, but now, as I took the necklace out of my kit, I couldn't believe how obvious it was. This sort of thing didn't usually make me nervous, but as I aligned the pyramid-shaped diamond with the letter Delta and pushed, my mouth felt dry and my heart was racing. I heard a soft click as I popped the diamond into place and a small portion of the wall slid open.

A rectangular space, about the size of a jewelry box, had been cut into the wall. I expected to find money or jewels or some other valuables, but discovered only an unsealed manila envelope with an assortment of papers inside. The papers must have held secrets vital to our national security for someone to go this far to hide them.

I swallowed and pulled out the contents. At the top of the stack were several sets of income tax returns, only they didn't belong to Trammell. They were Ellington's. As far as I knew, Trammell wasn't a CPA, so why would he have anyone's tax papers other than his own? I also found some other paperwork that had to do with Ellington's dental practice.

The next thing I found was a report from a clinic in Santa Monica, almost twenty-five years old, assuming the date on it was accurate. While I couldn't decipher Ellington's documents, this sheet of paper left little to the imagination; it was the result of a paternity test, addressed to Richard Spencer. Trey may have shared Richard's last name, but not his DNA. There was no mention of who the father was, just that it wasn't the senior Mr. Spencer.

I let that sink in. Not only had Richard raised a kid he knew wasn't his, but Trammell knew as well. What about Mrs. Spencer? Did she know too? My money was on yes, even if she'd been doing the deed with two guys at the same time. Women usually had a sense about these things. The question was: Had she told her husband he wasn't the father, or had she kept that bit of news to herself? It was easy to imagine a woman so concerned with her image taking that secret to her grave, which would mean something, or someone, had given Spencer reason to question the paternity. But what? Or who? And what in the world was Trammell doing with a copy of the test results?

Whatever the reason, I wasn't going to figure it out here, in Trammell's bedroom closet. Using my phone, I took pictures of everything, returned the envelope to its hiding place and slid the panel shut. I stuffed the necklace back into my clutch. I had to admit, using a diamond as a key was pretty smart.

On the way to the stairs, I passed the bedroom I'd gotten trapped in by Spencer and his boy toy, Thor. That was still a tough one to wrap my head around, but I smiled at the thought of Niles walking in on their suddenly not-so-secret rendezvous. I wished I could've seen the look on his face. Setting him up like that might have been a tad cruel, but it was no less than he deserved. As if the possibility of being given a part in his cheesy movie would be enough to coax any right-thinking girl into the spa in the bowels of the … the sub-level!

As quietly as I could, I hurried to the ground floor and searched for the way down to the sub-level. The television cast just enough light down the otherwise darkened hall for me to make out several doorways along either side. The first, on my left, opened to a bathroom, and the one across from it led to an office or a library. Then came the kitchen, a closet, and the doorway leading to the family room. Amelia was nestled into the corner of the couch with her back to me, watching one of those dating shows on cable. It's true. The rich really are just like the rest of us. Their flat screens are just four times bigger.

The back of my neck tingled, warning me I'd already been in the house too long, but no way was I leaving now. I grabbed the doorknob. As I eased it open, I heard the faint beginnings of a squeak. Great. The volume on the TV was up to a decent level, meaning I could've possibly opened the door without tipping Amelia off, but I didn't like it. Remember, to a thief, silence is a girl's best friend.

I crept back down the hall to the kitchen and, near the stove, found a pair of matching oblong glass bottles. I picked one up and sniffed. The tang of vinegar hit the back of my throat. I grabbed the other one — olive oil — and went to work on the hinges. Once they were lubed, I tried the door again, opening it inch by inch. No squeak this time. I returned the olive oil to the kitchen and then proceeded down the stairs to the sub-level. With the door closed behind me, the stairwell was shrouded in darkness. Though there was probably an over-head light, I opted for my phone's flashlight instead.

At the bottom of the stairs, I reached another door that was closed — and locked. A close-up inspection revealed that the lock was shinier than the rest of the knob, and it didn't have the scratches that came from the repeated insertion of a key. Someone had just had the lock installed, and odds were that someone was Trammell.

I sized up the lock, guesstimating how long it would take to pick. If it were a woman, she wouldn't be saving herself for marriage, but she wouldn't be going home with just any smooth talker from the bar either. But there was a wild card in the equation: How long could Lucas keep Trammell tied up at the restaurant? Maybe his story was so riveting that Trammell wouldn't be able to tear himself away, or maybe he was already about to leave. For all I knew, Lucas could've been a no-show. That was the problem with depending on addicts.

My phone was on the ground, shining its light up at the knob. I kneeled next to it, taking out my tools so I could get to work. The lock proved to be more of a challenge than I'd thought. Perspiration gathered on my forehead as I manipulated the pins, trying to coax them into position. I stopped for a breather but knew I couldn't rest for long; I'd already overstayed my welcome. No matter what though, I was opening that door.

It took several more minutes, but I finally got the last pin to click. The door opened and the swirl of air told me the area was large and open. I closed the door and ran my hand along a tiled wall until I found a light switch. I flicked it on, and there in the far corner, across from a square-shaped spa with columns at each corner, was a kennel with Whimsy inside.

"Whim!"

She'd been asleep but sprang awake at the burst of light. Her tail whipped back and forth, and she barked at the sight of me. I sprinted across the room, in disbelief that I was seconds away from holding her again. I also needed to quiet her down. I threw open the cage door and scooped her into my arms. She squirmed against me, licking at my face, and I laughed like a kid.

Scratching her ears and chin, I looked her over. She didn't look too much worse for wear. Next to the kennel were two bowls: one half-full bowl of water and an empty one for food, I guessed. A leash sat on top of the kennel. At least she'd been fed and walked, although probably by someone on staff. I couldn't picture Trammell standing next to a tree, holding a plastic bag, waiting for Whim to finish her business, but none of that mattered now.

As soon as Whimsy got over her excitement, I turned off the lights and carried her back to the main floor. I peeked inside the family room. Aside from changing ends on the couch, Amelia was where I'd left her. I stroked Whim's coat and felt her shake as I shouldered the door open. She twisted her neck back and forth rapidly, taking in her new surroundings.

"Easy," I whispered, praying for her to keep quiet while I snuck back toward the kitchen. Nearing the doorway, I spotted the iron giant standing just across the hall. Whim locked onto the empty suit of armor looming in the darkness. She shrank back, a growl building in her tiny gut.

"It's okay, Whim." I held her closer, hoping to make her feel safe. "We're almost out of here."

I crossed the kitchen and paused at the door. How was I supposed to climb the fence at the back of the yard while holding on to Whimsy? A quick search of the pantry turned up a nice, big canvas shopping bag, plus the last couple of bottles of some really expensive water. I wasn't thirsty, but any chance to annoy Trammell was too good to pass up, so I took them.

Outside, I moved along the edge of the yard with Whimsy in tow, and at the wall, I stuck her in the bag. The load tugged on my shoulder as it swayed back and forth, making Whim seem heavier than she really was, but if I could just clear the wall, we'd be home free.

I pushed aside the ivy, located a grip, made a final check over my shoulder, and saw the cat an instant too late.

29

W him sprang from the bag and darted across the lawn at full tilt.

"Whimsy! No!" I shouted, but it was useless.

Her barking and yapping shattered the peaceful night and ruined a perfect getaway. The only one making an escape was the cat, and all I could do was give chase, even though I knew what was coming next.

I tripped one of the motion sensors, and just like that, the backyard lit up like Vegas. The cat made a beeline for a tree on the opposite side of the yard and shinnied up the trunk to safety. Sitting on one of the branches, it looked down with disdain as Whimsy barked and jumped against the tree.

I scooped her up and urged her to knock it off, but my words fell on deaf ears as she kept right on barking. I looked at the house. Amelia, wearing sweats and a scowl, stood in the middle of the picture window, staring back at me with a phone to her ear.

"That can't be good."

Hustling for the wall, I dropped Whimsy in the bag and held

it closed as best I could. Somehow, I made it over the wall while juggling my dog and hit the ground running. The car was a block away. I preferred to save my running for Nordstrom's semi-annual sale, but this was no time for sloth. When people in Holmby Hills called the cops — what I guessed Amelia was doing — it was like Commissioner Gordon picking up the Batphone.

Once we were in the car, I drove up into the canyon rather than down the hill. If the cops were coming, that was the direction they'd be arriving from. I meandered along a series of narrow, twisty paths until I thought we'd traveled far enough from Trammell's place to venture back onto the main roads. For her part, Whimsy stayed put inside the bag on the passenger seat, her head poking out just far enough for me to see what looked like a remorseful expression.

"Whatever," I grumbled, but I couldn't stay mad at her. At the first red light I came to, I leaned over and gave her furry, brown face a kiss. "I'm sorry it took me so long to come get you."

She gave my nose a lick to let me know it was all good.

On the way back to the hotel, I stopped for food and some bowls. Then I snuck her into my room — unlike the Westcott, this hotel wasn't pet-friendly — where she curled up beside me on the bed.

My visit to Trammell's had been more profitable than I'd expected. The value of the necklace wasn't in its stone, but rather in the secrets it was protecting. How many other people knew about Richard Spencer III's paternity? Why were the test results only addressed to Mr. Spencer? Maybe because he was the one who filled out the paperwork or something simple like that. Less easily explained was Trammell's possession of said test results. Were he and the Spencers so close that they'd trust him with such sensitive information? Given what I knew about him, I had trouble buying it. There was also the matter of

Ellington's tax papers. While I couldn't make heads or tails of it, I knew who could.

AUBREY STOPPED TYPING AND BROKE OUT INTO A HUGE SMILE AT the sight of Whim and me entering her office the next morning.

"I'm surprised you're not sporting a prison jumper," she said.

"Huh?"

"Last time I saw you, you were four-inch stilettos deep in misery."

I shut the door behind me and took a seat while Whim made herself comfortable on the floor. "Was not."

"Oh, please. You were moaning like it was the end of the world and talking about handing yourself over to the cops."

"I plead the Fifth."

"Fine." Aubrey peeked over her desk at Whimsy. "I take it this is the little one you were after?"

I nodded. "This is Whimsy."

"Hi, Whimsy!" Whim looked up at Aubrey, her tail beating against the carpet. "So cute. Where was she?"

Memories of skulking about Trammell's residence flashed through my mind. "That's probably one of those need-to-know kind of things."

Aubrey raised her hands, opting not to pry. "So you're here because?"

"I need your professional expertise."

After calling up the photos of Ellington's paperwork, I handed her my phone. At first, the pictures made no impression, but a minute or so after looking at them, she frowned. "Kate? Is this what I think it is?"

I shrugged. "What do you think it is?"

Aubrey's voice dropped to a whisper. "Doctored books and income tax fraud?"

"Really?"

"Where did you get this? Or is that another need-to-know kinda thing?"

"Most definitely."

So, Ellington was cooking his books, possibly to keep assets from Virginia, just like she thought. At least that explained why he had money to invest in Trammell's movie. But Spencer? He was having money trouble. That was why he and his wife had sold their house, so how was he coming up with the money to invest? And when would either of them see a return on those investments?

As far as I'd determined, cameras had yet to roll on this production, and an actual movie was nowhere in sight. That couldn't have made for happy lenders. If it were me, I would've quit writing checks a long time ago, but Aubrey's records had the project dating back almost a year. Why on earth was the money still coming in? Was their friendship that strong? Possibly, though it pained me to believe they could actually care about anything other than what car someone drove or which zip code they lived in. Ellington and Spencer had chosen to trust Trammell with secrets that could've been disastrous if made public, so why wouldn't they invest a little money?

I sat up in the chair, startling Whimsy. Because they hadn't *chosen* to trust him with anything. "Aubrey! This isn't a movie. It's blackmail."

"What?"

"Think about it: There's a bunch of people supposedly working on the movie — like Lucas Blaisdale and Denise before she died — but none of them are doing anything ... except for you. And your job is to make the whole thing look legit. Meanwhile, Ellington and Spencer keep dumping money into Trammell Preston's bank account. Aubrey, there is no movie. It's hush money. It has to be."

She sat back in her chair, thinking through what I'd said. Part of me wanted her to poke a king-sized hole in my theory, to say the stress of the situation had gotten the better of me, but instead, she exhaled and a look of resignation came over her.

"Let's say you're right. That would mean Trammell's blackmailing Ellington over his finances, but what does he have on Spencer?"

I broke off eye contact. Telling her about Ellington's books was one thing—that was just money—but getting into Spencer's paternity test was different—personal. It felt like a betrayal. Aubrey, though, wasn't having any of it.

"All right, Kate," she said. "Give it up. And none of this need-to-know business."

She sat perfectly still, letting her stare weigh me down until I couldn't take it.

"Richard Spencer isn't Trey's biological father."

Aubrey's eyes bulged. "You're kidding!"

"I wish." I showed her the photo of the paternity test results. "Spencer must've gotten an inkling, because he submitted to a paternity test, which basically told him he wasn't baby daddy. Somehow, Trammell got his hands on the results—"

"And he's using that to blackmail Spencer."

I nodded.

"Geez, with all the people he's screwed over, I'm surprised Trammell's not the one who ended up dead."

She was right. He'd blackmailed his friends, planted bugs in their offices, and if his interaction with me was any indication, he wasn't above playing the bully either. If anyone should've been marked for death it was him.

I was back where I'd been a few days ago: nothing made sense. I reached down to scratch Whim's ears. For now, she was back with me and not on her way to Montana. Tomorrow I'd go see Alvin Klein, but today Whim and I were going to play tug-of-war with her rope, visit the dog park, and make a stop at the place that made doggie ice cream — all of her favorite things — just in case it was my last chance to do them.

"Is there anything you haven't told me?" Aubrey asked.

"Well ... I have a date."

30

I felt myself smiling as I stepped out of my car and handed the keys to the valet. Getting asked out while I was the subject of a citywide manhunt (Womanhunt? Person-hunt?) felt especially weird, but really, the timing couldn't have been better. It felt good to be doing something normal for a change instead of hunting for clues or keeping a step ahead of the police.

When I entered, Mel was holding down the host station. He must've taken our little chat to heart and given Komar the night off, because she was nowhere in sight. He smiled and was about to greet me when I spotted Connor sitting on a bench just to the right of the podium. His outfit was straight out of the first-date playbook: navy blazer, white shirt, and jeans. The smile and awkward shift of his weight, however, was all him.

"Hey, Theresa," he said. "Good to see you again."

I peeked at Mel and saw confusion on his face. I gave him the tiniest shake of my head, praying he'd get the signal.

"It's good to see you too," I told Connor. "I hope I didn't keep you waiting."

"No, I just got here," he said and then addressed Mel. "We have a reservation under Andrews."

Mel took a moment to size my date up. "Of course, Mr. Andrews. Right this way."

Andrews—a simple, but strong name that suited him. Without me thinking about it, the letters started bouncing around in my head like those balls the lottery machine spits out. Just that quickly, I realized his name could be reshuffled to spell "wardens," as in the guys who ran prisons. I shivered, hoping there wouldn't be any of those in my future.

Mel guided us past the bar, where several customers were chatting, or watching the television mounted overhead, and stopped at a cozy table near the end of the dining area. He placed the menus on the table and pulled out my chair, giving me a quizzical look as I sat.

Connor must have noticed, because once Mel had returned to the front of the restaurant, he leaned in across the table. "Was he giving you the stink eye?"

"Who? Mel?" I waved the suggestion off. "He's the owner, and he's probably just wondering why I haven't been here in a while."

That seemed to satisfy Connor, as he relaxed back in his chair and turned his attention to the centerpiece—a small arrangement of red and gold flowers inside a crystal, cube-shaped vase. The other tables had similar vases, but some had purple and orange flowers instead.

"Nice," he said.

I nodded. "Mel always comes up with interesting arrangements. It's one of the things I love about this place."

"So he's into horticulture as well as food?"

"Actually, what he's crazy about are ..."

Mention of Mel's obsession with eighties cinema never made it past my lips. Something about the way Connor had said horticulture reminded me of the joke Trey Spencer had told just yesterday, the one about leading a whore to culture. It hadn't been funny then and it still wasn't now, but the meaning hit me like an avalanche. He hadn't said, "lead a whore to culture," but *horticulture*. And then there was the line he'd used when he'd gotten home early from playing golf: *Back by poplar demand*. I thought it had been an alcohol-induced pronunciation of popular, but it was another one of his jokes—a play on words. I started giggling. It all made sense now. He liked making bad plant jokes.

Connor eyed me as though I'd come unglued. "Are you okay?"

I told him Trey's horticulture joke. The light wasn't the best, but I swore I saw a hint of blush on his neck. Once I'd stopped laughing (mostly at myself—the jokes were average), I asked Connor to excuse me while I went to thank Mel for giving us such a good table. I waited briefly at the host stand while he seated another party, and when he returned, it was with a frown he'd probably turned on his daughter more than a few times. I got the distinct feeling that a lecture was coming.

I reached out to shake his hand. "Mel, you're the best. Thank you for taking such good care of us!"

As he took my hand, his face softened and then lit up to maximum brightness. That was because I'd used the handshake to pass him the ring I'd picked up at Sterling-Ross.

"I can't believe you did this, especially with your ... troubles. You're amazing."

I could've argued, but why? We hugged, my heels making me just tall enough to see over the top of his head. I was glad I'd come through for him, and I promised myself I wouldn't put him in a position like that again. Mel stepped back, holding me at arm's length. His stern look was back in place. Lecture in three, two, one ...

"Why does your young man call you Theresa?"

I sighed. "It's a long story that started with a patio heater the night I stole the necklace ... the first time. But he's nice, right?"

"He's ducky."

"Yeah? So you like him?"

Mel grunted. "No, Duckie. Jon Cryer's character from *Pretty in Pink*. And you're Molly Ringwald. He's a nice boy, but you're all wrong for him."

"I'm going to chalk that up to your unfamiliarity with the phrase and assume you meant to say *he's* all wrong for *me*."

"I know what I say. Look at him." Across the restaurant, Connor, his lips pursed, was studying the menu. "Look at that face."

"I have. He's cute."

"He's upstanding. He should be dating a school teacher."

Well, that stung. I liked to think I was pretty upstanding, once you got past the whole acquisitions thing.

"I wanted to be a school teacher once. Doesn't that count?"

A party of five entered the restaurant. Mel gave them a smile and collected a handful of menus from the podium.

"If there's one thing I learned from John Hughes," he said to me, "it's how to tell when boy is wrong for girl ... and I should've moved to Shermer, Illinois."

"Not a real place, Mel. Besides, that's two things," I said, but he'd resumed the role of charming host and was paying me no attention.

Taking the hint, I made my way back to the upstanding Connor. Mel was right about one thing: dishonesty was no foundation for a relationship. I couldn't continue to hide what it was I did for a living. What was the worst that could happen? Maybe one day we'd look back on it and laugh.

Connor looked up from his menu. "Is everything okay?"

"Oh. Yeah. Fine." I retook my seat. My stomach felt like Jell-O, and it was me, not him, struggling to maintain eye contact. "It's not a huge deal, but there's something I have to tell you."

In an instant, worry clouded his face. I'd intended to down-play things, but I'd done just the opposite. I might as well have given him the old *we need to talk*. I glanced at the centerpiece, and when I looked back up, it was with the full intention of clearing up that little misunderstanding, but my eyes drifted past Connor to the television suspended above the bar. My driver's license photo was plastered onscreen in HD with "Kate Albertson wanted for questioning" captioned beneath for good measure.

This was Trammell's work; it had to be. He was probably pissed because I still had his necklace *and* I'd gotten Whimsy back, so he'd totally put me on blast. This was so not good.

"Connor? Would you hold that thought?"

Once again, I excused myself from the table, this time heading for the bathroom. My neck was burning, and I swore half of those around the bar turned to watch me as I passed by.

A tall redhead was coming out of the bathroom as I entered, and we narrowly avoided a collision. I did a quick stall check and was relieved to see I had the place to myself. I was about to have one of the most famous faces in town, and it wouldn't be long before somebody tipped off the police. I couldn't hang around here, not unless I wanted get arrested over Mel's biko — this sticky rice dessert that was nothing short of sinful.

Good thing I hadn't been planning something dramatic like slipping out the back door, because Connor was standing right outside the bathroom, with a crease in his forehead that I feared might be permanent. "Are you sure you're all right? You looked like you were about to get sick."

Handsome and observant. Another check mark in the plus column.

I took him by the arm and led him toward the front of the restaurant. "I'm fine, but ... I think I need to go."

"What's wrong?"

It would have taken entirely too long to answer that questions, and people were definitely looking in my direction, so I quickened my pace for the front door. Mel gave me a "I told you so" look as we breezed by the podium. Outside, I handed my valet ticket to a young man in a red jacket. He searched a metal cabinet full of keys, found mine, and dashed off to retrieve my car.

"Will you tell me what's going on?" he asked again. "What's the big hurry? And not just tonight. You're always running off, like at the jewelry store, and now you're doing it again. What's up with that? If I'm doing something wrong, just tell me."

My mouth dropped open. He thought he'd ... of course he did. Because Mel was right; Connor was decent to his core, which put him on the endangered species list in L.A. And because he liked me, it was beyond him to imagine that I might actually be some kind of nut. His only conclusion was that the problem must have been with him.

I stepped closer to him. "Connor, I'm so sorry. I'm kind of in a mess right now, and I haven't been honest with you. You're right, I do owe you an explanation, and I'm going to tell you everything as soon as I sort all this out. Really. But for now, just know that you haven't done a single thing wrong, okay?"

The valet pulled up with my car. As he held the door open for me, I stood on my tiptoes and kissed Connor's cheek. Then I hurried into the car before either one of us could say another word and drove off.

I thought about casting fate to the wind and going back to my apartment. If the cops were there, they could arrest me. If not, I could take it as a sign that things would be okay. But Whim was waiting for me back at the hotel. I couldn't risk getting tossed in jail and leaving her there all alone, especially after what I'd gone through to get her back. D was right. It was time to meet with his lawyer friend. Maybe he could keep me out of prison long enough for me to find Whim a good home.

Just after I'd redirected my car toward the hotel, my phone

rang. It was D.

"Hey," I said. There was a hitch in my voice, and a tear was literally hanging on by an eyelash, blurring my vision.

"Problem?" he asked.

I cleared my throat. "No. It's all good."

"If you say so." He paused, possibly waiting to see whether I'd change my mind and spill my guts, but I didn't. "I have news."

The classification of said news was conspicuous by its absence. "Is this good news or bad?"

"I'll let you decide. The analysis on that drink came back. My guy at the lab said it would've been a lot easier if you'd put it in a cup and not on your shirt."

"I would've placed a to-go order if that had been an option. I got it out of there the only way I could."

"I can only imagine. Anyway, it tested positive for andromedo, a poison found in certain plants."

"No kidding?"

"No kidding. It metabolizes in the digestive system without leaving a trace. It's lethal, though, if you get enough in you."

How much was "enough?" The amount I'd spilled on myself? "What about the pill from Trey's medicine cabinet?"

"Straight up placebo."

"No way! He's on risperidone. That's for people with—"

"Paranoid schizophrenia," D said. Like me, he'd done a little homework.

"So if you aren't on your meds—"

"No telling what you might do."

I shook my head at the possibilities. Under everyday circumstances, that kind of knowledge had the potential to be disastrous, but add an emotionally unstable person to the mix … I checked the time. All golf pros had gone home for the day.

"D? You wouldn't happen to have Jimmy's cell number, would you?"

31

Whim was so excited to see me when I got back to the hotel room that she let out a bark. I quickly shut the door while she ran circles around my legs. If management found out I was violating their no-pets policy, we'd be living out of my car. Poor thing. Being cooped up in a small room couldn't have been much fun for a bundle of energy like her. And I was about to leave again. I gathered up her leash and, after peeking down the hall to make sure there was no one around to ID either one of us, used the stairs to sneak her outside for a walk.

When D had loaned me his car, I'd joked about using it to leave town if things got out of hand. That was looking far less like a joke now, only I'd be hitting the road in a dreary sedan instead of his Mustang. I didn't want to leave L.A. The weather was almost always beautiful, and it was a target-rich environment for someone in my line of work. Best of all, I knew great people like Mel and Shrevie. I'd made new friends too, like Aubrey and D. Without their help, I never would have come close to figuring this thing out. Aside from the occasional aftershock, I'd never felt more at home. If I could just get the police and Trammell Preston off my back and make things right with Connor ... Right. And if I stood here long enough, maybe I'd get sideswiped by a pair of Tom Fords.

Whim and I returned to the hotel, and I'd just put away her leash when my phone rang. The prospect of letting it go to voicemail was tempting, but I picked up.

"Kate? It's Shawna Larson." Her voice was trembling. "You said you were an investigator, but ... I saw you ... online. The police want to question you."

Her, too? At this rate, leaving town might not be good enough. I'd have to go completely off the grid. "Shawna, it's complicated and right now isn't the best time—" On the other end, I heard labored breathing and then a sniffle. "What's wrong? Are you okay?"

"No ... I'm horrible ... I lied to you."

"About what?" I asked, as gently as I could.

"The other day when I said I didn't know anything. You asked if Robin was happy. She was; super happy. I think she was in love ... with Trey Spencer."

"Seriously?"

"Yeah." Shawna cleared her throat. "She didn't say the words, but just the way she talked about him all the time, saying he was so sweet and so fun and took such good care of her."

All the time? The morning I spoke to her in the parking lot, Shawna told me she'd lost touch with Robin, but it sounded now like that hadn't been the case.

"I ... I was jealous. How come her? I mean, I would've understood if she'd come from a rich family like he did, but Robin was like me — not really poor but not rich either, just sort of in the middle. I tried to hide it, but Robin must've known. She started hanging out with me again; not as much as before, but it was good. A couple days before she died, she told me she had big news. She was writing a novel and she'd put it on this website where people post manuscripts and stuff. An agent saw it and wanted to represent her, even though it wasn't finished."

"That is big news."

She sniffled again. "I think you should read it."

"Okay, what's the website?"

"The story's not there anymore, but I saved a copy. I can send it to you."

I gave her my email address and minutes later, she replied with an attachment. The story was about a small-town Hispanic girl who moved to New York City and made friends with a group of kids who loved the fast life. They came from prestigious, old-money families, but the boy she was falling for had a secret: the man he called his father really wasn't, at least not biologically. The girl swore that that didn't matter to her, and at a country club Christmas party, they promised their hearts to each other forever. He was planning to propose on New Year's Eve, but instead, he called that night to break things off.

That was where Robin had stopped writing, and part of me felt cheated; I wanted to see how it ended. No wonder an agent wanted to represent her. It was riveting stuff.

To my favorite Spencer man. As if.

That was what she'd written on the back of the picture I'd found in Trey's bedroom. As if. As if he really was a Spencer.

She'd known Trey's secret, that someone other than Richard Spencer was his father. My guess was that he'd confided in her — about his paternity, his invalid Delta legacy, maybe even his father's sexuality — but one thing was clear: someone didn't want her writing any more of that story. Despite cosmetic changes like giving the characters different names and moving the setting from the West Coast to the East, the identities were apparent.

Jimmy had told me that Trey had brought Robin to Briarwood once, and Celeste had made it clear he wasn't to make that mistake again. That was why she'd suddenly had time for Shawna again. Had that been the impetus for her novel as well?

I called Shawna back. "Why didn't you tell someone about this? The police or the private investigator?"

She burst into tears. When she first tried to speak, her words were unintelligible amongst the sobbing, but after several attempts, she managed to say, "I couldn't. It was too late."

"It wasn't. It's not. Murder doesn't have a statute of lim—"

"I already took the money."

Every muscle in my body tensed. I don't think I was even breathing.

"I was on my way to class one morning a few days after Robin died, when this guy started walking beside me. He smiled at me and said he wished he were on his way to the beach instead of class. I just thought he was flirting or something, but then he took me aside and told me I needed to be very careful not to say anything to anybody about Robin. He put his fingers to his lips and turned an imaginary key before walking away.

"The whole thing was so scary I was shaking. I found a bench and sat there, thinking about what he said and wondering why anyone would do that. Finally, I convinced myself to go home, even though I was still freaked out — I must've looked over my shoulder for that guy at least a dozen times. When I got to my apartment, there was a FedEx box addressed to me on the doorstep; one of those big ones, but it was still heavier than I thought it would be. When I opened it, all these bundles of money fell out on the kitchen table; more money than I'd ever seen. I knew right away it was no coincidence, that guy and the money both showing up on the same day, and I knew I shouldn't keep it but ... God, I was just so scared. That guy knew where to find me ... and Robin wasn't coming back no matter what ... so I did it. I kept my mouth shut. I even left school. I spent a semester in Tahoe until things calmed down."

Tahoe. No wonder D hadn't found her.

"I promised myself the money was just for school, not so I could go out partying, but now I feel ..."

Shawna lapsed into more sobbing, but the blanks weren't hard to fill. She'd justified taking the money because she'd felt as though someone owed her something; Robin had gotten a taste of the good life, so why not her? Or maybe because, deep down, she just wanted the money. Whether or not she'd spent it wisely didn't matter; what mattered was that she'd fattened her bank account by helping her friend's murderer escape justice.

"The guy who approached you when you were walking to class, did you know him?"

"No, he was wearing a cap and sunglasses. I might recognize his voice if I heard it, but I'm not sure."

I looked at the clock. I had to hurry. "Okay. Thank you, Shawna. Really."

"Do you think this will help?"

There was no mistaking the desperation in her voice. Shawna Larson was in dire need of a lifeline, some sense that she'd at least tried to make things right. She'd already lived with a horrible decision for three years, and at no more than twenty-three, she had a lot longer to go.

"Yes," I said. "I think so."

After ending the call, I did another search. It took longer than I would've liked, but I finally found what I was looking for.

I gave Whim a snack and apologized for leaving her again, but promised to be back soon. Her tail fanned back and forth, and those big brown eyes of hers sparkled as if to tell me she knew I had this.

That made exactly one of us.

32

The Getty Museum sits atop a hill above Brentwood and has some of the best views of L.A. that anyone could ask for. The entire basin fans out to the south and, looking west across the ocean, on a clear day, you can catch a glimpse of Catalina Island. On clear nights, the city lights seem to go on forever. Every year, more than a million people, tourists and locals alike, come to see works by van Gogh and Renoir and Monet, or to walk through gardens bursting with color thanks to more than five hundred of types of plants.

It was hard to complain about the Getty as a location for a fundraiser to build a sea lion habitat, with a couple of exceptions. One, if you're looking to make a quick getaway, don't forget to BYOH—Bring Your Own Helicopter. The only way to get between the museum and the parking garage at the foot of the hill is via a tram that moves at glacial speed, and there's usually a line for it too. Two, because of the small fortune in artwork that calls the venue home, there's a ton of security as well, and not just the latest in video surveillance and heat-sensing monitors, but the old-fashioned, two-legged kind as well.

It was tough to move very far in any direction without spotting a guy who resembled a tree trunk sporting a black jacket and an earpiece.

A couple hundred members of L.A.'s elite society were on the grounds, all frocked up in their formal best. I was still in my date dress, and I hated being underdressed for any occasion. If there was any consolation, it was that I hardly knew anyone here, and I hoped those I did know wouldn't recognize me, at least not right off. I'd pulled my hair back and thrown on a pair of thick, black frames I'd grabbed at the drug store right after swinging by my apartment building to reclaim the tracking device Broussard had attached to my purse.

The steps leading up to the main rotunda were jam-packed, and I had to wedge my way through the crowd while keeping an eye out for Celeste. She was nowhere in sight out front, so I made my way through the exhibition buildings. A handful of TV reporters were on hand to cover the event, although based on the snippet of conversation I overheard, the event was a snooze as far as they were concerned. I found lots of people munching on hors d'oeuvres, sipping champagne, and pretending to appreciate art they likely didn't comprehend at all. At one point, I spotted Trammell and immediately doubled back. He was busy talking to a couple of women a good twenty years younger than him and probably wouldn't have noticed me, but why take a chance? I ducked a couple of guys in LAPD uniforms, who were on hand in addition to the regular security guards. I could not believe I was going through this much trouble without even planning to steal anything.

Finally, in the gardens, I spotted Celeste. Her new hairstyle looked great with her strapless white gown. She and Virginia Ellington were engaged in deep conversation, and I would've given anything to know what that was about. I waited a few minutes, and when it didn't look as if their chat was going to break up anytime soon, I snuck back to the main building and asked the woman at the information desk to page Celeste.

I was doing my best to stay in the background, when a guy in a tuxedo approached me, sipping from a champagne flute. He was fortyish, with an average build and just enough hair to run your fingers through.

He greeted me with a smile. "Is this your first visit to the Getty?"

"No, I've been here a few times," I said.

"Excellent. Have you seen the new Tiberius exhibition? Phenomenal."

He seemed harmless enough, and under different circumstances, I wouldn't have minded him chatting me up, but the saying is true: in life, timing is everything.

"You're probably going to think I'm awful, but there is zero chance of this happening right now."

He shrugged, downed a little champagne, and went in search of someone else to put under his Tiberius spell, which I appreciated. Had he been clueless, like that guy Niles, he would've taken my response as a challenge and kept trying instead of realizing it was time to fold 'em.

Celeste arrived at the information desk a couple minutes later. She was trying to get the attention of a staff member when I stole up behind her and touched her shoulder. She turned, startled. It took her a moment before she recognized me.

I nodded to the area where I'd been waiting. "Can we talk?"

She followed me away from the crowd, and even though my back was turned, I could feel the iciness of her stare.

I'd intended to get the first word in, but the second it was just the two of us, she said, "Kate?"

Her arms were crossed, and her eyes were cold.

"You're no more Virginia's daughter than I am. And you're

no TV show producer, like you told Virginia. I don't know what brought you into our lives, but I know you're a liar. You've been lying to all of us."

No one likes being called a liar, but what I found interesting was what she hadn't accused me of being, because she knew the truth.

"You're right, Celeste. I did lie, but you know what? The punishment for lying isn't being murdered. You should be happy for that."

"And what is that supposed to mean?"

I left her question hanging. Her stare wasn't quite as piercing as it had been a moment earlier.

"How many people have you lied to over the years? Passing off Trey as you and Richard's son. You probably knew Richard wasn't the father from the minute the doctor told you you had a bun in the oven, but if that news had gotten out, it would've torpedoed your reputation. Celeste Spencer couldn't have that, could she?"

Celeste put a hand to her mouth as she teared up.

"Who's the father, Celeste? Tad Ellington? Trammell Preston? No one would blame you. I mean, we both know Richard prefers the other team."

"Don't you dare breathe a word of that, or—"

"Or what? You'll have Trey the botanist fix me up another one of his special cocktails? Like he did for Robin Castro? Or Denise Ladd?"

Celeste reeled and I was prepared to catch her, but she righted herself. "Denise? No. He ..."

Jimmy hadn't been especially happy to hear from me — and he'd had to make a phone call before getting back to me — but he'd confirmed that Trey had majored in botany before dropping out after Robin died.

Quite the mixologist was what Richard had called him. And some of his concoctions were fatal. Celeste had just tipped her hand. She knew her son had killed; she just didn't know — or didn't want to believe — that he'd done it twice. And I was a spilled drink away from being victim number three.

"He did, Celeste. Think about it. Two young, perfectly healthy girls, both friends of his, just drop dead? That's no coincidence. Neither is Trey knowing which poison won't show up on an autopsy."

Celeste closed her eyes and shook her head as if that would keep her from hearing me.

"He can't help himself," I said. "He's ... he's not in control. Combine that with being scared ..."

"What do you mean, scared?"

"Scared of getting expelled from the order of Spencer men, like Lawrence."

Lawrence Spencer was Trey's cousin and, according to the information I'd dug up, had never met a party he didn't like. The family put up with his behavior for a while, even through two stints in rehab, but getting arrested in a San Francisco hotel with a pile of cocaine and an underage girl had been more than they could bear. The article, which I'd found on an alternative newspaper website, claimed Lawrence was last seen living in Baja. None of the mainstream media sites were reporting anything about Lawrence—the Spencer family influence at work, no doubt.

"I know this isn't what you wanted for your son. I know you didn't raise your son to be a killer. He needs help, Celeste. Forget all this Spencer family stuff. *You're* his flesh and blood. If he can't count on you ..."

She was crying and made no attempt to hide it. "He has problems, but ... his medication ..."

"I don't know how this is going to shake out, but from now on I think you should keep a close eye on those pills. You can't let anyone else die. You have to do the right thing, for Robin and Denise. And for your son."

She nodded. There were no more words between us, but I trusted she'd do what needed to be done. She composed herself as best she could under the circumstances, and the last I ever saw of her was as she vanished into the stream of people gathered to admire precious works of art from centuries past.

At the start of the night, I thought I'd be having a nice dinner with Connor, and maybe even a drink by now, but clearing my name wasn't a bad alternative. In a perfect world, I'd know exactly how to make up for running out on him, but one step at a time.

The crowd had more than doubled since I'd arrived, and I began feeling claustrophobic as I attempted to make my exit. It was slow going, and suddenly, the wall of people in front of me halted. The pack was so dense that even on my tiptoes I couldn't see anything. Getting fresh air became a challenge as well. I stood on the small concrete barrier lining the walkway to make myself a few inches taller. I never saw the cause of the holdup because I immediately made eye contact with Trammell across the way. He did a double take, but then must've seen through my disguise, because he started pushing his way through the crowd toward a police officer.

I hopped to the ground and doubled back the way I'd come. I was so close—so close to setting things right—but as far as the cops were concerned, I was still wanted for questioning. Trammell, fearing that I'd expose his blackmail scheme, would do anything to put me out of circulation. If the police got their hands on me, it might be enough to convince Celeste to keep her mouth shut in the hopes that I'd be the one taking the fall for Denise's death.

More than a few unhappy looks were thrown my way as I brushed aside three or four guests and bounced off a few others. My head was on a swivel, looking everywhere for her, while also keeping an eye out for Trammel or a security guard. She had to be here; the temptation was too great for her pass up. A trio of servers passed by with trays of empty glasses, and as they cleared my view, I saw Broussard. In jeans, of course. At least her tee shirt was black.

A moment later, she spotted me and hustled over. "I *knew* you were on to something big," she said, keeping her voice low. "But the Getty? Wow, I totally didn't see that coming. All right, what's the play?"

I sighed, feigning exasperation.

"Come on, Kate. We're partners, right? And it's bound to take two people to pull off a gig like this."

After giving her words time to sink in, I said, "Fine. Follow me." We threaded our way back through the museum to the wing that housed the Tiberius exhibit. Fortunately, the guy who'd approached me earlier wasn't among those in attendance. The centerpiece of the exhibit was a life-sized, bronze statue of the emperor draped in robes. Pockmarks and scars littered the statue which, according to the story, had been damaged in a volcanic eruption. There were also paintings and numerous artifacts, most of which looked hundreds, if not thousands, of years old. Sitting in a square display case off to the side was a gold band. I nodded toward it. "See the ring? It's worth almost two million."

"Nice."

"Yeah, and the best part: it's got a dedicated security system. There's a backup, but the lag is almost sixteen seconds. You can take down a Triad Millennium, can't you?"

Her eyes widened. "A what?"

"The security system. Do you know how to disable it?" I had no idea whether any of the stuff I'd rattled off was true, but it didn't matter. I knew how Broussard would answer before I asked the question.

"Um ..."

"Never mind. I'll take care of security, you grab the ring ... discretely. I can trust you with the ring, can't I?"

She smirked. "Kate, it's me."

Exactly. "There's a lock on the display case—"

"No worries," she said. "I got it."

"Okay, give me your number. I'll text you the second the security system is down."

After making sure the coast was clear, I took refuge among some plants sculpted into miniature towers just outside the exhibit area, and started counting. If this didn't work, I could start thinking about the best ways to accessorize a prison onesie. When I got to a hundred, I sent Broussard a text: *Go!*

At first there was nothing, then a screeching alarm shattered the air. I peeked out from my hiding place just in time to see the exhibit room door slide shut. There was a mad scramble of guards as they converged on the area, shouting back and forth into the communications units attached to their lapels. Initially, the assembled guests were happy to look on from afar, but as curiosity spiraled, they edged closer, hoping to catch a glimpse at what had caused the commotion. The chaos gave me the perfect opportunity to slip out unnoticed and make my way to the tram.

"Did you have a good time?" the operator asked me as I climbed aboard.

"I don't think it could've been much better."

Halfway down the hill, my phone buzzed. Broussard had texted me: *I'll get you for this, Kate.*

Have a nice day, eighteen to twenty-four months' worth, I replied. *And tell Greg Whittaker I said hi ... girlfriend.*

lvin Klein wasn't what I'd been expecting. At all. Blame it on too much television, but I'd pictured a guy in his mid- to late-thirties, tall and athletic, with an even tan, a thousand-dollar suit, and a three-hundred-dollar haircut. Instead, judging by the creased forehead, thick glasses, and white, thinning hair, I got a guy pushing sixty who favored off-price department stores. That said, he had a wise face.

He welcomed me into his office, which was in a Mid-Wilshire high-rise. The building wasn't like the gleaming, sprawling law offices on TV, with dozens of young associates hustling back and forth, researching cases, defeating injustices, and whatnot. Alvin's was a one-man operation, and his space could best be described as cozy. The office had enough room for a large oak desk that was clean except for that day's *Times* and a cup of coffee. A row of filing cabinets took up the right wall. Diplomas from the University of San Diego and Stanford hung above the cabinets. Behind him, a window running the length of the rear wall gave a view of downtown, and to the left was literally an entire wall of books. He also had excellent taste in chairs. The ones across from his desk had sturdy legs and arms and broken-in leather that was more comfortable than my bed.

Given that it was my first time inside a lawyer's office, I naturally had questions.

"Have you actually read all those?" I pointed to his books. "Or are they more like props?"

He looked at me the way people do when they're waiting for the punch line, then it dawned on him that I was being serious. "I can't honestly say I've read them all cover to cover, but they're not those kinds of books. They're mostly for reference, and I can assure you, they are not props."

"Got it. Can I ask one other question before we get started?"

"No relation." When he smiled, his blue eyes danced as though they were full of mischief. I liked him right away. "Well, Ms. Albertson, you've had quite the time of it."

"You can say that again."

"How about we take it from the top?" He put his elbows on his desk and rested his chin on his steepled fingers. "Tell me everything, and I do mean everything."

And that's what I did. Starting with Trammell's party, I told him the entire story — the necklace, Trammell, Denise, the Ellingtons, the Spencers, the Deltas — everything (I'd marry attorney-client privilege if I could).

When I finished, Alvin said, "My word. I'm ready to call it a day, and all I did was listen."

Instead, he picked up the phone and began making calls. He did a lot of listening and mm-hmm'ing, making it hard for me to piece together what was going on. He also scribbled a lot of notes on a legal pad. After ending the second call, he simply said, "Well."

I all but jumped across the table. "Well what?"

"Mrs. Spencer and her son have met with the district attorney. They're in the process of working out a plea deal."

"Is Trey going to jail?"

"That's still up in the air. Between his condition, the Spencers' standing in the community, and what's certain to be some fancy lawyering, my guess is that he'll be spending some time under court-ordered medical supervision. The shenanigans with his medication could also be a mitigating factor."

Shenanigans. What a great word. Did I mention how much I liked Alvin? "So I'm not a person of interest any more?"

"You are not."

"Meaning, I'm in the clear?"

"You are."

It was over. After all the running, hiding, sneaking, and detecting, it was over, and I could go back to being me. I sprang from the chair, not sure what to do first. I moved in to give him a giant hug but didn't know whether that violated some sort of lawyer ethics thing, so I thanked him. Two or three times, actually.

"Ms. Albertson?"

"You can call me Kate."

"Certainly. Kate?"

"Yes?"

"You will stay out of trouble from now on, won't you?"

"Come on, now. Do I really look like the kind of girl who goes around getting into trouble?"

He neglected to answer, but he did show me to the door and wish me all the best. I was waiting for the elevator to head down to the parking garage when it occurred to me that if this were a movie, the elevator doors would part and Connor would be standing there. I would've apologized for giving him a fake name, ditching him at Mel's, and basically being a total flake from the minute we met, and he'd shut me up with a great, big kiss.

But this wasn't a movie. When the elevator dinged and the doors opened, the only person standing there was a woman in a pair of mom jeans.

I checked out of the hotel, and Whimsy and I headed home. Once I returned the Chevy to its hiding place in favor of the Karmabile, things would truly be back to normal, although that skylight was in need of some serious burglar-proofing.

I pulled into my apartment building's parking garage, feeling as if I'd been gone a month. As we got out of the car, I glanced down to make sure I had the door key, and when I looked up, Richard Spencer was standing beside my car.

"Hello, Kate. It is Kate, not Theresa, right?"

He'd always been fairly gregarious and outgoing, but his expression was one I hadn't seen before. Frankly, it rattled my nerves, and I suddenly wondered whether the man I'd met before was the real Richard or if I was just now seeing him.

"Might we have a word?" he asked.

"I don't think we have anything to discuss."

He moved quickly, stopping only inches away from me. "Oh, I very much think we do."

Funny how I'd gone my whole life without having a gun jammed in my ribs, and yet I knew that's exactly what it was when it happened.

Whimsy's barking and growling rebounded off the walls of the parking garage. She jumped at Richard, and only my grip on the leash kept her from getting to him. Richard aimed his gun at her.

"Kate, one of us is about to silence that dog."

That was when I realized the look in his eyes was one of real desperation, meaning there was no sense in pointing out that a gunshot would be noisier than Whimsy. Logic tends to fly right over the head of a desperate person. At the restaurant, when Ellington told me I didn't know who I was dealing with, he'd been referring to this lunatic.

I kneeled down and stroked her, telling her everything would be all right. That got her to dial it down a little, but no doubt she still would've tried to take a piece out of Richard if I'd let go of the leash.

"Put the dog back in the car," he said.

"Are you serious?"

He answered by pointing his gun at me.

I gathered Whim up. She was scrambling to get free, and I needed both arms to hold on to her. "Will you at least pretend to be a decent human being and open the door?"

Richard sighed but did as I'd asked, and I put Whim in the back seat, rolling down the window enough for her to get fresh air. She whined and her eyes pleaded for me to open the door.

"I'll be back for you real soon," I said.

"You shouldn't make promises you can't keep." Richard snatched me by the arm and forced me into his SUV, then he hurried to the driver's side, making sure I saw that he had the gun trained on me. Once inside, he fired up the engine and drove us out of the garage, heading west on Wilshire.

I sat there without a clue about what to do next. Keep quiet and let him think? Or make conversation and distract him just long enough for me to get my hands on the pistol? It didn't take long to rule that one out. While someone like D could've snapped Richard in half, the odds of me overpowering him were supermodel slim.

He drove to a quiet motel in west L.A., near Culver City. He parked close to the middle of the building and got out, ordering me to do the same. I did but apparently not fast enough, because he snatched my wrist and pulled me toward the building.

My feet skittered across the gravelly pavement, stirring up dust. "Shoes! Shoes! Watch the shoes, you Klingon! They're Gabbana!"

Richard produced a plastic key card from his pocket and tossed it at me. "Unlock the door."

I did and got a face full of cold air, courtesy of the window unit humming away with the grace of a jackhammer. The small room contained a bed, a dresser, and a chair in the corner. Straight ahead was a sink with a doorway on the left that led to the bathroom. He nudged me into the room with the gun and shut the door behind him.

He pointed at the bed. "Sit."

The comforter featured a drab blue- and green-diamond pattern and a half dozen cigarette burns. There was also a sponge-sized mystery stain in the middle, so I bypassed the bed in favor of the chair in the corner beside the lamp.

"What am I doing here?" I asked.

"Did you really think I would just sit there and take it while you ruined me and my family? That is not how Spencers do business."

"You won't get away with this," I said, and he laughed. "Seriously. My partner is expecting me, and if I don't check in pretty soon ..."

Richard snorted. "What then?"

"He'll go straight to my place. He'll find Whimsy in my car and know something's wrong because I'd never leave her like that. A little while later, the cops will find your fingerprints on the door handle, and you'll have a ton of explaining to do."

My mouth went dry as I waited to see whether my words had any effect. Clearly, he was making things up as he went along. He stood with his weight against the wall, contemplating his next move.

"You don't have a partner," he finally said.

"You're wrong. You might even remember him: Darius James, a private investigator. He looked into Robin Castro's death a few years ago after the police didn't get anywhere. You know, the *first* time Trey killed someone?"

"Right," he muttered. "James."

"And I told him everything."

"Did you?" Richard looked up D's website on his phone.

Then he took mine, dialed, and handed it back to me. "Let's invite him to this little get-together, shall we? I can kill two problem children with one gun. And don't try warning him or anything like that. You're a pretty little thing. Just be nice and playful as you tell him to meet you at a hotel, and let his male libido fill in the blanks, got it?"

As I did what he asked, it occurred to me that my life now rested squarely in D's hands.

Satisfied, Richard made himself comfy on the bed. He turned on the television and flipped past a woman hawking bad jewelry, a soccer game, and a Spanish soap opera before settling on a gardening show. We sat in silence through two segments of a landscaping show until the hosts demonstrated how to use trellis mirrors to create the illusion of space.

"Now that's cool," he murmured.

"Whatever."

He looked over at me. "Why so hostile?"

"Wouldn't you be hostile if someone had a gun on you and forced you to make a tacky phone call? Or are you going to blame my hormones?"

"I thought your hormones would've been churning at the thought of a hook-up with a young stud like Mr. James, no?"

I ignored him. Dignifying his comment with a response and all that.

"I guess destroying—" The air conditioner shut off, so he lowered his voice. "Destroying families is more your speed."

"What?"

"Destroying happy families? Is that what gets you off?"

I had a pretty good idea what got him off — I'd nearly been an ear witness to it on the night of Trammell's party — but I didn't see any benefit in mentioning that. "You're blaming me for destroying your family?"

"We were doing just fine until you came along."

"What about Trey?"

"Trey was doing fine too."

"Until you switched his medication."

Richard sat up and gawked at me, losing his grip on the gun for a split second. That confirmed my suspicions. He'd substituted Trey's schizophrenia meds with placebos — what Alvin had referred to as shenanigans.

"He was sick, Richard, and you knew it. You knew what he was capable of because he'd done it to Robin Castro. You managed to keep him out of jail and get him on medication, but when you wanted Denise Ladd out of the way, that was when you made the switch. Then it was just a matter of pushing his buttons, right? All you had to do was make him think Denise was a threat to the good Spencer name and let things play out the way they had before. It wouldn't surprise me if you arranged for her to be at Briarwood that night so Trey could make her one of his famous drinks. Robin Castro died because Trey is sick. Denise Ladd died because you are."

He got up from the bed and approached me. Seeing the gun in his hands, my heart ramped way up.

"You think you're pretty smart, don't you? Got it all figured out. But why would I do all that? Why would I mastermind the murder of a perfectly innocent girl?"

"Because she ..."

He had the gun by his side, but the hand holding it shook. "Go on. Because why, Kate?"

"Because she knew about you and Lance Waltrip ... and a gay Spencer just won't fly."

Sweat formed on Richard's forehead. He looked at himself in the bathroom mirror and mopped his brow.

"Well, aren't you the clever girl? A gold star for you, Kate." His eyes were locked on the mirror while he spoke to me — a discomforting way to have a conversation. "I don't know how you figured all that out, but no matter, because when Mr. James shows up, ready to get his freak on, I'm going to shoot him and then I'm going to shoot you. After that, I'll wipe my prints off the gun, put the weapon in your hand, and all my problems are solved."

Earlier, I thought he was making things up on the fly, but now I wondered whether all of this had been calculated. Everything was lining up perfectly for him, as if he'd planned this whole motel thing from the start. If he was improvising, he was doing a good job. I was about to ask whether he'd been playing me since the parking garage, when someone knocked on the door.

"Housekeeping," a woman outside said.

"We don't want any!" Richard shouted.

The knock came again. "Housekeeping."

He stuffed the gun into his waistband and covered it with his shirt. He marched to the door, looked through the peephole, and yanked the door open. Standing on the other side was a woman holding an armful of towels. "For you, sir."

Richard huffed, took the towels, hung the Do Not Disturb sign on the knob, and promptly shut the door without even a thank you. Muttering something I didn't quite catch, he tossed the towels aside and returned to the bed. No sooner had he made himself comfortable than there was another knock. "Housekeeping again. Very sorry, sir."

"For the love of Christ!" He leaped from the bed and crossed the room. He yanked the door open just as D swung in from the overhang like a gymnast from a high bar, planting his feet right on Richard's chest and launching him backward. Richard crash-landed flat on his back. He reached for his gun, but D rushed into the room, snatched the gun away, and cracked him over the head with the butt, knocking Spencer out cold.

"You all right?" D asked, while the woman from housekeeping looked on from the doorway, eyes bulging and her hand covering her mouth.

I waited for him to finish cuffing Richard and then asked, "Figured out I wasn't inviting you over for a tryst, huh?"

"Something had to be up, because when I answered the phone, you called me Spyder."

"Well, don't get used to it, because it won't happen again. Except for next time, of course."

"Next time?"

"The next time the you-know-what goes down. It'll be like our own private bat signal."

D shook his head. "Oh no, no, no. No next time. You're dangerous."

"That's not nice, D, especially considering I was about to mention that there's still an outstanding reward for any information leading to the capture of Robin Castro's murderer. I already told Alvin you were instrumental in that regard."

"No shit?"

"Just do me a favor and spend some of the money on new office chairs." I stood and fanned myself. This sort of excitement would render even the best antiperspirant moot. "I need some air."

"Oh. Right." D made sure Richard was secured and followed me outside. He plucked a black cable from inside the air conditioner unit.

"What is that?" I asked.

"A camera, see?" He held it up and showed me what looked like a regular piece of cable, except for the tiny lens attached to the end. "I threaded it through the grate in the back and got Spencer on video. Should make the D.A.'s job real easy, but I had to disable the AC unit first, or the motor would've drowned out Spencer's confession. Sorry if it got a little warm in there."

"I'll survive. Literally."

34

It wasn't quite a return to the scene of the crime — more like a return to the scene of the chase — although this visit promised to be more serene. At just after nine o'clock, the street was thick with traffic, but the tourists hadn't fully descended on Hollywood and Highland. I got coffee and sat at a table where I could see Trammell coming up the escalator — the same escalator I'd slid down just a few days earlier to give those cops the slip. The video of me scooting downhill while hopping over the speed bumps already had almost four hundred thousand views on YouTube. Not too shabby. And best of all, because it was a shaky cell phone video, no one could make out my identity.

The news media had quickly lost interest in me too. Some starlet had a wardrobe malfunction on the red carpet, and just like that, I wasn't even fit for the back pages, which didn't stress me one bit. The only famous burglars are the ones in jail.

Alvin had been right about Trey. He was sentenced to five years of medical supervision, but Richard wasn't nearly as lucky. He got eighteen years for orchestrating one murder, attempting a second one (me), and aggravated kidnapping (me again).

Trammell arrived, but when he got to my table, he realized there was only one chair, and I was already ensconced. He scanned the area for another one, but I said, "No need to get comfortable. This isn't social, and you're not staying."

I reached in my purse and dropped his necklace on the table. I couldn't have been happier to be rid of it. "You're kind of sleazy, you know that?" I told him.

He chuckled as he scooped up his uninspired piece of jewelry. "There are plenty of people in this town who would eliminate the 'kind of,' so thank you."

His candor shocked me, and I certainly had never expected to hear him utter those last two words. Blank you, maybe, but not thank you.

"Those people would be right. Putting the squeeze on your so-called friends? I don't know the words to express how low that is, and I know a lot of words." I wanted to ask how he'd even gotten his hands on some of those documents, but I was better off not knowing.

"Look at it like this," he said. "By keeping things quiet, I allowed them to keep their dignity."

"Right, just not their money." I paused to sip my coffee. I loved the smell of French roast in the morning. Wait. That sounded like a line from an old movie. Was Mel having undue influence on me? "Look, I don't care about you or Tad Ellington or Richard Spencer. As far as I'm concerned, you guys all deserve each other. But Denise Ladd is another story. You may not be joining Richard in prison, but that doesn't make you innocent either. Not in my book anyway."

He started to interrupt, but I put my hand up. "Have you heard of Pacific Coast Haven?"

He shook his head.

"It's a no-kill animal shelter."

"And you're telling me this why?"

"Because it's about to get a hundred thousand dollar donation. From you."

"A hundred thousand dollars? Are you—"

"*A year.* Otherwise, the whole world will find out what a lowlife scumbag Trammell Preston is." He staggered and grabbed a nearby handrail for balance. Confusion clouded his face, so I cleared things up for him. "I've got multiple copies of everything in the safe that your little necklace opens, Trammell."

"But ... that's—"

"What? Blackmail? Funny how that works, huh?" I took another drink, giving him the chance to respond, but he had nothing. "Let's skip to the fine print, shall we? If you don't stick to the deal, or if anything happens to me, copies will be sent to the media, everything will come out, blah blah blah. But you already knew that, right?"

Just down the street, the side of a building was being turned into a billboard for the latest superhero action movie that was bound to be a rush, with explosions and fight scenes galore, but the only movie in my future was a nice, quiet chick flick. I'd had enough action to last me a while.

When I turned back, Trammell was still standing beside the table, looking several times less full of himself than when he'd arrived.

"Off you go," I said.

I finished my coffee in peace, poked around some of the shops, and then drove down to Santa Monica to meet Aubrey for lunch at Pelican Flats, this little seafood restaurant on the beach. Despite a light haze over the sky, the midday escape had been a great call on her part. When I arrived, she was seated at a table on the patio, looking downright cozy in a pair of navy wide-leg pants and a loose fitting white linen top that billowed in the breeze.

Any other time, the primary topic of conversation would've been my date with Connor, but she'd caught my photo being flashed all over the news, so I gave her the rundown on my big adventure, from the Getty to the motel showdown. At one point, she accused me of embellishing, but I insisted, "Your entire life really does flash before your eyes when someone points a gun at you."

"Okay, fine. But how'd you figure out that Richard Spencer was involved?"

"Things started making sense when I found that kernel of dog food the second time I was at the Spencers' house. It's no big deal for me to find stray pieces of dog food around my apartment, but you'd expect that from someone who has a dog. The Spencers didn't. And then when Richard caught me walking out of Trey's room, I couldn't help but notice his shoes. I recognized them — particularly because of the Louisiana-shaped stain right near the Nike swoosh — from the day I got caught in Denise's apartment and hid under the bed."

"Why'd he go to the apartment?"

"For the necklace. I think he and Ellington were working together to get it. They'd figured out that Trammell was hiding the blackmail secrets using the same method as the Deltas. But Trammell was on to them. He overheard the same conversation that I had and sent Lucas to Denise's apartment to get the necklace before they could. When Spencer got there and saw that someone else had turned the place inside out, he thought he was too late. He left without realizing he was taking a piece of Yoda's food with him. It must've gotten stuck in his shoe or something."

"Wow, Kate. If I ever need a detective, I'm calling you."

I shook my head. "But let me know if you ever come across a target ripe for acquisition."

We talked and laughed over crab cake salads and margaritas, and before I knew it, we'd been there close to two hours.

Aubrey joked that she needed to get back to work because her boss was a total pain.

The valet attendant arrived with my car first, and Aubrey broke into a huge smile at the sight of the Karmabile. It was freshly washed and waxed and looking especially yellow. "Is that really yours?"

"Yeah, it's how I roll when I'm not working undercover."

The valet exchanged my keys for a tip, and he set off to get Aubrey's car.

"Do you like living in the Marina?" I asked her.

"You're not thinking about moving, are you? I thought you loved your apartment."

"Meh. There're too many criminals hanging around that place."

In fact, I'd already cleared all my stuff out of there. All things considered — two hostile intrusions in the same week on top of a bad breakup — it just didn't feel like home anymore. For now, the Westcott Hotel would have to do. After all, I was kind of flush at the moment. D insisted I take half of the reward money for solving Robin Castro's murder, because I'd been Richard Spencer's abductee. D said they called it "imminent danger" pay in the military. So why not splurge a little?

Whimsy was fresh from the Westcott's spa for pets. They'd groomed her head to tail, turning her into an absolute diva, complete with a miniature white hoodie. I settled for a nap and then a marathon shower, after which I draped myself in a robe and sat on the window ledge with Whim. The sky was littered with stars that night, as if someone in a hurry had dropped a bag full of diamonds. Hundreds of years ago, high priests in some cultures used diamonds to determine a person's guilt or innocence. A diamond was placed before the accused, and the brighter it shined, the more truthful they were considered. But if the diamond was dull, the priests assumed the person was lying.

As I admired the heavens, I thought of Robin Castro and Denise Ladd. Were they totally innocent? Denise had taken part in an affair, and Robin had planned to cash in on a thinly disguised story about the Spencers, so maybe not. But who was I to judge? One thing was certain: they hadn't deserved the hand fate dealt them. Anyway, I took those glittering stars as a sign that Robin and Denise were out there somewhere, letting me know that, all in all, I'd done well.

I don't know, maybe that was crazy, but a girl could hope.

Made in the USA
Las Vegas, NV
12 July 2023

74594674R00164